Christmas in Port Berry

ALSO BY K.T. DADY

Christmas in Port Berry

K.T. DADY

Choc Lit
A JOFFE BOOKS COMPANY

Choc Lit, London
A Joffe Books company
www.choc-lit.com

First published in Great Britain in 2025

© K.T. Dady 2025

Cover art by Dee Dee Book Covers

ISBN: 978-1781899076

Love changes the world.

CHAPTER 1

Alice

The scent of seafood wafted over to Alice Dipple as she stood outside Seaview B&B, gazing up at her business. The large chalky white building needed some Christmas spirit. It was late November, and she still hadn't decorated for the season. She didn't have any guests booked in for the big day, but she had a few now, and there were some due for New Year's Eve, so even if she wasn't in the mood to celebrate, it would be nice for them to see a tree covered in tinsel, at the very least.

Peering over the road at the dark sea, she wondered if it was just the heavy salty air that made her think of cockles and mussels. That or someone nearby was having some for a late breakfast. Not something she'd ever considered before lunch, even living by the harbour all her life.

She sighed, then glanced at the stained-glass window of a boat at the top of the wide arched front door. That could do with a wipe. She really needed to get some motivation. It was her first Christmas in her new business, only having bought it from Mabel in the summer. Perhaps if the elderly woman hadn't died soon after, life at the B&B would feel happier.

1

For years, Alice had dreamed of owning her own B&B along the harbour in Port Berry. She had grown up just around the corner and helped Mabel out at the B&B since she was in her teens. Never in a million years did she expect Mabel to retire and offer her first refusal of the place. It was more than a dream come true — it was everything. And Mabel had been so pleased her family home was being passed down to someone who cared so much about it and wanted to keep the premises as a B&B.

Looking at the building now, Alice wondered how something so old still stood so strong. At the age of only thirty-one, Alice often felt more like a hundred, especially when her fibromyalgia flared up.

Bell of Blood. She laughed to herself, trying to visualize when her new home was a tavern with that name. She could just see the pirates of Penzance popping in to sup some ale and cause havoc. 'If only you could talk, eh?'

She wondered what Mabel's ancestors would now think about her at the helm. So far, no ghost had tapped her on the shoulder or kept her awake throughout the night, so she figured if one was floating around, they seemed to be okay about the exchange.

'Morning, Alice,' came a voice, breaking her from the trance she appeared to be in with the sea-facing balconies.

She turned to see a local fisherman walking by. 'Morning, Jed. I thought you'd still be out there.' She pointed over Harbour End Road at the calm sea.

'I caught what was needed for the shop first thing. Now I'm off on a walk for a bit of exercise for the old knees.' He scuffed back his salt-and-pepper hair as he grinned at his legs. 'Your grandmother was supposed to join me, but reckons she was needed by your mum in the newsagents.' His slate-blue eyes twinkled. 'I think we both know that was an excuse.'

Alice laughed. 'Yes, well, Nan isn't known for wanting to exercise. Anyway, with you both being seventy-one now, isn't it time to relax?'

'Pfft. While there's life in you, use it. I'm fitter than your Benny, and he's, what? How old is that nephew of yours now? I can't keep up.'

'He turned fifteen this year.'

Jed rubbed his wiry grey beard. 'Soon goes, doesn't it? Only feels like yesterday he was knee-high to a grasshopper.'

Alice smiled. 'He's not that tall now. I'm thinking he'll have a growth spurt soon or stay on the shorter side like his mum.'

'Aw, bless your Lisa.' Jed gestured at the cold-blue sky. 'It's tough this time of year when they're not with us, eh, my girl?'

Following his gaze, she agreed. 'My sister has been gone eight years now. Sometimes it seems like yesterday.'

'I know the feeling. Not a day goes by I don't think of my wife and son.'

Alice reached for his hand. 'I feel sadder this year, Jed.'

'Because of this place? And Mabel?'

She nodded. 'Yep. Doesn't feel right. I know we have to get on with life, but sometimes it feels tainted.'

'Yeah, I know what you mean.'

'Mabel still had so much life in her. She was all set for the next phase and just like that, she dies.'

'And that is exactly why we live our best life in the time we have, because we just don't know how long that will be.'

Alice leaned into his shoulder. 'Blimming heck, Jed. What do we sound like? Not the cheeriest of conversations.'

'All part of life, Alice. The ups, downs, we can't avoid it or pretend these things don't exist. It's okay to talk about such matters. Best not to dwell though.'

She motioned to the door. 'Best for me to make a start on adding some holly and mistletoe.'

'And we've got a lot of events to look forward to this December.'

Alice squealed quietly. 'Ooh, yes, Sophie and Matt's wedding on the twentieth. How are her nerves holding up?'

Jed chuckled. 'Not sure my granddaughter has nerves. But Matt might need his hand holding if you see him. He can't wait for their big day, but I think his excitement overwhelms him some days. He keeps going out for early morning swims in the sea.'

Alice shivered at the thought. 'It's freezing out there.'

'Ah, you get used to it when you do it every day.'

'I prefer snuggling in front of my wood burner this time of year.'

Jed pointed at the B&B. 'Do you want my help with the decorations?'

'Thanks, but I'm okay. You get back to your walk. Demi's in the kitchen, prepping for the lunch guests, so I can always grab her to lend a hand if need be.'

'Well, you just give me a shout if you need anything.'

Alice waved as he headed off. Just that brief chat with Jed had lifted her a touch. Life was short, Christmas was around the corner, and Mabel would want her to put the tree up and show the guests some festive joy.

'Right, that's it. Holly jolly time.'

It was nice and warm inside the small foyer, helping Alice's stiff bones to relax. She approached the light-wood reception desk and rummaged around in a box beneath for the key to the storage room, where the Christmas decorations were kept.

Each year, she'd help Mabel with the task of giving the B&B a slight touch of Santa's Grotto, so she knew where everything went. Perhaps this year she might add something of her own.

It was heart-warming looking through Mabel's ancient garlands and tree ornaments, and Alice was pleased Mabel had left so much behind for her to keep.

'Some of these bits and pieces have been with this place before my time, Alice,' Mabel would say each year.

Alice felt blessed to have had such a wonderful woman as her friend.

4

Pulling out the stepladder, Alice held back tears and composed herself. Mabel would tell her off for all the doom and gloom. Not one to grumble about the bad things that happened, Mabel kept her chin up and her head in the game. Alice needed to take a leaf out of her book.

It was hard not to think about Mabel while climbing the ladder to pin one end of a foil garland in place. The only joy the woman really had was the B&B, until she met her girlfriend who she'd been about to join in Jersey. Her son had been a rotten drunk, hardly ever home, and her grandchildren never seemed to appreciate the fact their grandmother raised them after their mum had died when they were six.

Alice was so grateful to her mother and nan. They had always been there for her, even more so when she adopted Benny. It was nice having such a close, loving family. She was lucky, she knew that and could never take them for granted. Mabel's grandchildren were the same age as Alice, but age made little difference. The granddaughter lived in Australia and didn't come back for the funeral or send flowers. She never wrote or contacted Mabel. And as for the other twin, he was still in prison.

Jamie Stark was never far from her mind, but he needed to be, as there was work to be done.

Alice smiled as a young couple came down the stairs. 'Enjoy your day.' She waved, remembering how they had told her at breakfast that they were off to Penzance for the day to visit friends.

'Thanks, bye.'

Alice wondered if she should put the radio on low behind the desk. There was an older gentleman still in his room, and a middle-aged woman typing away on her laptop in the small lounge area. She didn't want to disturb her guests, so opted for silence. Perhaps later, when the writer had left, she could add some festive tunes to the foyer, ready for the lunch customers.

She climbed down the ladder and dragged it across the room so she could pin the other end of the garland. At least she had made a start, and she was feeling a bit better in herself.

Moving a potted leafy plant out the way, Alice settled the ladder along a wall, checked it for sturdiness, then climbed once more, stretching for the ceiling, grateful for her long limbs. She started to hum a Christmas song while blowing strands of her long dark hair out of her eyes, then giggled to herself as the garland slipped and landed on her head.

'Hello, Angel.' The male voice startled her.

Only one person in the world called her by that name, but he wasn't being released from prison until early next year.

In a tizz, Alice swirled on the ladder, lost her footing, and tumbled straight down into athletic arms that caught her. She stared up into soft blue eyes. 'Jamie?'

A moment of silence passed as they stared at each other.

'You're here,' she managed.

His mouth parted slightly, and she watched his gaze fall to her lips. 'Yeah,' he said, sounding just as surprised.

6

CHAPTER 2

Jamie

Jamie found he couldn't stop staring at Alice. She was in his arms, her face so close to his. It was all so surreal.

'I thought you weren't being released till next year,' she said quietly, not attempting to move from his hold.

'I lied. I didn't want to tell you in case something went wrong.' He dipped his head. 'After eight years inside, I guess I was finding it hard to believe I'd ever be free.'

'But you're free now?' It was as though she needed the confirmation.

'Yes. I've served my time.'

'I would have come got you.'

He met the kindness in her light-brown eyes and smiled. 'You've done enough for me.'

They stayed staring at each other as another beat passed.

'Jamie, I—'

Demi came walking out from the dining room. 'Alice, I've . . . Oh, erm . . .'

Jamie gently lowered Alice to her feet, then turned to the woman in her late-thirties gawping his way.

'Demi, this is Jamie. Mabel's grandson.' Alice cleared her throat, and Jamie watched her paste on a smile. 'Demi is the chef here. Makes brekkie, and we are now open to the public for lunch.' She brushed her hands down her jeans.

Demi stepped closer. 'Pleased to meet you. I'm sorry about your gran. I hadn't known her long. She was always so lovely.'

'Thank you.'

Demi thumbed towards the door. 'I'm just heading to the pub to grab some carrots, only we've run out. I live a couple of doors down at the Jolly Pirate with Robson. Not sure if you know him.'

Jamie nodded. 'I remember Robson.'

Demi smiled softly. 'Pop over whenever you like. I don't drink myself, but I'm happy to buy you one. Welcome you home.'

He wasn't expecting that, but then again, Demi didn't know the old version of him. 'Thank you, but I'm sure Robson wouldn't want me in his pub.'

'Look,' said Demi, 'I won't beat around the bush. I've heard about you, and I know you standing here means you've just got out of prison, right?'

He nodded, wondering what was coming next.

She tapped her chest. 'I was in prison once, so I know what it feels like to step back outside and feel a little lost. We need people to believe in us. To give us a second chance.'

Jamie stole a glance at Alice before returning his attention to Demi's brown eyes revealing nothing but friendliness.

She smiled softly. 'There's a place I go to that helps ex-offenders. It's called The Butterfly Company. They got me my first job when I was released. I could take you over there one day, if you like.'

'Thanks. I know the place. I'm already booked in to go there tomorrow.'

'That's brilliant,' said Demi. 'They're so good. Would you like me to come with you?'

'You're very kind, but I'll be fine by myself, thanks.'

'Just know I'm around if you ever need another friend.' Demi headed towards the door. 'Are you staying close by?'

'He's living here,' said Alice.

'Till I get sorted,' he added, not wanting to put her out. Seaview B&B wasn't his home anymore. Hadn't been for years, and now it belonged to Alice.

'Okay,' said Demi. 'Well, I'll see you in a bit.'

Jamie turned to Alice as soon as Demi left. 'Thanks for letting me stay here.'

'It's your home.'

'We both know that's not true anymore.'

'You don't have anywhere else to go.'

He looked up through his dark lashes. 'I'll sort something soon.'

'There's no rush. Erm, back when you lived here, I know your family used the top level as your home, but a few years back, Mabel moved down here, and the top rooms are rented out.' She glanced at the door behind the desk and moved her head in that direction. 'Benny and I are back there now. It's just two bedrooms, but you can have a room on the first floor. One with an en suite and a sea view.'

'You'll lose money if you give me one of the best rooms.' He lowered his gaze.

'It's winter. You know we won't have many guests this time of year.'

He knew. He had grown up watching his grandmother run the place single-handed.

'I'll get a job soon enough and start paying my way.'

'How about we get you settled and worry about that another time.' Alice went to fetch a key. 'Are you hungry?'

'A little.'

'Let's put your things away, then we can see what's in the kitchen.' Alice glanced at his feet. 'Oh, you don't have much.'

'I never went in with a suitcase.' He grabbed his one carrier bag and followed her to the first floor and into the bedroom.

9

The air smelled of furniture polish, and the fresh sheets on the bed looked inviting, but it was the sea view that captivated him for a moment.

'I used to love looking out at the sea.'

'We can ask Jed to take you out on his boat.'

He stared over at the red-and-white lighthouse in the near distance. 'I think we both know that you, and now Demi, will be my only friends around here.'

Alice stepped to his side. 'You're not that person anymore. In time, they'll see.'

'I terrorized the neighbourhood. Brought nothing but trouble to my nan's door.' The memory was raw, made worse by the fact he couldn't make it up to his grandmother now. 'I couldn't even face her funeral, and I was allowed to go.'

'It's in the past, Jamie. Things are different now.'

He could tell she was being hopeful, rather than certain, and he needed her to know that he had changed, and that she'd get no bother from him. 'I just want peace.'

'And you'll have that here.' Her sweet voice went straight to his heart, as always.

He turned to face her. 'I'll skip the food and stay in here, if that's okay.' Not only did he feel like a burden, he felt like a failure. And a pity party for one was heading his way.

Alice frowned. 'No, it's not okay. You've just spent years confined to a room. I want you to walk around freely. Head to the kitchen to eat whenever you want. No timings, no routine, no restrictions.' She took his hand, looking down at the connection. 'I know it's going to take time for you to adjust, and I don't want to force you to do anything, but I honestly believe it will do you the world of good to show yourself you're free by acting that way.'

Jamie heard her words, but his concentration was on their joined hands. 'Angel, I—'

'Please, Jamie, come to the kitchen and eat. Let's try to be normal again.'

He met her eyes. 'Were things ever normal between us?'

She gave a small smile. 'Not sure what to call it.'

'I don't deserve someone like you in my life.'

'Yes, you do. None of it was your fault.'

'Don't make excuses for me.'

Alice let go of his hand and headed for the door. 'There were excuses. Big fat ones. But right now, all that's important is you eating. So, come on.'

Jamie followed her to the kitchen. Every step feeling surreal. He used to dream of the day he'd go home to Port Berry, rebuild his life, but being there didn't feel real. Being so close to Alice was unbelievable on every level. 'I see not much has changed about the old place.'

Alice opened the fridge. 'Mabel was stuck in her ways, but I plan to do a bit of an upgrade here and there.' She waggled a packet of ham. 'Sandwich, or would you rather wait till Demi comes back to make some hot lunches?'

'Sandwich is fine, thanks.' He was happy to eat anything she offered, just happy to be around her.

'Coming right up.'

'I can help you with this place. I'm okay with a paintbrush.' He smiled when she glanced his way.

'That'll be nice.'

'After this, do you want me to put the Christmas decorations up? You know, what with me not being allowed to hang out in my room.'

Alice's giggle was one of his favourite sounds. 'I'm not going to be the boss of you.'

'Oh, you've always been the boss of me.'

She placed a plated sandwich on the table where he sat. 'Not true. If I had been, I would have kept you out of prison.'

Jamie reached for her hand. 'You kept me alive in prison.'

A beat passed.

'You had no one writing or visiting you,' she said quietly, water pooling in her eyes until she blinked it away.

Jamie pulled back. 'Erm, shall I make us a drink or something?'

'There's juice in the fridge, or you can put the kettle on.' She glanced over her shoulder as she headed to the breadbin to put the bread away. 'Or did you mean something stronger?'

'Juice is fine.' He went to the fridge, putting the ham away at the same time. He needed something to do other than keep staring at her.

Alice sat down with her own sandwich. 'Do you have any plans?'

He joined her side, passing her a glass of orange juice. 'I have that appointment tomorrow at The Butterfly Company to talk about finding a job. So I'll go from there.'

'Anything else?'

'Not just yet. What about you? I know you didn't tell me everything about your life.' He bit into his sandwich, wondering if she might mention a boyfriend.

'Just this place occupying my mind. And now you.' She gave him a friendly nudge of the arm.

Jamie swallowed hard. 'So, erm, you don't have a partner?'

'No.'

'Right.' He took another bite of his sandwich.

'I did have one a couple of years back. Thought I'd give it a try, but it didn't work out, so I went back to focusing on myself and family.' She looked his way. 'Not something I wanted to write to you about.'

'I understand.'

'I made a mistake,' she said quietly, cupping her glass of orange juice.

'No, you didn't, Angel. You just tried to have a normal life.'

'I just regret it, that's all.'

It was the way she said it that had him meet her eyes, searching for clues as to how bad the relationship was.

'You okay now?' he asked gently.

Alice smiled widely. 'I'm so happy.'

That was good enough for him, because the thought of some bloke making her unhappy was enough to land him back in prison if he caught up with the man.

Jamie went back to his food, wiping away the image of Alice in bed with someone. He had always believed she might one day move on with her life. Fretted she might stop writing to him. Pretend he didn't exist. It wasn't in her nature, but insecurities hit hard when locked up in prison. He would stare at her photo stuck to his wall, the selfie she'd sent of her smiling with the sea and lighthouse behind, and he would wish so hard he could rewind time and start over.

CHAPTER 3

Alice

Decorating the artificial Christmas tree in the foyer with Jamie wasn't something Alice had expected to do. It was a little strange, but Jamie looked relaxed, while she wasn't quite sure how to feel. She hoped she'd made the right decision about letting him stay at the B&B. It was a lot easier when they would just talk about his release, but here he was, out. She needed to remind her heart to be still around him. And that helping him out was one thing — being too involved with him again was another. She would simply show some support and be the good friend she was.

'Customers will be in for lunch soon.' Alice glanced at the door. 'We could go for a walk afterwards. I'll show you what's what around here now. Although, I do need to speak to my mum first.'

Jamie raised his brow. 'Tell her I'm here, you mean?'

'Yep.'

'How much of a problem is this going to be for you?'

Alice shrugged. 'It's their problem. I'm getting on with my life, and so are you. We've got no problems.' She hoped.

He took the red bauble she handed him. 'Hmm.'

'I'll take you to see the Happy to Help Hub. Finally get to show you our setup there.'

'I'm looking forward to that. I liked hearing about your success there.'

Alice smiled. 'We all pitched in, so it's more a success story for the community. It may be small, but it sure helps a lot of the locals, especially the food bank part.'

'I'm surprised you have time to volunteer.'

'I don't have that much time since owning the B&B, but Demi has been brilliant around here which means I still get to put in a shift or two each week. Even Benny staffs the reception at times.'

'I take it he's in school.'

Alice nodded. 'Yeah, and I want you to know that even though I didn't mention you to Mum, I did talk to Benny about you staying here. I just thought it would be in the new year. Anyway, he was okay about things, so he won't be any trouble.'

'But your mum will?'

The thought alone made Alice grimace. 'She won't be best pleased, but she'll come around. Listen, Jamie, not everyone is going to expect you to be the same person you were eight years ago. We all change.'

Jamie gestured at the dining room as they placed the last of the tree decorations onto branches. 'Do you want my help in there?'

'No, that's fine. But I do want to give you something before I get back to work.' She waved him towards her living quarters and invited him inside.

Jamie glanced at the kitchenette. 'It's quite nice back here.'

Alice nipped to her bedroom and pulled a white envelope out of a top drawer. 'It does the trick.' She met him by the wood burner, her favourite spot in the B&B.

'What's this?' he asked, taking the envelope.

'Money for you.'

'Whoa!' He quickly handed it back. 'I'm not taking your money, Angel.'

'It's not from me. It's from Mabel. She had it stashed with her will and other important documents. Strict instructions for me to give this to you on your release.'

He peered inside, flicking through the notes. 'Bloody hell, there's about five hundred quid here.'

'Yeah, it's so you can replace your clothes she gave to charity.'

His face was filled with amusement. 'She gave my clothes away?'

Alice thought it best to be honest. 'It was after you were sent away. She had a moment where anger took control, so she gathered your things and, well . . . Erm, you do have a couple of boxes of your other stuff in the storage room. She felt bad afterwards. Anyway, she wanted you to have that.'

He was staring at the notes. 'I hadn't expected her to leave me anything. I know she hated me for so long.'

Alice reached for his hand. 'She never hated you.'

'Both Shannon and I weren't good to her. I caused trouble, and Shannon was, well, Shannon. I never know which word fits her best.'

Alice had quite a few to describe her, but she remained silent.

Jamie raised the envelope. 'I'll take this to my room. Let you get on with your day.'

'I won't be too long, then I'll come find you.'

'You won't need to look far. I'll be the one finishing off your Christmas decorations.'

'Oh, I don't expect you to do that. I can sort it later. It takes so long, doesn't it?'

Jamie shrugged. 'First time I've helped.'

'Really?'

His head dipped a touch, then he made his way back out to the foyer.

Alice went to say something but froze on seeing her mum's beady blue eyes glaring at her from the other side of the reception desk. 'Mum!'

'Hello, Lizzie,' said Jamie politely — not that it mattered. Lizzie's glare remained firmly in place.

'A word,' she said flatly to Alice.

'Not now, Mum.' Alice gestured to the lunch customers starting to enter the dining room.

'Kitchen,' said Lizzie through gritted teeth.

Alice watched Jamie head over to the stepladder as she walked away with her mum.

Lizzie huffed, ignoring Demi who glanced up from the stove to see what was going on. 'Have you lost your mind?' she whispered urgently to her daughter. 'Were you even going to let me know?'

'I was coming to tell you after lunch.'

'Well, the Port Berry grapevine beat you to it, girlie.'

Demi bit her lip. 'Sorry, that might have been my fault. I told Robson.'

'Who told Spencer, who told me when he came to the shop for some chocolate. Assumed I knew. You know, what with me being your mother.' Lizzie shook her head in annoyance.

Demi went out to the dining room to take some food orders.

Alice took a calming breath, wishing her mother would do the same. 'Mum, this is his home,' she said quietly.

'Not anymore.'

'Well, I told him he can stay.'

'Tell him you've changed your mind.'

Alice clenched her fists behind her back. 'No.'

'That boy has been nothing but trouble since he was fourteen years old. I never liked you hanging out with him. You know that.'

'You know his story, Mum. You know why he ended up that way.'

Lizzie sat at the table, taking Alice with her. 'Now you listen to me. Plenty have a rotten old drunk of a dad, but they don't grow up committing crimes left, right, and centre.'

'It wasn't just his dad.'

'Don't you bring the excuse of him losing his mother to cancer when he was six, because our Benny lost his mum to the same thing when he was seven, and do you see him tearing up the town? No, you don't. Our Benny is a good boy.'

Alice sighed. Keeping her voice low, she said, 'It was a combination of things for Jamie, but mostly his own cancer. Mum, he was in and out of hospital from the age of eleven thanks to leukaemia. He never had a proper childhood. Hardly attended school for a good couple of years. He was messed up in many ways, then that Gregg came along with his gang, making Jamie feel like he was part of something, and that's why it all went wrong.'

'Oh, love, listen to yourself. You make it sound like Jamie had no mind of his own. He had a good nan, a solid enough home — once his loser of a dad kicked the bucket — and he was cured. He did what he did because he wanted to.'

'It's not as black and white as that, Mum. Everyone knows psychology plays a part. And anyway, that was in the past. He's been punished, and now he's back to rebuild his life and just find some peace and quiet.'

Lizzie pointed at the doorway. 'And I'm sure he can do that elsewhere.'

'He has nowhere to go.'

'This isn't on you, Alice.'

'He's been my best friend since primary school. I've been making his life part of mine since he got sick. The other kids stopped bothering with him after a while, but I stuck around.'

'Fat lot of good it did him. Shame your ways didn't rub off.'

Alice held her mother's hand, wishing she would understand the bond she had with Jamie, even if it was a little unusual. 'Mum, I know he's changed. I've been witnessing it happen over the years.'

Lizzie frowned. 'What do you mean?'

It was now or never, and seeing how Alice was obviously helping Jamie, she figured she might as well tell the truth.

'I've been writing and visiting him all these years.'

Lizzie sat back, eyes wide and mouth gaping.

Alice waited for the information to sink in.

Demi came back to plate some orders, keeping herself to herself.

The silence was unnerving, and it wasn't long before Alice found herself saying something.

'I know you don't like him, Mum, but I know him better than anyone. I'm telling you he's changed. And he's staying here in the B&B.'

'With you?' Lizzie sounded deflated.

'No. He has his own room.'

Lizzie slowly got up to leave.

'Mum . . .' Alice reached for her arm, but Lizzie moved away.

'You've got lunch to sort.' Lizzie stopped by the door, her expression having switched to anger again. 'But I'll tell you this, girlie. If one bit of trouble comes here, no matter how tiny, I'll be taking our Benny home with me, because there's no way I'll have him subjected to that.'

Alice's blood was boiling. 'I would never do anything to harm Benny.'

Lizzie closed in on her. 'No, but you're fool enough to let a scumbag into his life.'

'That was one time, and I didn't know Alan was a narcissist, did I?'

Lizzie stabbed a finger towards her. 'You're too soft, Alice. Makes you an easy target for these losers.'

'Jamie is not a loser, and Benny will be perfectly safe around him. Just give him a chance. He's a thirty-one-year-old man. He's changed.'

Lizzie waved off the comment and left.

Alice flopped back to the chair, placing her head in her hand.

Demi sat by her side. 'Hey, Al, don't be too hard on your mum. She's just worried. My family were, too, when I got out. Assumed I'd go straight back on drugs, start robbing shops again. What I'm trying to say is, it takes time to build trust, but if Jamie is serious about starting a new life, he'll show them. Trust is all about action, not words.'

Alice looked up and smiled weakly. 'Thanks, Dem.'

'No worries. Now, best get these lunches out.'

Alice stood to help. 'Yes, sorry about all this.'

'No apology needed. I've had plenty of rows with my lot, but you know what? I believed in myself, and that's what really counts. Do you think Jamie is at that stage?'

'Yes. The first couple of years he was inside, he got into all sorts of trouble, but then he started having therapy and had a mentor. Everything changed after that. He even took up studying.'

'And you really believe in him, don't you? I can see that clearly enough.'

Alice nodded. 'I do. I always have. I know he has a huge heart, and I know he's sorry for the trouble he caused around here.'

'Was it that bad?'

'Yep. Theft, fights, vandalism, racing stolen cars.' Alice shook her head. 'He was drinking heavily, missing for days on end, served a shorter sentence before this last one. But there were times when he'd take me up to his room and just hold me and . . .' She didn't want to tell Demi about his tears, breakdowns, his moments of tenderness with her.

The memory of them laying in each other's arms, not doing anything but holding each other, hit hard. Every single time she would try to stop him leaving her arms, going back to that gang, being someone he wasn't.

Demi rubbed her shoulder. 'It's okay, Alice. It's all okay now.'

'Give me one sec to wash my face, then I'll get serving.' Alice dashed to her quarters, avoiding Jamie in the foyer.

The cool water gave some respite, and the soft towel was a good place to hide her face for all of a minute. A warm presence came from behind, followed by a soft voice.

'Angel, are you all right?'

She pressed the towel harder against her cheeks, then, straightening, took a silent breath and pasted on a smile. 'Sure, just got a bit hot in the kitchen.' Turning, she met curious eyes.

'I don't want me being here to cause you stress.'

'I'm not stressed,' she lied.

He lightly brushed back a piece of her hair that was stuck to her lip. 'Tell me what to do. I should have listened to you years ago. I should have stayed with you.'

Alice glanced at his mouth, her heart pounding in her ears. 'Put the fairy lights up out front.'

His smile was small, but as beautiful as ever. 'I can do that.'

'I'd better get back to Demi.'

Neither of them moved for a moment, only the scrunched towel between them.

Alice swallowed hard, lowering her gaze. 'See you in a bit.' She quickly headed to the kitchen, his touch still very much with her.

CHAPTER 4

Jamie

It was nice going for a walk with Alice, getting reacquainted with his old neighbourhood, visiting all the places they used to hang out as kids.

'Let me show you the Hub now.' Alice led the way along Harbour End Road.

He smiled on the inside at just how hard she was trying to make him feel comfortable.

There was a smiley face sticker stuck to the Hub's front door, and as soon as he stepped inside, the scent of the lavender potpourri by the window hit his nostrils.

No one was inside the small cosy space, so Alice went to a room out back, leaving Jamie to gaze around at the framed affirmations on the wall. A small Christmas tree twinkling in the corner by the window caught his eye, before he promptly refocused on the muscular man following Alice out of the back room.

'Jamie, this is Will Pendleton. He was friends with Mabel.'

Jamie stepped forward to shake Will's hand.

'Sorry about your gran,' said Will. 'Bit of a character, that one.'

Jamie smiled softly. 'Yes, she was.'

Will gestured at a green high back chair. 'I lived at the B&B when I first arrived here, and Mabel took me under her wing, bless her.'

'Will is Ginny's partner,' said Alice, sitting to his side.

Jamie nodded. 'I remember Ginny. How is she?'

Will almost glowed as he replied. 'She's good. At home at the moment with our son, Robert. He's almost three months now.'

Alice splayed a hand at the Hub. 'Thought I'd show Jamie what we've done here.'

Will smiled at him. 'You can volunteer if you like.'

Jamie glanced at the street door. 'Not sure that would be a good idea. It would be nice to do some sort of voluntary work to repay my community for all the damage I caused though.'

'From what I hear, you've served your time,' Will said. 'Your gran told me about you. Simply not being that person anymore is good enough, and if you help out here, people will see the new you.'

Jamie was intrigued. 'I'm surprised my nan spoke of me at all. I wasn't exactly her favourite topic.'

Will held a sympathetic look. 'She told me you had a big heart, and she was going to write to you. Make amends. So I guess maybe you were one of her favourite topics.'

No one had written to him but Alice, who was currently gazing his way, looking hopeful. Should he mention that his grandmother hadn't sent any letters? He had no idea what to make of Will's information.

'I told your gran I'd look out for you,' added Will. 'I'm no mentor, but what with me being around ten years older than you and ex-navy, I think Mabel thought I'd be a good role model.' Will smiled warmly. 'So, you let me know if you need any help. I can always give you some shifts at Harbour Light Café, or there's our tea shop, Ginny's Tearoom. The baby keeps us busy, so another set of hands at either of our businesses is always welcome.'

'Thanks. I'm seeing someone tomorrow about work, but I'll keep that in mind.'

'I can take you over to the Sunshine Centre as well, see if it's somewhere you'd like to join,' Will said.

Alice turned to face Jamie. 'It was built not long after you went away. It's designed for people with disabilities and those needing emotional support or respite. Lottie goes there for art therapy.'

Jamie stopped staring at the light-wood table on hearing Lottie's name. 'I need to see Lottie. I owe her an apology.'

Alice offered a sympathetic smile. 'You don't have to go around saying sorry to people.'

Jamie stood. 'I do. She was a friend once, and . . .' He headed for the door. 'Do you think she'll be in her flower shop?'

Alice nodded. 'Yeah, she should be. Do you want me to come with you?'

'No, it's okay, but thanks. Will you wait here for me, though?'

'Sure.' Alice turned and smiled at Will. 'I'll put the kettle on.'

Jamie went back into the cold and walked a few doors down to Berry Blooms. He inhaled the salty air, then opened the door, looking up as a small antique bronze bell jingled above his head.

Lottie was sat in her electric wheelchair at a small table to the side of the shopfront, making bows from silver ribbon. Her sea-blue eyes and rosy cheeks lost all sparkle when she recognized who had entered. 'Jamie.'

'Hello, Lottie. I'm here to apologize,' he told her softly. 'The last time I saw you—'

'Was when you threw a brick through that window.' She stabbed a finger towards where he stood.

'I didn't know you were inside until you came out the door. I'm glad you didn't get hurt by the glass.'

Lottie pursed her lips. 'I was working late, and it scared the living daylights out of me.'

Jamie dipped his head but kept eye contact. 'I'm sorry, Lottie.'

'I always thought we were friends until you did that.'

'I was an idiot. Drunk and acting on a dare.'

She flicked back her strawberry-blonde locks. 'Well, you certainly paid for your stupidity.'

'I'd like to repay you somehow.'

'Mabel paid for the repairs at the time.'

No one had told him that. Had his nan gone around fixing all his damage? He wished he could ask her. Apologize to her. But Mabel was gone. All he could do was try to make amends where he could. Let them all see his remorse. His shame.

'Perhaps there's some other way I can make it up to you. Sweep the floor, deliver some flowers—'

'Clean the window you smashed?' Lottie quirked an eyebrow.

Jamie nodded. 'Yeah, even that.' He glanced over at the doorway leading to the back room as a tall dark-haired man appeared.

Lottie immediately followed his gaze, and judging by the glare in the man's amber eyes, Jamie figured he'd overheard their conversation and was probably Lottie's partner.

'Sam, this is Jamie Stark. Mabel's grandson.' Lottie turned back to Jamie. 'This is Samuel Powell, my partner.'

'I guess you heard us just now,' said Jamie.

Lottie spoke before Samuel had a chance. 'Yes, he did, but you've said sorry, so we're going to wipe the slate clean and leave it at that.' She gave Samuel a knowing look, which he seemed to understand.

'Thank you,' said Jamie.

'I'm not doing it for you,' she replied. 'When my brother came in earlier to tell me you were back and living at the B&B, I knew I'd have to give you a second chance for Alice's sake. If she's taken you in, then she must really believe in you. And I have full trust in her.'

Jamie glanced behind Samuel. 'Where's Spencer? I'd like to apologize to him as well.'

'He's out in the van, delivering Christmas wreaths.'

'I'll catch up with him later.' Jamie gave a slight nod, then turned for the door, glancing at the tinsel-adorned window.

'I really do hope you've changed, Jamie,' Lottie said.

'I have.' He closed the door.

A seagull swooped low to a mesh bin a little further along the pavement, gaining Jamie's attention for a moment. There weren't many people about, and cars were few as he crossed the road to stare out to sea. Some of the things he'd missed most while in prison was the sound of the waves, the scent of the harbour, and the cry of the gulls.

He didn't have many memories about his mum, but one was of them eating ice cream along the front, smiling, happy.

His grandmother had once told him that his dad only hit the bottle after the death of his beloved. Jamie had never figured out why his father had to be so cruel to everyone though. As he got older, he understood his dad being heartbroken, but hating his kids was something Jamie couldn't get his head around until he had therapy in prison and discovered what pain could do to a person.

He leaned on a wall, staring over at a white yacht in the distance. 'I was just like you,' he whispered into the wind.

I hated life.

He glanced over his shoulder at the Happy to Help Hub, knowing Alice was inside.

He realized it was stranger being home than being free. He could have gone anywhere to start over, but knew he had to return. For years he had planned his apologies. To help his community somehow. Not so he could stay, but because Port Berry deserved better.

A bitter breeze blew through his dark hair, taking his breath for a second, but he continued to stare out at the rolling waves, enjoying the sound, the smell.

'Hey, you okay?' came Alice's voice behind him.

He turned to see her shiver. 'It's cold, Angel. Go back inside.'

She snuggled into herself instead. 'I like watching the sea, too.'

He smiled softly, wishing he could place an arm around her, hold her closer to his body warmth. 'I'm having a weird day.'

Alice breathed out a huff of a laugh. 'You and me both.'

He turned to face her, then noticed the old lady standing behind them, her midnight-blue eyes boring into his soul.

Alice followed his gaze. 'Nan?'

Jamie turned fully. 'Hello, Luna.'

'You know me, Jamie. You know I see and hear things others don't. I'm here to tell you Mabel is happy you're home. She can see your truth and is proud of the man you now are.'

'Nan!' Alice snapped. 'This isn't the time for one of your psychic readings.'

'Yes, Alice, it is.' And with that, Luna marched off, swiping her white hair from her cheeks.

Jamie wasn't sure if he believed people could talk to the dead, but it would be comforting to think his grandmother could see into his soul and know he had changed. He wished so badly she had contacted him in prison, then he could have told her.

'Are you okay?' asked Alice.

'Alice, did you ever tell my nan you were in contact with me?'

'I never told anyone.'

He bobbed his head.

'I'm sorry she didn't write to you. Perhaps she was going to but didn't know where to start. You know what they say, the longer you leave something and all that.'

He saw her shiver as a gust of wind blew up. 'It's okay. Come on, let's get back to the B&B.'

'Yeah, Benny will be home soon.'

Jamie took a calming breath, all thoughts on Alice's nephew. He knew she'd raised Benny as her own for the past eight years, and even though she'd spoken to the lad about living arrangements, Jamie just hoped Benny really was okay about the setup.

CHAPTER 5

Alice

Benny came home just as Alice was dishing up dinner in the kitchen. As it wasn't a meal she had to prepare for guests, she could take her time and potter around at her own leisure. Only this time, she felt like a bag of nerves.

'What's the matter with you?' he asked, approaching the sink to wash his hands.

She smiled falsely. 'Nothing.'

There was laughter in his blue eyes. 'You've got a weird look on your face.'

Alice frowned. 'I'm just cooking dinner, that's all.'

Benny peered over her shoulder at the fish pie she'd taken out of the oven. 'Never play poker. You'd lose every time.'

She nudged him with her hip. 'Erm, excuse me, but I can lie, thank you.'

'Ah-ha! So, you are hiding something. Come on, Mum, tell me.'

It always warmed Alice's heart when he called her that, as mostly he called her by her name. She hoped her sister would approve. No one ever struck lightning on her, so maybe

29

Lisa was all right with it. Alice wished she knew for sure, but for some reason Lisa never sent messages to their psychic grandmother.

'I haven't got any secrets or lies to tell, Benny.'

'There's definitely something going on.'

She moved his hand away from the green beans she'd drained of boiling water. 'Something did happen today that I want to talk to you about.'

'Knew it.' He snaffled some food.

'Will you stop eating the beans? Go sit down, and I'll bring your dinner over.'

His dark hair flopped onto his brow as it crinkled. 'Why are there three plates?'

'That's what I want to tell you.'

Benny scrunched his nose. 'Oh, please don't tell me you've brought a date home and this is the meet and greet.'

Alice frowned. 'You once told me you'd be fine if I dated again.'

'I am fine about it, but I'm not too sure meeting your love interest over fish pie is the way to go.'

Alice chuckled as she dished him up a portion. 'I don't have a love interest. Anyway, there's nothing wrong with fish pie.'

Benny folded his arms, giving the impression he wouldn't eat a morsel until she got to her point.

She knew that he would last all of one minute and proved the point by handing him a fork.

Benny started to tuck in. 'Spit it out, Alice. Who is plate three?'

'Jamie Stark.'

Benny stopped eating mid-chew.

'He was released today.' She pointed at the ceiling. 'He's staying in room one.'

'Does Nan and Granny know?'

Alice nodded. 'Yeah. Your nan is still processing, but your granny seems okay.'

30

Benny glanced around the kitchen. 'I wonder what Mabel would think.'

'She would have put a roof over his head.'

'How are you feeling?'

'I'm all right. It was a bit of a shock at first, because I wasn't expecting him till next year, but he's here now, and he's going to find work and settle down. Show everyone he's changed.' She glanced at the door as Jamie walked in, looking sheepish.

'Sorry, I was outside and heard you talking about me, and I wasn't sure whether to come in or not.' Jamie smiled over at Benny. 'You've grown. Do you remember me?'

Benny shrugged. 'Not really.'

Alice manoeuvred Jamie to the table to sit, then set about bringing over their dinner. 'Ah, you were just seven when Jamie last saw you.'

'I wasn't around much, though,' said Jamie. 'Flittered about back then.'

Benny went back to eating. 'I've heard all about you.'

Jamie bobbed his head. 'Well, whatever you've heard, it's probably all true.'

'But that's in the past,' said Alice. 'This is Jamie's fresh start.'

Benny raised his fork. 'Hope life treats you better this time around, mate.'

Alice bit her lip, suppressing a grin.

'Thanks,' said Jamie, smiling. 'I hope so too.'

'So,' said Benny, still munching away. 'I see you put up the Crimbo bits. But why no lights outside?'

Alice was so glad of the subject change, but then frowned at the question. 'There are fairy lights around the bushes. Jamie put them on earlier.'

Jamie nodded. 'And I put some on that mini tree out there.'

Benny raised his eyebrows. 'Well, they're not there now.'

Alice jumped up. 'Oh no, you're kidding.' She dashed outside to see for herself.

Jamie came up behind her. 'Someone has had it on their toes with them.'

'Check the security footage,' said Benny, standing in the doorway.

Alice sprinted across the foyer. 'Good idea.' She fired up the laptop, then let Benny do the rest. He was much better at the technical stuff.

The time on the footage told them that the thief had untangled the lights about half an hour before Benny came home and had shoved them under a bush.

Jamie pointed at the screen. 'Look, there's someone.'

They all zoomed in to see the hooded, masked thug walking off.

'Now why would someone do that?' questioned Alice.

Jamie nudged Benny. 'Come on, let's go get them.'

Alice went to the main door, watching them as they rummaged around the bush. 'I've never heard of this kind of thing happening before.' She shook her head.

'I'll switch them on, see if they still work,' Jamie said.

'Do you think I should call the police?' asked Alice. 'I know we've got the lights back, and we can't identify the masked man, so I'm not sure what to do.'

Benny nodded. 'Yes, let them know. Even if they can't do anything right now, at least they know someone has done this. There might be other reports in the area.'

Alice nodded. 'True.' She smiled at Jamie, on his knees by the plug socket, then went to the desk to make the call.

'This one's working,' he said.

Benny took it from him as soon as it was unplugged. 'I'm surprised they didn't try to hide the extension lead.'

Jamie frowned. 'It's a lot of bother popping in here just to unplug fairy lights only to dump them in the bush. Anything else happened around here?'

Alice was half listening to the woman on the phone and half listening to Jamie and Benny.

'No,' said Benny. 'Oh, except that fire we had the other month.'

'What fire?'

Benny pointed to the entrance. 'Just a small one that burned the carpet. That's why we have wooden flooring now.'

'How did it start?'

'We think one of the guests was smoking.'

Alice got off the phone. 'They're sending someone over to see the footage. Not that it'll help, but at least it's been reported now.'

Jamie looked up. 'All the lights still work. Should we put them back up?'

'Yes. Let's not let them beat us.' She gestured to the front. 'Seaview B&B will look festive, whether they like it or not.'

It wasn't long before the lights were back in place, the police had arrived to check everyone was okay, and dinner was finally finished.

Benny had gone to bed, and all the guests were in their room for the night, so Alice locked up, hoping her fairy lights were still there come morning.

'Oh, what a day,' she said quietly as she climbed the stairs with Jamie.

He turned at his door, smiling her way. 'Is there any reason you've walked me to my room?'

Alice hadn't even realized what she had done. 'Oh, I'm too tired. I'm not thinking straight. Sorry.'

'Ah, and there was me thinking you were worried about me, what with the Grinch on the loose.'

Alice managed a chuckle. 'Let's hope tomorrow is less eventful.' She peered into the room as he opened the door. 'I reckon you'll get a good night's sleep.'

He glanced at the bed, then her. 'It'll be different, that's for sure.'

'If you need anything, you know where I am.'

'Same.'

Alice stood there for a moment, simply staring at him. It was all she could do to stop herself from reaching out and giving him a hug. 'Welcome home, Jamie,' she said softly.

'Sleep well, Angel.'

Part of her heart melted as she walked away.

CHAPTER 6

Jamie

Jamie walked into The Butterfly Company, not knowing what to expect. He scanned the large open-plan foyer, seeing colourful seating, a large Christmas tree, and a white reception desk. The big windows allowed a lot of light to shine across the room, making the area look warm and inviting.

'Hi, how may I help you?' asked the female receptionist, her beam showing perfectly straight teeth.

'I have an appointment with Henley Foster.'

'Please take a seat and I'll let him know you're here.'

An athletic man with amber eyes entered the foyer. 'No need. I'm already here.'

For some reason, Jamie had imagined the social worker to be a lot older than this fella who looked around his own age.

Jamie shook his hand and followed him to a side room. 'So, is this just about work? I've not been to one of these places before.' He remembered the last time he was in Penzance. Stealing cars with his mates wasn't the best memory to have while sitting in a centre designed to help ex-offenders.

'We do quite a few things here,' said Henley, flipping open a file on the table between them. 'I can help you find work, offer group therapy sessions, enrol you for further education.'

'Go back to the group therapy. I had some one-to-one in prison, but what do you do in a group? Is it like those sobriety ones?'

'It's more of a safe place for ex-offenders to talk about their life. How they're coping, what works for them, that sort of thing. It can be helpful for some to be around those with understanding.'

Jamie liked the sound of that. 'When's the next one?'

'Tomorrow evening, upstairs.'

'I'll be there.'

'Great. Now, let's talk work placement. I see here you did some courses at your prison.'

'Yes, I did GCSE English and maths, and desktop publishing. One of the men in my group used to create websites for a living, and I liked the idea of doing something like that.'

'Okay, with that in mind, I know of an evening course you could start in January to learn that skill.'

'Really? That would be great.'

Henley scribbled something down while humming, then glanced up. 'Meanwhile, what about a day job?'

'A friend just offered me some shifts at his café or tea-room, and they're both along the road where I live.'

Henley glanced at his file. 'Harbour End Road. Ah, was that Ginny Dean, by any chance?'

'Her partner, Will.'

'Kind of him. It might be worth taking him up on the offer. You'll have something for the day, then come the new year you can get stuck in to your course and, who knows, by springtime, you could start your own website design business. We can help with that too. There's a woman here who knows all about how to run a small business, tax accounts, that sort of thing. I can book you in for a chat with her after you've completed your course.'

Jamie felt a little overwhelmed. He'd made the plans, but now they actually seemed doable. It was quite exciting to have a glimpse of the future.

'We'll take it one step at a time, Jamie. Always the best way.'

'It feels a bit strange, if I'm honest. This day always felt so far away. You know, just dreams, hopes. But I can see how close it is to me now. How I can do this.'

'There's a difference between dreams and goals. You did the dream part, wishing, wanting, and now you're taking the steps that lead to your goals. It's the action that makes things work.'

'I'm ready to take action. I'm ready for my life.'

Henley smiled. 'I can see. Just keep your focus, and trust the process.' He raised a palm. 'Yeah, I know. I sound like a motivational bumper sticker, but it's true. If you know what you want, go for it, and don't let excuses get in your way.'

Jamie was already fired up to get started. 'It'll be December in a couple of days. So, not long now.'

'Christmas will be different for you this year.'

Even though the holiday was fast approaching, he hadn't thought about the big day. His mind had been occupied with building a future. And on Alice.

'It certainly will.'

The rest of the meeting flew by, and Jamie left feeling inspired and grateful.

He headed for the shops to buy some clothes, visualizing his grandmother in a frenzy clearing out his bedroom. It was so unlike her to do such a thing, but he understood her frustration and anger. It wasn't as though he had made life easy for her.

It was quite surreal, shopping. The last time he was in a clothes shop, he'd stolen a belt. He felt a tad proud of himself paying for his goods, even though it was his nan's money. It just made him feel like everyone else. Normal.

He wondered if he'd ever shake off the bad memories. If anyone had accomplished such a task.

With a handful of carrier bags, he jumped on the bus to head home.

'Hey, Jamie.' Demi waved a hand.

He smiled on seeing her and sat by her side. 'Hello. Excuse my bags.' He moved some to his lap so her feet weren't squashed with how many he had.

'Looks like someone had fun shopping.'

'I thought I'd get a bit done after my appointment at The Butterfly Company.'

'Ooh, how did that go?'

'Good. I'm going to be doing an evening course at college next year. So, I just need to get a day job, which I'm hoping to sort once I've dropped these bags home.'

'What kind of job?'

'In the café or tearoom along the front. The owner offered me some shifts. Thought I'd take him up on it.'

'Yes, definitely get involved there. Will's a lovely man. Very friendly. And, not sure if you know, but Harbour Light Café has two nights a week where it opens as a food bank café for a couple of hours, serving dinner to those in need. It's part of the Les Powell Trust. Not sure if you've heard of that. It's run by Samuel Powell.'

'Lottie's partner?'

'Yes, that's the one. See if you can do some voluntary work there. All looks good on a CV, you know. And let's face it, we need all the help we can get when we have a —' she lowered her voice — 'criminal record.'

Jamie nodded. 'Did you find it hard?'

'I was lucky, because I'm a trained chef, so I got placed quite quickly but then the restaurant closed down. Robson offered me a temporary job at his pub, then Alice gave me the role at hers.'

'Would you like your own restaurant one day?'

Demi scoffed. 'No thanks. It's too much stress. Anyway, with my menu at the B&B, and my online stuff, I'm happy enough.'

'What's your online stuff?'

'When I first got out, I lived on my own and was a little lonely for a while so, in my spare time, I started creating short videos showing how to make cheap and easy meals for one. I had no idea it would turn me into some sort of food influencer. I get paid to advertise on my socials now.'

Jamie breathed out a small laugh. 'You just never know where life will take you.'

'I know, right.'

'I joined group therapy at the centre as well, so that's something new for me to try.'

'I'll be there tomorrow for that.' Demi pulled out her phone. 'I go to sobriety ones as well, and you know how we have sponsors that help us when we're feeling on edge, so to speak?'

Jamie nodded.

'Well, we can have the same sort of thing at Butterfly. So, if you want, we could swap numbers, and any time you feel you might slip into your old ways, you can call me to talk you down.'

He appreciated her kindness. 'I don't have a phone just yet.'

'Let me write my number down for you. You can always ring from the B&B if you need me.' She removed a small notepad from her handbag and jotted down her number. 'It's up to you.'

He didn't feel he needed it but took the torn paper anyway, thanking her.

They got off the bus and headed towards their homes, saying goodbye at the Jolly Pirate pub.

Jamie was about to head inside the B&B when he spotted Will outside the tearoom just along the road. He called out, then made his way over.

'Hey, Jamie. Been shopping, I see.'

Jamie glanced at his bags. 'Yeah. Hey, listen, I was wondering if I could talk to you about any shifts going.'

'Sure, come inside. I'll grab you a coffee or something.'

Jamie followed him into the cosy tea shop and sat at the table near the window, pleased to see no one had swiped the tearoom's Christmas lights. At least whoever had taken Alice's didn't return for another go.

He leaned back against the exposed brick wall and placed a hand on the boat-print tablecloth, thinking how nice everything looked. The scent of fresh coffee filled the air, and a waft of chocolate cake came from a woman's plate at a nearby table.

'Tea or coffee?' asked Will. 'Or hot chocolate?'

'Black coffee is fine, thanks.'

Will brought the drinks over, then gestured at the glass counter by the till. 'You want some cake?'

'No, thanks. Spoil my lunch.' Jamie laughed.

'So, tell me, Jamie, what you've got in mind. Café or tearoom?'

'I'm not fussed. Wherever you need your floors mopping.'

'Oh, I'm sure we can get you doing a bit more than that.'

'I've got an evening course lined up to start in January, so I just need some daytime work until I get the skills I need to start my own business.'

Will beamed like a proud father. 'Brilliant. Doing what?'

'Website design.'

'Lottie runs the website for the Hub. She's self-taught, but perhaps she could give you a few pointers while you're waiting for your course to begin.'

It was a nice thought, but he wasn't too sure Lottie had forgiven him enough to sit side by side with him as his teacher.

He stayed awhile with Will, arranging shifts, mostly at the café, then headed back home, looking forward to seeing Alice.

Benny was behind the desk, reading.

'No school?'

'Heating went, so we got sent home.'

'Alice about?'

'Nope. She's gone to a bridesmaid fitting for Sophie's wedding.'

Just for a second, Jamie visualized Alice dressed as a bride. Any man would be lucky to have her, he knew.

'She said to tell you there's lunch in the fridge with your name on it.' Benny carried on reading his book.

Jamie went to his room and plopped his bags down, feeling he'd had a productive day so far. He couldn't wait to tell Alice how everything went with Henley.

Glancing down at the bed, he smiled at how it had taken him a moment to gather his bearings when he'd woken at six that morning. He still couldn't believe he was home.

He opened the balcony door and stepped outside to inhale the fresh salty air. Even though it was cold, it didn't matter. The sea breeze on his face lifted him higher.

'Oi, Stark!' came a voice from the street.

Jamie peered down to see someone from his past. 'Gregg?'

'I heard you were out.'

'News travels fast around here.'

The lanky man stepped closer to the B&B. 'Come down, I might have a job for you.'

Jamie shook his head. 'Not in that game anymore, mate. New life now.'

'Oh, come on, Stark. Easy money.'

'There's more to life than money.'

Gregg scoffed. 'Since when?'

Jamie waved one hand. 'Don't knock for me, Greggy-boy. I'm not playing out.'

Gregg grinned. 'You know how to find me.'

Jamie watched his past walk away, knowing that was where it was going to stay. He didn't blame Gregg for trying, reaching out in his own way, but unlike Gregg, Jamie had grown up and moved on.

Benny came into sight, first glancing down the road, then looking up at Jamie's balcony.

Jamie stared back, raising a palm.

Oh, so you heard that.

In a way, Jamie was glad Benny had heard the conversation, because at least it showed the old days were over. He went inside and caught a glance at himself in the mirror, feeling pretty pleased with life.

Yep, it's been a productive morning.

CHAPTER 7

Alice

Alice gazed at herself in the full-length silver mirror in the wedding shop. Her long crimson bridesmaid dress fitted her tall slim frame perfectly. She had never felt so pretty.

Lottie poured some champagne at a nearby table. 'It doesn't look like you need any more alterations done, Alice.'

Alice glanced at the hem. 'I agree. I think I'm ready.' She turned to Ginny. 'How about you, Gin?'

Ginny was checking out a row of shoes. 'I can't see myself losing any more baby weight before the wedding, so I'll stick with this size. I'm going to pick the four-inch heels though. Help give me some height.'

Alice pointed at the flat pair. 'I'll take those, then we'll level out a bit in the photos.'

Ginny laughed. 'You'll still be taller than me, Al. Everyone's taller than me.'

'Have you forgotten I'm in a wheelchair,' said Lottie, tapping her push rim.

Ginny took the glass of bubbly Lottie offered. 'Yeah, but you said you're going to use the chair that stands you upright.'

Lottie smiled. 'Only for going down the aisle. It shows off my dress better.'

Alice stepped away from the mirror. 'Good luck to you, Gin, wearing high heels all day. Honestly, I'm taking my slippers to change into once the lights go down and the party starts.'

Ginny raised her glass. 'That's a good idea, chick.'

Lottie beamed. 'How exciting is it that our Soph is getting married?'

'I'm so glad she met Matt,' said Alice. 'She deserves happiness.'

'Thank you,' came Sophie's voice from behind thick cream drapes.

'You ready yet?' asked Ginny, stepping closer to the changing area.

'One sec,' called back Sophie.

Ginny turned to Lottie. 'Are you sure you want to do everyone's hair and makeup on the day? We can always hire someone so you can just focus on yourself.'

'I love doing hair and makeup.' Lottie quirked an eyebrow beneath her full fringe. 'I was winner of Miss South-West Beauty Pageant, three years in a row, remember. If anyone knows how to apply foundation correctly, it's me.'

Alice glanced once more in the mirror. 'I'd love to be Miss Port Berry.' She looked at Lottie, sipping champagne. 'What was it like, Lott, representing your hometown in the competition?'

'Nerve-wracking at first, but then I got used to it. You tend to see a lot of the same faces in those contests, so I made a few friends during that time.'

'You should enter again,' said Ginny, trying on cherry-red shoes.

Lottie scrunched her nose. 'Nah, I prefer entering charity races now. Plus, I have my art. And my gorgeous nephew keeps me busy.'

Alice cooed. 'Aw, how is Archie? I can't believe he's one already. This year has flown by.'

Lottie smiled. 'He's doing great. Keeps Spencer on his toes. Oh, I can't wait to see Archie in his little pageboy suit.'

Ginny nodded. 'Robert has one too. It's beyond adorable.'

Alice ran a finger along the smooth texture of a shoe while thinking how wonderful it would be to have a baby. It wasn't something she mulled over too often, as Benny was her child, so she never felt she was missing out on motherhood, but with Jamie back in her life full time, lots of locked away feelings were starting to creep through.

'Your Benny will look a beaut as an usher, eh, chick?' Ginny nudged Alice out of her trance.

'Yes, he's so excited. But he won't tell me a thing about his outfit. Said I have to wait until the big day.'

'Speaking of which.' Ginny turned to the curtain. 'How's it going, Soph?'

The assistant pulled back the drape and Sophie stepped out, looking every bit the blushing bride.

The ladies all cooed as Sophie headed for the mirror, with the assistant splaying out the bottom of the floaty white dress.

'Oh, chick, you look amazing.' Ginny swiped away a tear, and Alice hugged her.

'I feel like a princess,' said Sophie, holding up her dark hair for the assistant to clip in place. Her green eyes sparkled at her friends. 'And you all look so pretty.'

Alice picked up a champagne flute and handed it to Sophie. 'Let's have a toast.'

Everyone raised their glasses.

'To love,' said Alice. 'And every happily ever after.'

'Cheers,' said Lottie.

The women laughed, then huddled together at the mirror.

'I love you lot.' Sophie sounded slightly choked.

'We love you too,' said Alice, water filling her eyes.

Ginny sat down on a cream loveseat. 'Have you decided on a honeymoon spot yet?'

Sophie nodded, turning so the assistant could pin the hem. 'Grandad is sailing us over to France on Samuel's yacht, then we're touring the country for a few weeks in a campervan.'

'Ooh, lovely,' said Alice.

Ginny chuckled. 'I reckon Jed will be in his element on that beauty.'

Lottie smiled. 'Sam wants to do the same thing one day. We're hoping to sail over to France next summer.'

'We're not going till after Christmas though,' said Sophie. 'We want to spend that with Grandad.'

'Will you be shutting up shop?' asked Ginny.

'No. We've arranged a roster while we're away. Beth is helping while the schools are closed for the holiday, even though I told her teachers should put their feet up. But it was her idea. Plus, we have Demi, Robson, and Samuel all signed up.'

Lottie laughed. 'I can't wait to see Sam behind the counter, selling fish. He reckons he's looking forward to being a fishmonger, but I told him there are skills to gutting fish.'

'Grandad will do that part,' said Sophie. 'Everyone else will just be shop assistants.'

'Sea Shanty Shack won't be the same without you, Soph,' said Ginny. 'But I'm sure your temp staff will cope.'

Sophie nodded. 'I have great faith all will be fine. Besides, Grandad could run that place blindfolded with one hand tied behind his back. And Robson's helped out before. Plus, he and Demi have hygiene and health-and-safety certificates under their belts.'

Alice raised her glass as she swirled. 'So, no more talk of fish, this is our last dress fitting. Let's speak about all things romantic.'

'Hmm,' said Lottie. 'Like you and Jamie.'

Alice stopped spinning. 'There is no me and Jamie.'

Lottie widened her eyes. 'Please try to remember we grew up together. I know you always had a thing for him.' She glanced at Ginny. 'In fact, it's quite possible you were the only true friend he ever had.'

'Well, that doesn't mean we have a thing now.' Alice downed the rest of her drink and sat on a velvet-covered chair.

'You've let him move in with you,' said Lottie.

'He's got one of the rooms, not my room.'

Lottie's face held a sympathetic look. 'Just be careful.'

Sophie approached them as the shop assistant went out back. 'I thought we were all about giving people second chances. It's why we set up the Happy to Help Hub, right?'

Ginny nodded.

'So, I think we should do our best to help Jamie settle back here, as I can only imagine how alone he must be feeling,' she continued.

Lottie sighed. 'You're right, Soph. And I will make more of an effort when I see him.' She turned to Alice. 'He came in my shop and apologized for smashing the window way back when. He did seem different. Just in the way he carried himself, you know.'

'Life has a way of changing us,' said Ginny.

'Okay, I have an idea.' Lottie reached for Alice's hand. 'How about we invite him for dinner with us at the pub one evening?'

Alice warmed at her friends' kindness. They all knew about Jamie's past, so she understood their concerns, but as Sophie had reminded everyone, they had created a Hub designed to give people a second chance or a helping hand.

'I'll ask him. See if he's up for a mingle.' Alice smiled a thank you at Sophie. 'Now, let's get back to this wedding.'

CHAPTER 8

Jamie

It was nice sitting in the kitchen with Alice and Benny, each talking about their day, and when Jamie shared his news of the upcoming college course and his shifts at the café and tearoom, it warmed him to see Alice so happy.

Benny went off to do some homework, and Alice asked Jamie if he'd like to go for a walk.

'You do like your walks.'

Alice chuckled, wrapping herself in a coat, hat, and scarf. 'I like to use my legs while I can.'

He followed her out into the brisk chill. 'While you can?'

She gave a brief nod. 'There's something about me I haven't told you.'

He felt his stomach flip. 'Should I be worried?'

'No, it's okay. It's just, well, I have a medical condition called fibromyalgia. Basically, I'm in some sort of pain every day, but I measure it on a scale of one to ten, and quite often I'm around two to four, so not bad. Some days my knees play me up, and I can't get around much. So when the going is good, I like to oil my joints, so to speak, by going for walks or doing some light yoga. In the summer, I jog round the block with Robson. It's more of a power walk, but still.' She grinned.

'I'm so sorry to hear that. Is there anything I can do to help?'

'Not really. Flare-ups tend to happen if I've been out in the rain or freezing cold too long or if I'm stressed, so as long as you don't stress me, my levels will stay low.'

He saw her smile but knew there was truth in her statement, and he vowed to himself to help bring peace to her life as much as possible. 'How long have you had it?'

'It started about six months after Lisa died.'

He lowered his head as they started walking. 'Yeah, that was a tough year for you.'

'You too.'

Jamie hated being such a mess back then. It was the one time he could have been there for Alice, but no. He had to go and get himself arrested and sent to prison. 'I'm sorry I wasn't there for you.'

'It's done now,' she said quietly, staring over at the calm sea.

Jamie sighed silently, keeping his focus on the multi-coloured Christmas lights on the windows of each house or shop they passed. There were some things in life that would always haunt him, and the year Alice needed him was one.

'Benny told me Gregg stopped by,' she said, breaking the silence.

He saw her arms tighten a little around herself, and he wasn't sure if she was just warming herself or feeling tense. 'That's right. Gregg was just testing the water.'

'Do you think he'll be back?'

Jamie stopped, turning to face her. 'I told him not to return. Please don't worry, Angel. Gregg doesn't get to live in this part of my story.'

She slowly nodded, then tucked her chin down into her dark scarf.

'You warm enough?' he asked, giving the wool a gentle tug up to her mouth.

'I'm okay. I've learned how to work with my body over the years, and I'm pacing myself so I won't be ill for the Port Berry Christmas tree lighting.'

'They still do that?'

'On the first Saturday in December every year.'

Jamie laughed. 'I think I was a kid the last time I went to that.' He stopped smiling. 'I never really cared about much in my teens.'

'No, you didn't.'

He met her eyes, seeing the regret he felt. 'Seems I have a lot to catch up with.'

'You want to go?'

Jamie nodded. 'Yep. I'm working at the tea shop that day, and seeing how it closes at four, I'll be able to pop along and watch the event. Is it still at Old Market Square?'

'Yep. Do you want to go together?'

He grinned as they made their way over to the short pier across the road. 'Are you asking me on a date, Alice?'

Alice blew out a laugh. 'No.'

'Ah, well, never mind. I'll still go with you.'

They leaned on a rail, listening to the hum of the water washing against the pilings.

Jamie looked up at the stars. 'It's absolutely beautiful out here.' He'd never been one to stop and smell the flowers, but since walking out of prison, he noticed everything, big or small, and so much about life now made him smile on the inside.

'It's peaceful when the sea is calm.'

'I'm a big fan of peace and calm nowadays.'

Alice smiled. 'Me too.'

They stared down into the dark water.

'Jamie, is there anything you haven't told me?'

He gazed her way, frowning. 'Is this about Gregg?'

'No. I just know that when we used to write to each other, we kept it light. So, I wondered if anything might have happened to you that you'd like to talk about now you're out of that place.'

He shook his head, then went back to looking out to sea. 'No. I pretty much told you everything in those letters. I know there wasn't much to tell during the first couple of years, but once I settled down, I was happy to share all the positive things going on with me.'

'I was worried more about the negative stuff.'

'I didn't get into any more fights after I started therapy.'

Alice leaned a little closer. 'I was thinking more about your health.'

'Ah.' Now it made more sense what was playing on her mind. 'I never had any health scares.'

'Would you have told me?'

He nodded. 'Yes. I never hid any of my cancer worries from you. Why would I? You've seen me at my worst. Mopped my brow and read me to sleep. You were always there throughout my treatment. I remember you trying to keep me up to date with school work, and the times you'd just sit and hold my hand. You're my angel.'

'It's what friends are for.'

He wanted to place his arm around her shoulder and give her a gentle squeeze, but thought it best to keep his arms to himself. 'You went above and beyond. We both know that.'

They shared a warm smile, then Alice looked away.

'I'm surprised you never went into nursing or something along those lines, especially after Lisa,' he added. 'Have you got any more presentations lined up before the schools break for Christmas?'

'No. No one's going to want me educating them about smear tests just before Christmas. I've got my next talk booked in at a uni in the springtime.'

'It's good what you do.'

Alice smiled at the black sky. 'I do it for my sister. Raising awareness is important to me. Perhaps Lisa's story can help save someone's life. And so many young girls come up to me after my talks to tell me they didn't know women could get cervical cancer that young. They're shocked when they discover Lisa was only twenty-seven.'

'I reckon you've saved lives. It's what the angels that walk among us do.'

'You are getting mushy in your old age, you know that?'

Jamie smiled. 'I realized a long time ago, life's too short to be angry all the time. I like my softer side.'

'You're softer than you act.'

He raised his brow. 'Is that right?'

Alice shivered, snuggling further into her scarf.

'Time to get back,' he said, pulling off the rail. 'How about some hot chocolate? It's almost Christmas, so I'm thinking, cinnamon, and a candy cane on the side of the mug, perhaps.'

Alice nodded as they made their way over to the B&B. 'Not sure I have any candy canes yet, but there's definitely cinnamon.'

'I remember Nan used to put a bowl of sweets at reception each year for guests.'

'Ooh, yes. I'll buy some. And candy canes.'

'You could put them on the tree.'

Alice nodded. 'With some chocolates. I haven't got many guests staying, but you never know who might pop in. Plus, we get lunch customers now, so they might like that.'

'Are you booked in for Christmas dinner at the pub again?'

'Yes, but I'm only going there now if you come, too. Otherwise, we'll eat at home.'

Jamie didn't want her changing her traditions because of him. 'You just do what you always do.'

Alice grinned. 'What, look after you?'

'Hmm.'

She nudged his side. 'You've been invited to eat at Robson's with us beforehand. So, you could try it out if you like?'

He helped her remove her coat in the foyer. 'Who invited me?'

'It was Lottie's idea.'

Even though she was faffing with her hat and scarf, he could see her eyes held hope. He didn't want to let her down.

'Okay, well, I have group therapy tomorrow evening, so how about the evening after?'

'Sure. I'll see if I can get that arranged.'

Jamie headed for the stairs. 'I'll just put my coat away, then come make those drinks. You can put your feet up.'

Alice called after him. 'Bring your new clothes down with you, and I'll pop them in the machine for a wash. It's always nice to wash new stuff before wearing.'

'I'm not fussed. And anyway, I can sort that tomorrow. I know where the washing machine is. If it's still in the same place?'

She grinned. 'I think it's the same machine.'

Jamie laughed to himself as he entered his room. His nan always seemed to make things last. He hung his coat up in the oak wardrobe, then tipped his clothes out of the shopping bags and onto the bed.

She kept some of my things.

The memory had him shoot off to the storage room. It was locked, so he called out the back to Alice to ask where the key was.

Benny came out and opened a drawer beneath the desk. 'Alice is just in the bathroom. Here you go.'

'Thanks. I'll put it back in a minute.'

Benny went back to his room, and Jamie entered the storage section to search for anything he recognized.

Within a minute, he noticed two cardboard boxes with his name on, so he picked them up and moved them to the reception desk so he could lock up and put the key away.

He had no idea what his nan had saved so was a little intrigued.

As he placed the boxes on the floor in his room, he pondered over opening them there and then, but Alice would be waiting for him to make hot chocolate, so he decided whatever of his past was tucked away, it could wait.

CHAPTER 9

Alice

All morning, all Alice could think about was the night before. How she'd snuggled on the sofa in her living room with a blanket and hot chocolate and Jamie. They'd pretty much talked all night, bringing up funny memories, and Alice catching him up on any local news since her last letter.

She hadn't known at the time it would be the last time she'd write to him in prison. She wondered if she might have written something other than the usual Port Berry updates.

None of it mattered now. He was home, and she could just speak to his face whenever she wanted. No security checks, no PO box usage, and no missing his voice.

The phone rang on the reception desk, disturbing her thoughts.

'Hello. Seaview B&B. Alice speaking. How may I help you?'

There was no reply, so she waited a moment, then tried again, but still no one spoke, so she hung up. The phone rang again immediately, and once more no one was on the other end.

54

Alice hung up while reaching for her mobile phone so she could test the landline. For a whole week last month, she'd had calls where she couldn't hear the other person. The last thing she needed was the business phone to give up the ghost. Lots of her guests liked to book that way.

She called the B&B number and all seemed to be well, so at least she knew the problem wasn't her end.

Heading for the laundry room, Alice wondered how Jamie was getting on with his first shift at the café. She was dying to go over for a nosey. He hadn't seemed nervous at all last night, but she knew he was good at hiding his true feelings.

Alice pulled out her phone again and sent a message on the group chat, asking her friends for some sort of welcome home dinner at the pub the following evening for Jamie.

'It will be good for you to hang out with positive people doing good in this world,' she mumbled, transferring white towels from the washing machine to the tumble dryer.

'You talking to yourself, Al?' asked Demi, poking her head around the door.

Alice breathed out a small laugh. 'I think I spend half my life talking to myself. I have a busy brain.'

Demi grinned. 'Mine's usually occupied with recipes.'

'Were you about to head off?'

'Yeah, I'm going to take Champ over the park for a walk before I have to get ready for lunch.'

Alice smiled, thinking of the rescue dog Demi had saved. 'He's doing so well now, isn't he?'

'Oh, yes, he's loving life, especially his bed. That dog does like his sleep.'

Alice yawned. 'I know how he feels.'

'Late night?'

'Jamie and I were talking way past our bedtime.'

Demi smiled. 'You're really close, aren't you?'

There had never been a way to describe the bond Alice had with Jamie, so it was hard to explain to others. She simply nodded.

'Right, I better head off. See you later.'

Alice creaked to a stand and followed Demi out to the foyer, waving off a guest as well who was off out.

Benny was off school for another day while the school's heating was fixed, so he was out the back, playing a computer game.

'I'm just popping out,' she told him. 'Won't be a minute.'

Benny laughed, not stopping his game. 'I'm surprised you lasted this long.'

Alice frowned, amused. 'What's that supposed to mean?'

'I'm dreading my first day at work. I can just see your face squashed against the window or something or casually bumping into my boss, then asking how I'm doing.'

'I wouldn't.'

Benny scoffed. 'You totally would. And you're about to do the same thing to Jamie.'

'Am not.'

'Fibber.'

Alice bit back her laugh. 'Okay, so maybe I was just going to take a small peek at the café.'

'Just like when you took a small peek in the playground on my first day at secondary school.'

She remembered the day as though it were yesterday. Her stomach had churned all night. She'd stayed up late, meticulously ironing every crease out of Benny's new uniform. Come morning she felt sick, worried he might get bullied by the bigger boys.

Alice had nothing to say on the subject. It didn't stop Benny continuing to grin. Leaving him to his game, she put on her coat and hat and figured a short walk would do her legs some good. She often passed by the café, so what difference would it make if she walked that way today?

Telling herself to act normal, to stop fretting, and to not under any circumstances enter the café, she headed out the door.

Dark clouds filled the sky, and the waves were high, rolling the boats along the harbour. Hardly anyone was about, which wasn't surprising, seeing how cold it was.

Alice stopped at the café, peering out to sea, sure it might snow any day. She hoped for a white Christmas. Something magical for Jamie's first one back home.

Just for a moment, Alice forgot she was checking on Jamie, as thoughts of tartan pyjamas, a crackling fire in the wood burner, festive wrapping paper, and the jingle jangle of holly-jolly music occupied her mind. She was going to make sure he had the best Christmas ever.

'What you doing out here?' came Sophie's voice.

Alice turned, surprised to see her. 'Oh, erm, I was . . .'

Sophie grinned. 'Staring into space?'

'Something like that.'

Sophie gestured towards her shop. 'Come inside with me. I've only been outside one minute and my lips are chapped.'

'Ooh, that won't do. Your wedding is almost here.'

'Another three weeks to go, and I want kissable lips for Matt, so come on.'

Alice followed her into Sea Shanty Shack, closing the door on the gust of wind that pretty much helped push them inside. 'Hi, Matt,' she said, giving a slight wave to the tall dark-haired man behind the cold counter.

Matt's pale blue eyes held a sparkle as Sophie kissed his cheek. 'Were you in the Hub as well, Al?'

'No, I was just going for a walk.'

Matt grimaced at the window. 'In this?'

Alice shrugged. 'Stretch the legs.'

Sophie put on her white work coat. 'I found her outside the café when I came out the Hub. Staring out to sea, day-dreaming, by the look of things.'

Alice frowned.

'Although,' added Sophie, 'I happen to know it's Jamie's first shift in the café this morning, so she was probably spying on him.' She turned to Alice. 'Will was in the Hub with me.'

Alice motioned towards the door. 'As you just pointed out, I was staring at the sea. So, no snooping at all.'

Sophie chuckled. 'Alice, we all know how much you worry about people. It's obvious you'd be thinking of Jamie today. And if it helps, Will did say Jamie was doing just fine.'

It did help, but she refused to admit that fact.

'Ask Lizzie to read his cards if you're that concerned about how his life will go from now on.'

'My mum's not talking to him, let alone whipping out the tarot for him.'

'Why isn't Lizzie talking to Jamie?' asked Matt.

Alice sighed quietly. 'She thinks he's still a rotten egg.'

'Doesn't sound like your mum to not give someone a second chance.' Matt looked at Sophie.

Sophie shrugged. 'Jamie was no angel last time he was here. It's natural for Lizzie to be wary. She'll see in time he's changed. We all will.'

'I don't need time,' said Alice. 'I already know he's a different person.'

Sophie waggled her phone. 'And we're going to do our best to help settle him back into the community. I got your dinner request, and Matt and I will be there.'

Matt nodded. 'Sophie texted me straight away. I'd like to meet him.'

Alice smiled at her friends. 'He's going to group therapy tonight with Demi at The Butterfly Company. Do you go there, Matt? I hope you don't mind me asking, but I know you spent some time in prison, so I wasn't sure if you go to those chats they have for ex-offenders.'

Matt shook his head. 'No. I've never been, but that's not to say I wouldn't. I know about those things. They help others struggling with life back out here. January Riley told me about the centre.'

Alice slapped a hand to her mouth. 'Oh, perhaps I shouldn't have mentioned it. I'm pretty sure Jamie won't mind, but still, me and my big gob.' Alice glanced at Sophie. 'I wonder if Jan will be there. She would help Jamie if he needed any extra support. She's the best therapist I know, not that I know loads. I just know she helps so many around here.'

'My advice,' said Matt. 'When it comes to people and their healing journey, it's best to let them get on with things their way.'

Sophie raised an eyebrow. 'Basically, Matt's politely telling you not to poke your nose in.'

Matt frowned. 'I'm not being rude about it, Alice. I'm just saying it's okay to offer help, by all means, but don't arrange anything for him. Let him guide you.'

Alice dipped back to one heel. 'I don't want to do anything that would harm him in any way. I just want him to, well, to stay on the straight and narrow.' She sighed, scratching beneath her hat. 'I trust him. I do, but I'd be lying if I said it didn't enter my mind, especially as he's staying at mine.'

'We're only human, Al,' said Matt. 'Soph and I talk a lot about my mental health, how I'm coping with being in recovery from addiction. I'll always have my battle with alcohol, but with the support I get, and love, I lead a good, happy life.' He smiled at Sophie.

'Jamie will too,' said Sophie. 'It's probably a bit overwhelming for him right now. The man was away for years. And if he's turned his back on crime, then it might take a while for him to find his feet doing a proper day's work. Just talk with him about his day, like we do, and give him help when he asks.'

Matt placed his arm around Sophie as she snuggled to his side. 'From the moment I met you, Alice, I could tell you were the motherly type. So, all I can say to you is, don't fuss the fella. He's a grown man, and he needs to be your equal not a project or charity case or treated as a child in need of care.'

'He's flown the nest, Alice,' said Sophie. 'Time to sit back and watch him soar.'

'You two make it sound as though I'm going to pamper him. Wrap him in cotton wool. Take charge and . . . God! I do that, don't I?'

They both nodded.

'It's not a bad trait,' said Sophie. 'You care too much, that's all.'

'I don't want to suffocate him.' She gazed out the window, wondering if she should take the long route home to avoid the café now.

'Walk by his side, Alice,' said Matt. 'No pushing, no leading, just side by side. We all need those kinds of mates.'

'He knows I fuss.' Alice chewed on her bottom lip. 'But I'll take your advice, and not get myself too involved. If Jan is at the centre tonight, she can introduce herself.' She looked at them both. 'I just want him to have good people around him.'

'He has that,' said Sophie. 'And once we've all had dinner together tomorrow night, he'll have some more.'

Alice smiled softly. 'Thanks.' She headed for the door. 'Benny reminded me what I was like on his first day at secondary school.'

Sophie laughed. 'I remember that.' She turned to Matt. 'She was worried no end. Alice does tend to overthink.'

Alice nodded. 'I do, but I'm going to go about my day now, not thinking at all. Jamie is fine. I am fine. Everything is fine.' It was worth drumming it into her head.

'It'll get easier as the days pass,' said Matt.

'You're right. He's only been out five minutes.' Alice smiled, reaching for the door handle.

'And, Al,' said Sophie gently. 'Please try to remember it's not your job to fix him. Help out like you would anyone who walked in the Hub, but don't exhaust yourself.'

Alice nodded, said goodbye, then went back outside to face the bitter wind.

If it wasn't her job to be there for Jamie, whose was it? She'd been there for him since they were kids. It was hard to hold back. But Matt was right. Jamie was a grown man, and he would want to be treated as one. He was finding his feet, and one day, those feet might take him somewhere else. Maybe far away.

Deciding not to peer in the window of the café as she passed, Alice scurried by, thinking it for the best. There was no way she wanted to act as though she were Jamie's mum.

It was so hard though, as the need to at least wave if she caught his eye was strong. But she dipped her head and carried on her way.

'Hey, Angel,' called Jamie.

She turned to see him leaning out the door of the café, tea towel slung over one shoulder.

'You not going to pop in to say hello?' He was smiling.

Alice rushed up to him, quickly stopping herself from giving him a huge hug. 'I have to get back.'

Jamie seemed to be studying her face. 'Not checking on me then?'

Alice went for her best innocent look. 'Me?'

'Let me make you a coffee.'

'Oh, no, I don't want to get in your way. I have to . . .' Alice found herself suddenly in the warmth of Harbour Light Café. She glanced up at the fishing nets hanging above and the fake seagulls, then looked down at the seat she was placed onto.

'I've got a ten-minute break,' he told her. 'So I'll join you.'

Alice smiled as he set about making them coffee, but Matt's advice whirled in her mind, and Jamie had seemed to know she was only by the café because he was working inside. Now she didn't know how to act.

Jamie put the mugs on the table and sat by her side. 'You look frozen.' His smile was soft. 'You been fretting?'

She met his eyes and decided not to lie. He always knew when she was anyway, so there really wasn't any point. 'I was going to look in on you, but then I changed my mind. You're a grown man, and you don't need me fussing.'

Jamie mocked hurt. 'But I've always loved your fussing.'

She figured she could still do a little, just hold off when it came to things like his therapy. 'How's it been?' she asked quietly, glancing around at the three customers huddled at a back table, tucking in to an all-day breakfast.

'I haven't stolen the cutlery. So, so far so good.'

'That's not funny, Jamie.'

He lightly tapped her knuckles. 'I've had a good morning. No more worrying.'

Alice felt her neck heat a little at his touch. 'If I come on too strong, please say. I don't want you to ever feel smothered by me.'

Jamie frowned. 'Where's that coming from?'

She didn't want to tell him she had just been talking about him to her friends, so she simply shrugged.

Jamie brought his hand to his heart and held it there for a moment. 'You, Angel, have never done anything but show me love. And it all sits right here. I don't want you looking at me and overthinking. Let's just be the us we know.' He lowered his hand. 'Have I ever told you to back off?'

'No. You used to just walk away.' The memory hit of the times she'd try to stop him from going off with Gregg.

'I won't be walking away again, Angel,' he said softly.

Not knowing what to do with that snippet of information, Alice drank her coffee.

CHAPTER 10

Jamie

Jamie had the feeling someone had got into Alice's head. When she had sat with him in the café earlier, he could see her concerns. Not for one moment, even when in prison, did he expect her to automatically believe he was now a good person. She couldn't see into his mind, know what his plans were for the future. It was obvious he would face some doubts, even from her.

He walked into The Butterfly Company, thoughts only with Alice. He didn't want her to back away from him. To start acting like a different person. It was unsettling.

Part of him was ready to turn and head home just so he could talk to her. Get more to the bottom of her thoughts and feelings. Make it perfectly clear he had no problem with the way she showed how much she cared about people. About him. Some days, he felt it was only her belief in him holding him up.

'Jamie! Over here.' Demi waved from the staircase.

He smiled, heading her way. His chat with Alice would have to wait. 'I thought I might have seen you on the bus.'

63

'I was visiting my brother, so I came from a different direction. How you feeling? Nervous?'

Jamie shook his head. 'Nah, I'm okay.'

They went into a large room, windows lining one wall. The air smelled of furniture polish, and the carpet looked as though someone had not long given it the once over with a vacuum cleaner. Chairs sat in a circle, and Jamie straight away noticed Henley sitting on one.

Henley stood as Jamie and Demi sat with the others already there. 'Please welcome newcomer Jamie to the group.'

A few people said hello while others nodded.

Jamie felt far from new. Surrounded by ex-offenders was something he was quite used to. Although, in prison, they were inmates, and not everyone had the desire to go straight when they got out.

He sat and listened to a couple of men talk about their experiences since being released. One seemed to struggle with his family, and the other with holding down a job.

Working in the café for the best part of the day gave Jamie a real sense of purpose. Not once had he got bored or thought about faster ways to make money. Not that money was ever the reason he did anything.

It was a bit of a relief hearing stories similar to his own, and even though he felt sorry for the people in his group for all they'd been through, he was glad he wasn't alone, because quite often, that's exactly how he felt.

'Jamie, would you care to share anything today?' asked Henley. 'Don't feel obligated. No one is expected to talk on their first time, but just know you can.'

Jamie wasn't sure what he could add that hadn't already been mentioned. Demi was giving him a reassuring smile, and the others seemed friendly enough. He thought for a moment, then decided to get something off his chest.

'In your own time,' said Henley softly.

'Well, I guess what I want to know is, do you reach a point where you feel like chucking in the towel and going back to your old life because no one is willing to believe you've changed?' Jamie noticed Demi frown slightly at him. 'I'm not at that stage myself,' he added. 'I've not been out five minutes, and I'm hopeful for my future, but I am curious.'

Demi's hand lifted a touch. 'May I answer?'

Henley nodded. 'Of course, Demi.'

Demi glanced around the group before placing her gaze on Jamie. 'I had a tough time with my family at first. I didn't blame them. How could they just believe me when I'm a recovering addict? But it was hard not having that belief, I won't lie. However, I found it made me believe in myself extra hard. I had to be the one in charge of what happened to me next. You can't live your life worrying what everyone else thinks of you. You have to think highly of yourself.' She looked around the circle. 'So anytime you feel like giving up just because someone else doesn't believe in you, that's your alarm letting you know you need to up your game and believe in yourself.'

Jamie smiled warmly while one woman quietly clapped and a young man gave Demi a fist bump.

'And those are the wise words we'll end this session with,' said Henley. 'Thank you, Demi.'

Jamie followed her over to the table where tea, coffee, and biscuits were set up. 'You've really got it together, haven't you?'

Demi poured herself a tea. 'Had to fight for myself, Jamie. It didn't happen overnight, and though I have the most amazing man in my life now, I would still fight for myself even if Robson left me, because the one thing life has taught me is, this is my journey, and I get to call the shots.' She looked up and smiled. 'It would break my heart if Robson left me, but I wouldn't let it break me. Do you understand what I'm saying?'

He nodded. 'Yeah. Be in control of yourself.'

'For your own sake. We humans can be quite fragile. Best to build on our independence. If we gain support along the way, that's okay, but never let go of being the hero of your own story, because, trust me, being the damsel in distress in the tale sucks.'

Jamie breathed out a quiet laugh. 'I know what you mean.'

Her words had made him think back to how he'd found unhealthy ways to cope with his stress. Allowing others to take the wheel, guide him into the danger zones.

When he'd discovered he could study in prison, possibly make something of himself on release, parts of him fell into place as though they should have been there all along. It was a major turning point in his life.

But his thoughts went back to Alice. His rock. The only constant in his life. Demi was right with what she said, and he knew he shouldn't rely heavily on Alice's kindness, but he felt so attached to her.

Unlike Demi, who would clearly survive no matter who left her, he was quite sure he'd crumble away to nothing if anything happened to Alice. Nobody knew how strong their bond was but them. He needed to speak to her tonight to straighten a few things.

The bus ride home with Demi seemed to take longer than normal, not helped by the driver stopping to remove two drunk women dressed as elves singing Christmas songs at the top of their voices while pressing the bell over and over, annoying everyone.

Demi gave him a hug outside the pub, then entered the front beer garden to cuddle up to Robson, collecting glasses.

Robson glanced over her shoulder, spotting Jamie. It was obvious he wanted to say something, so Jamie remained on the pavement, waiting.

'Long time no see,' said Jamie.

Robson approached with Demi holding his hand. 'Hello, Jamie. I would ask how you're getting on, but Demi hasn't stopped singing your praises.'

Demi beamed his way. 'Jamie deserves praise.'

He smiled at how encouraging she always was. 'I've not done much yet, but I'm getting there.'

'Glad to hear things are looking up.' Robson's piercing blue eyes were almost boring into him. 'I'll see you here tomorrow for dinner.'

Jamie figured that was his way of saying goodnight. 'Yes, I'm looking forward to it.'

'So are we,' said Demi.

Unlike Demi, Robson had lived in the Jolly Pirate all his life, so he knew Jamie well. And being a few years older, Robson remembered more about the Stark family, so Jamie had to wonder why Robson was being friendly now.

With little thought, Jamie blurted, 'Sorry about my dad.'

Robson's head bobbed slightly as Demi frowned.

'I know he caused a lot of trouble in your pub,' Jamie added. He looked at Demi. 'He was a nasty drunk.'

'Who got barred in the end,' Robson told Demi.

She turned to Jamie. 'No need to apologize for him. It wasn't your fault.'

'Just felt the need to say sorry.' Jamie gestured at the B&B. 'Anyway, best get back.'

Robson took a step forward. 'Well, like Demi said, what your dad was like wasn't your fault. Feel free to come inside anytime you like. You're more than welcome.'

Jamie noticed Demi give her partner a gentle squeeze of the arm as she smiled his way. 'Thanks.'

They went their separate ways, and Jamie couldn't help but stare at the pavement, thinking of the times his father had walked the short route from the B&B to the pub. He could hear his slur and smell the stale fumes of booze mingled with cigarettes.

He stopped at the front of the pathway, frowning at Benny bent over by the bush. 'Benny, you all right down there, mate?'

Benny shot up, startled. 'You made me jump.'

'Sorry. What you doing in the bush?'

'Picking up Mr Pilkington. Well, what's left of him.'

Jamie chuckled. 'Nan's gnome. Blimming heck, I didn't even know that old thing was still about.'

Benny straightened, holding up a headless gnome. 'He went missing last month, then came back tonight. But look what's happened.'

Jamie went closer for a better look. 'Is his head down there?'

'Nope. Just this.' Benny frowned. 'Why would someone do this?'

'Have you just found it?'

'Someone banged on the door, so I came out and noticed the gnome on the doorstep. I was looking to see if the rest of it had been dumped nearby.'

Jamie glanced up the street. 'Bit weird.'

'Yeah, like the phone calls Alice gets.' Benny held up the gnome. 'Is this place haunted?'

'Not sure I believe in ghosts. Whoever did this was alive, you can bet on that.' Jamie went to go inside, when it dawned on him what else the lad had said. 'Hang on, what phone calls?'

'Started last month. Went on for about a week. The phone at the desk rings, no one replies when Alice says hello. Happened a few times today as well. Alice checked the line. Everything's working okay.' He passed the gnome to Jamie. 'What do you think Mabel would want us to do with Mr Pilkington?'

Jamie took the garden ornament over to the desk, his mind more on the phone calls Alice was receiving.

She came out from the back, glancing at the gnome with curiosity. 'Where's that come from?'

Benny answered. 'It was on the doorstep. Whoever was banging left it there, no doubt. I'm going to check the footage.'

Alice lifted the old thing. 'Oh, what a shame. Mabel loved him. I'm sure he's as old as me.'

Jamie turned to her. 'What's this I hear about dodgy phone calls?'

She sighed. 'I don't know. If it's someone messing about, I'm sure they'll get bored soon enough.'

'Do you know if that sort of thing was happening when Nan owned the place?'

Alice shook her head. 'She never mentioned anything. And I'm sure she would have told me.'

Jamie hoped it was kids messing about. Perhaps one of Benny's friends trying to prank him.

'I don't think anything went wrong when Mabel was in charge.' Alice blew out a short laugh. 'I think I'm jinxed. Maybe Seaview doesn't like me. Let's face it, since I've been here, we've had a fire, the gnome taken — now brought back headless, the phone calls where no one speaks, and our fairy lights taken down and stuffed in the bush. How's that for luck?'

It wasn't his thought process. 'Has Benny got any enemies you know of?'

Alice laughed. 'Enemies? Who do you think he is, a gangster? He didn't pay up so they beheaded our gnome.'

'I just meant kids can do silly things when they fall out with each other.'

Alice glanced over her shoulder at the opened door to their living quarters. 'Benny is one of those people who has magic about him. No matter who he meets, they love him. Seriously, he has that many friends, I've lost count. Anyway, I did ask him if he had fallen out with someone back when we had the small fire, but he said he hadn't.'

Benny's voice called out as he approached the desk. 'It's that man in the balaclava again.'

Jamie and Alice quickly joined him to home in on the laptop.

'Who the bloody hell is he?' snapped Alice.

'Local idiot, judging by what he keeps doing,' said Benny. 'Should we report him again?'

Alice shook her head. 'And say what? He returned our gnome.'

'Have you got the footage of him taking it in the first place?' asked Jamie.

'No,' replied Benny. 'We didn't notice it was gone until someone passing asked where it was. Could have been gone weeks for all we knew.'

Alice groaned. 'If I see him do one more thing to this place, I'm calling the police again. Bloody nuisance he is.'

Jamie placed the gnome beneath the counter just in case the head showed up at some point and they could glue it back on. He could see Alice was annoyed so thought it best to leave his deep and meaningful with her to another day. Right now, she needed a hot chocolate and a snuggle with her blanket.

'I'm going to save a file just for unexplained and weird behaviour around here,' said Benny, taking his laptop to his bedroom.

Alice turned to Jamie. 'Well, never mind all that. How did it go this evening at group?'

Jamie smiled softly. 'It went well. Now I'm thinking PJs and a funny film.'

Alice's expression softened. 'Ooh, I like the sound of that.'

'And hot choccy with marshmallows.' He winked, then waited for her to go out back before heading to his room. He was going to do more than build a file on the masked man. One way or another, he was going to make it his business to expose the thug.

CHAPTER 11

Alice

Alice had no idea how Jamie was feeling as they entered the Jolly Pirate for his welcome dinner. All she knew was how nervous *she* felt. She had told herself numerous times all day not to worry. Her friends were lovely people and they were giving Jamie a second chance.

She glanced at Robson behind the bar, then at the Jolly Roger flag pinned to the wall behind him. Normally she'd walk into the pub with a big smile on her face, ready to greet everyone, but a lot of the regulars had stopped supping their drinks and were now staring at Jamie.

Jamie, at her side, seemed relaxed enough, but he was good at hiding his emotions, and each time she had asked him since his release from prison if he was okay, he had told her he was just fine.

Red hair caught her attention as Spencer made his way through the small crowd by the bar to come her way.

His hand shot out towards Jamie. 'All right, mate.'

Jamie shook Spencer's hand. 'Hello, Spence.'

Alice swallowed hard, wondering if Spencer was going to follow up with talk of the past, mostly the part about the smashed window of his family's flower shop.

'I hear you're doing well,' said Spencer, his blue eyes not moving from Jamie's face as he lowered his hand.

'I am,' Jamie replied.

Alice smiled as Beth joined them. 'This is Spencer's partner, Beth.'

'Pleased to meet you,' said Jamie.

'You too. Come and meet our little one. Not so little anymore. He's just turned one.' Beth gestured across to a quiet corner where two prams sat side by side. 'He's asleep at the moment, but come and take a peek.'

Alice watched Jamie go off with Beth to meet Archie, then she turned to Spencer. 'Thanks for being kind. I know you don't owe him anything, and you could have made things difficult, but—'

'Hey, Al, stop stressing. Lottie said he's turned over a new leaf, so I'm willing to give the bloke a chance. We all know what he used to get up to around here, but that was years ago, so I'm not going to judge him on his past. Lord knows I'm not the same man I was two years ago, let alone eight.'

'A lot of people are saying the same thing.'

'If we only judge people on their mistakes, it wouldn't exactly encourage anyone to change, would it?'

'No, I guess it wouldn't. And most of us do change as we get older. Live and learn, and all that.'

Spencer lightly stroked her arm. 'You always were a good mate to him.'

'I always knew he had a good heart, that's why. When I look back, I think if he'd had some sort of therapy as a child, perhaps he wouldn't have gone off the rails.'

Spencer glanced over at Jamie and Beth talking by the prams. 'Maybe.'

Alice chastised herself as she remembered that Spencer had a tough childhood for a while. 'Sorry, Spence. I know you went through a lot as a kid as well, and you didn't go around breaking the law.'

'No, but I had my aunt to ground me.' He sighed, then smiled softly. 'Anyway, we're all different. As long as he's doing good now, that's what matters. Not a lot we can do about the past, but at least we get a shot at being the best we can be today so we can have a better future.'

'I know he really wants to just settle down and have a peaceful life.'

Spencer breathed out a small laugh. 'Don't we all.'

Lottie came over with Samuel. 'All okay?' She was looking at her brother.

Spencer nodded. 'I shook the man's hand. I'm giving him a chance.'

Lottie smiled. 'Good. The more I've had time to think about Jamie, the more of a chance I want to give him. He's one of us, and I want him to feel welcome in his home.'

Alice felt so relieved, she almost flopped onto Sophie as she approached with Matt.

'When are we eating?' asked Sophie. 'I'm starved.'

The change in conversation made Alice's smile grow. There was no way she wanted to talk about Jamie's past all night, or his new life, for that matter. All she wanted was a bit of normality for him.

Out of the corner of her eye, she could see Ginny and Will chatting to Jamie and Beth, so she decided to join them. She didn't want to be away from Jamie's side for too long in case he needed moral support. But just as she went to speak, Demi came over to let them know a roast with their names on it was ready to be served.

Jamie's hand brushed against Alice's as they made their way over to a long table, and she wasn't sure if he wanted her to hold his hand.

They sat side by side, and he leaned into her slightly. 'You stopped stressing yet?' he whispered, adding a small smile.

Alice chuckled. 'Am I that obvious?'

'To me, yeah.'

'I just want them to like you.'

'I know.' He glanced at the group settling into their chairs. 'So, how's the Hub going? Running smoothly?' His tone was confident, friendly.

Sophie answered first. 'Yes, we're doing so well. I can't believe how needed it is around here.'

'We weren't expecting to help as many as we do,' said Ginny, taking a napkin Will offered her.

Robson and Demi came over, serving the dinner.

'The food bank is used the most,' said Samuel. 'And now the café is open some evenings for free meals, we get a few people come in there, too.'

Will nodded. 'You wanted to do some voluntary work, Jamie. You can help out one evening there if you like.'

Alice started to cut her roast chicken as talk of the Hub continued. It was one of her favourite things to discuss, and even though they weren't having one of their meetings about the place, it still felt a tad strange that her mum wasn't there to join in.

Lizzie, Luna, and Jed were all missing from the group. She knew Jed was at choir practice with the Berry Buoys, singing sea shanties, and the only reason Will wasn't there with him was because he had a bit of a sore throat.

Benny was with his grandparents for the evening at the B&B, as Luna had offered to sit at the front desk while Lizzie and Benny cooked dinner.

It was the Port Berry way to lend a hand, so there wasn't anything odd about looking after someone's business. Alice had helped Mabel no end throughout the years, and she often jumped behind the bar to serve when Robson's pub got busy and there wasn't enough staff for the rush. One time she even worked in Berry Blooms, as both Lottie and Spencer had flu. That was her biggest work challenge, as making up bouquets wasn't as easy as it looked.

The conversation switched to Sophie and Matt's upcoming wedding, and Alice smiled to herself at the glow on Sophie's face each time she spoke of her big day.

It was so nice sitting with her friends and Jamie. It was something she had wished to happen for so long. Looking at him happily chatting to Matt as though they had known each other for years brushed away the last of her concerns.

CHAPTER 12

Jamie

Jamie briefly placed his hand over Alice's beneath the dinner table, showing her he was doing okay. He'd noticed she kept checking on him with her eyes every five minutes. He knew her inside out and could tell she was fretting about him fitting in with her friends.

The group around him was nothing but friendly, inviting him to join in with their Hub work, asking after his well-being, and Sophie and Matt even inviting him to their wedding.

He had no expectations when he first stepped off the bus to meet Port Berry again. All he had thought about at the time was putting one foot in front of the other, and taking one day at a time. If it hadn't been for Alice, he probably wouldn't have returned at all.

Looking around the pub, he could remember being inside as a lad, ready to help his dad walk home. They weren't the best memories, but inhaling the scent of alcohol brought it all back as though it were yesterday.

His nan would be shouting, his dad slurring curse words, and his sister would be staying put in her room. Shannon never did mix with any of them much after their mum died.

He wondered for a moment if his twin was happy. The last time he saw her was the day he got arrested. Her face was blank, her eyes as empty as ever. She simply stared at him as the police placed him in handcuffs and took him away.

Mabel was in tears, pleading with them to give him another chance, and Alice looked ready to pass out.

Jamie clenched his jaw and raised his chin as he glanced at the woman by his side. She was trying her best to bring joy to his life so the horrible memories had to go. If only they could leave him forever.

One of the bar staff turned the music up a notch, and Ginny and Lottie started singing along to the Christmas tune playing, livening up the group.

Jamie looked over at the Santa's sleigh ornament on the fireplace, then smiled at the large twinkling tree nearby, lop-sided at the top, making the angel look as though she were as drunk as the two men at the far end of the tinsel-adorned bar. He laughed to himself, then turned back to Alice as a chocolate dessert was brought out.

'We can leave early if you like,' she whispered close to his ear, her breath warming his skin.

'What, and miss out on hot choccy fudge cake and custard?' He winked, pleased to see her smile. Making her smile had the ability to raise his spirits. He only wished he had done it more often, rather than let her down so much. Things were different now. Now he was a better man; one determined not to waste any more of his life going in the wrong direction, having everyone hate him. Hating himself.

'Are you coming to the Christmas tree lighting tomorrow night?' Beth asked Jamie. 'We'll all be there.'

'First Saturday in December as always,' said Lottie.

'Will's supposed to be singing with the Berry Buoys,' said Ginny. 'But don't let that put you off.'

Will chuckled, nudging her arm. 'Oi!' He looked over at Jamie. 'I have a great voice, I'll have you know. I'm saving it for the event. Last year we raised money to buy some chickens to add to hampers for the food bank. Hopefully, we'll get some more this year, and if my voice isn't up to scratch, I'll mime like I had to last time.' He shook his head. 'I always seem to catch something this time of year.'

Ginny grinned. 'That's why we've stuck you in the corner out of everyone's way.'

Will touched his neck. 'It's just a sore throat.'

Ginny pointed at his bowl. 'Eat your pudding while it's warm, that'll help your pipes.'

Jamie bobbed his head their way. 'I'm going tomorrow, with Alice and Benny.' He met Alice's gaze, looking for confirmation.

Alice nodded. 'Hmm.' She had a mouthful of food so couldn't say more.

'Do they still put the wishes on the tree?' he asked the group.

Lottie nodded. 'Yep, and I'll be there with a Christmas wreath stall, so feel free to pop over and make one.'

'Then buy it,' said Samuel, grinning at Lottie.

Jamie chuckled. 'Will do.' He turned to Alice. 'Want one for the front door?'

'Yes, that would be lovely.' She leaned a little closer, her smile as warm as ever.

The conversation went on for another hour, coffee and brandy was offered, then the couples with babies headed home first.

Jamie couldn't resist spinning Alice into his arms for a short dance to the festive tunes as soon as they got up, making her giggle, but then he held back, chastising himself for acting as though nothing major had happened between them. What right did he have to be so tactile after the hurt he had caused his best friend? It was for the best if he just showed gratitude for her kindness, rather than thinking things could ever be the same again.

When it was time to leave, they thanked everyone for the lovely night, then took a slow stroll back to the B&B, Jamie wishing he could hold her hand like they used to, even as friends.

'Apparently, snow is due tomorrow,' said Alice, glancing at the dark sky.

'Let's hope it holds off for the event.'

They stopped smiling at each other as soon as they entered the foyer and saw Lizzie behind the desk.

'Benny's in his room, and your nan went home an hour ago.' Lizzie got up and grabbed her coat. 'Right, I'm off.'

'Thanks for tonight, Mum.' Alice gave her mother a hug before closing the door behind her, locking it up for the night.

This isn't right. I need to make amends. Say something. 'I need to talk to your mum,' said Jamie.

'Best to leave her for a few more days. She'll warm to you soon.'

He had to laugh, not that he found the situation funny. 'Not sure about that. She hates my guts.'

'My mum doesn't have hate in her. She's just concerned, that's all.'

'I know she is, and that's why I need to talk to her. Let her know I've changed.'

Alice touched his arm. 'Not now, eh, Jamie?'

It was late, and seeing how Lizzie had just ignored the fact he was there, he agreed now wasn't the best time, but one day he would have to speak with her. He couldn't let it carry on too long. More so for Alice's sake.

Alice yawned. 'Oh, I'm whacked.'

'Yeah, come on, time for bed.'

A cheeky smile hit her eyes, and he wondered if she was about to hit him with the line, 'yours or mine?'.

'Goodnight, Angel,' he said softly, not giving her the chance to say anything.

She gave a small wave, then went to her quarters.

He waited until she was gone before making his way up the stairs, feeling wide awake and content from his night. It was still so surreal being home, even more so that people were being nice to him. It wasn't anything like he had imagined, but then again, Alice was involved so he should have known she'd try to make things easy for him. It was her way.

Trying to fight off any negative memories lurking, he entered his room and took a deep calming breath. The boxes in the corner still hadn't been opened, so he decided to put on his PJs, sit on the floor, and have a nosey at what his grandmother had kept of his belongings. At least it was something productive to do.

Peeling back the cardboard flaps, he braced himself for photographs of his mother, as he figured his nan would put something like that inside. He hadn't seen a photo of his mum in years, feeling it was for the best he didn't have one in his cell, as it hurt to see her beautiful smile so full of life.

The first thing he saw were some old drawing pads, which brought a quirk to his lips. He used to love sitting on the pier when the weather was nice, sketching the boats and lighthouse.

He smiled at the good memory as he flicked through the pages, stopping at a doodle of Treasure Chest newsagents, drawn by Alice. He couldn't remember her doing it, but it didn't surprise him, as she often sat by his side along the harbour.

A few of his old action figures were still unwrapped in their boxes, which came as a surprise. He reckoned they might be worth a few quid now, especially as they were untouched. He put them to one side, then peered inside the box to see what else he would find.

He laughed quietly at spotting a picture of Alice as a girl sitting next to him on the wall outside the B&B. His childhood seemed like a lifetime ago. Sighing, he reached for another photo, and his heart paused as he gazed at his mum. She looked so happy, her hair blowing across her face, laughing, perhaps at that. Silently, he thanked his nan for the pictures as he carefully placed them to one side of the box.

A few letters were bunched together by an elastic band. Nothing he recognized. They weren't any he or Alice used in their correspondence.

Filled with curiosity, Jamie opened the one on top, widening his eyes as soon as he saw it was written to him from his nan.

There was no date marked, so he had no idea when she had decided to write to him. His main question was why hadn't she posted them.

Reading through, it was clear she had things to get off her chest, and an apology for not contacting him in prison was explained in great length.

She didn't need to say a word, he already knew it was difficult for her, not to mention how disappointed she was. He remembered it all.

But something had triggered her to write the letters, and as he read through each one, it became clear she had regrets, and that she had guessed Alice had been there for him as usual, which she was pleased about.

Jamie raised the paper to his nose, hoping he could smell his grandmother's scent, but there was no whiff of lavender. Nothing but her words, so he closed his eyes for a moment, absorbing all he had left of the woman who had tried her best to raise him.

'Oh, Nan,' he murmured, a lump clogging his throat.

The pain ripping into his heart was made worse by not being able to speak to his grandmother, to say his own apologies. All he wanted was to hold her, tell her how much he loved her, but she was gone.

A light tapping came at his door, taking him from his guilt. He creaked to a stand, knowing it would be Alice, no doubt checking on him once more.

'Hi, I came up to see . . . What's happened, Jamie?'

He glanced at her pink dressing gown as he let her in, then pointed at his things on the floor. 'My nan wrote to me, but she didn't send the letters.'

Alice knelt to his side as he went back to sitting on the floor. 'What did she say?'

'She's making amends.' He covered his face with his hands and lowered his head as his emotions got the better of him. 'I can't do the same.' Alice's arms curled around his shoulders, and her head gently rested upon his. 'I don't know what to do.' He sniffed, rolling back tears, not wanting to fall apart on her. Not wanting to cry at all.

'Just keep doing what you're doing, Jamie. She's watching over you. And I know she's so proud.'

He raised his weary head to meet her eyes, all walls a pile of rubble. 'I feel so alone, Alice.'

'You're not alone. I won't leave.'

He stared at her for a while, having one of his moments where he wondered if she was real. He had those moments when he was poorly as a child, when he was depressed in his teens, when he was spinning out of control as a young man. This angel was always somewhere close, offering a ray of light.

'How about we get you into bed?' she suggested, reaching for his arm as she stood. 'Sleep will do you some good right now.'

Not knowing what would be good for him, he let her lead him over to the bed and tuck him in.

'Stay awhile. Please.'

Alice settled by his side, taking his hand in hers. 'Close your eyes, Jamie. It's going to be okay.'

Those were the words she used to say to him when he was unwell as a child. Round about now, she'd pick up a book and start reading, but this time, she lightly stroked her thumb across his hand, and once more his angel soothed his soul.

CHAPTER 13

Alice

Old Market Square was buzzing with visitors for Port Berry's annual Christmas tree lighting. Food stalls lined the cobbled area, selling delicious snacks and beverages, and over in Anchorage Park a small funfair jingled and chimed, illuminating the green with twinkling lights and colourful sparkles.

The steeple of a beautiful stone-built church peeped over a small hill, no more than a two-minute walk away, where Alice and Jamie headed first.

The door to All Saints Church was wide open, welcoming guests inside, and the attached hall had tables outside, selling an array of Christmas gifts and ornaments.

Alice gazed up at the stained-glass windows either side of the tall building as she sat along the back pew while Jamie went to light a candle down by the altar.

He'd slept soundly throughout the night, peering at her only once during the early hours as she shuffled off the bed to go back to her own quarters. His smile had been small as she'd taken one last look his way before closing the door.

The B&B had kept her busy all day, and Jamie had worked in Ginny's Tearoom. Benny had gone to the supermarket with his nan, then helped out in the newsagents for most of the afternoon, so there'd been no chance to stop and chat.

Looking up at the ornate ceiling of the church, Alice hoped Mabel was somehow able to see Jamie. She wished his grandmother had found it in herself to send those letters or visit him, but it was never her place to interfere in Mabel's life choices, so she never did, but now she regretted not being a voice in the dispute. Perhaps she could have changed the outcome for them both.

If you can hear me, Mabel, I'm sorry I never told you I kept in contact with Jamie. I just couldn't bear the thought of him being alone. I wish we could all speak properly. I miss you.

She smiled softly as Jamie came to sit by her side, his face a lot happier than last night. 'Nice in here, isn't it?' she said.

'Yeah, but cold, eh?'

'Shall we grab a hot chocolate, then go make a Christmas wreath for our door?'

He nodded, putting on his gloves as he stood.

'I always wanted to get married in here,' she told him absentmindedly while looking down the aisle. 'It's so beautiful.'

'I just heard a couple by the candles talking about renewing their vows in here.'

Alice shared a warm smile with him as they headed outside.

Snowflakes started to gently fall as they made their way along a winding road leading to a row of quaint cottage-style shops and a small lopsided pub called The Crooked Hole.

'Ooh, how pretty is that?' said Alice, holding out a hand to catch the snow.

'As long as it doesn't get any heavier.' Jamie tapped her fingers, reminding her to put on her gloves.

Alice giggled. 'Now who's the worrywart?'

'I only worry about you. You, however, worry about the world and its sister.'

'What can I say, I have a big heart.'

They entered the square, scanning the stalls for the hot beverages trailer, while listening to the bell-ringers playing a tune over by the entrance to the park, their table lined with big and small brass hand bells, and the church choir was close by dressed in Victorian clothes, holding storm lamps and hymn books.

Children ran around the tall green Christmas tree in the middle of the square, eagerly awaiting the lighting ceremony, and a small queue had already formed to write wishes on stars, ready to hang on the tree.

Jamie ordered two cinnamon hot chocolates with cream, then walked with Alice over to the park to sit by the pond for a moment. 'We'll get that wreath sorted as soon as we've finished these.'

Alice was in no rush. Even the racket of the fair behind them had become white noise. Sitting on a bench staring at the calm water while light flurries of snow fell was nothing short of tranquil.

'Hello, Alice,' came a familiar voice from out of nowhere.

A shiver ran down her spine as she glanced back to see her ex-boyfriend, Alan. She had no words for him, not even a polite smile. She turned back to face the pond, knowing full well Jamie was staring at her.

'Bye then,' said Alan, walking away.

The chinking music of the funfair filled the air while Alice quietly sipped her drink, pondering over whether or not to go home, as all her peace had vanished the moment Alan appeared.

He had the ability to do that to her. Suck all positive vibes out of the air just by existing. She hated that she had let him into her life. To steal away time and make her miserable with his narcissistic personality. His controlling, bullying behaviour was all too much. At least she'd got away from the energy-sucking vampire in the end.

'Are we going to talk about what just happened?' asked Jamie.

'That was Alan, my ex. I don't talk to him.'

Jamie glanced behind them. 'Not sure he realized that.'

'Oh, he knows, but he doesn't understand the concept of boundaries, so whenever he sees me, he thinks it's okay to come say hi.'

'Do you see him often?'

'Not if I can help it, but he's one of those people who pops up every so often like a bad penny.' She shivered just thinking about him, and Jamie's arm suddenly came up around the back of the bench as if to block out the cool breeze.

'Do you want me to have a word with him if he pops up again?'

She met the seriousness in his eyes. 'No. I find ignoring him works best. In fact, I prefer to pretend he doesn't exist.'

'That bad, was it?'

Alice shrugged. The last person she wanted to talk to about Alan was Jamie. She could sense his tension already. 'It was a long time ago now, and I'd rather leave that section of my life in the past. Dead and buried, as far as I'm concerned.' She took one last sip of her drink, then tossed the cup into the nearby bin as she stood.

Jamie reached for her arm, gently turning her to face him. 'Look at me, Angel. Tell me if he's a problem.'

'He's not, honestly. It took a little while to get rid of him at first. He wouldn't take no for an answer, then he kept showing up until Mum threatened him with the police. After that, he stayed away, but every so often we cross paths — he only lives next door in Penzance. But it's been a long while now, and I've not had any bother from him. There's nothing for you to worry about, okay?' She watched him studying her eyes.

'Okay,' he said, finally.

'Jamie, I mean it. I don't want you back inside. No fighting. You just saw what happened. He said hello, I ignored him. He walked away. Done.'

'I'm not going to fight. Just so we're clear, I haven't had a fight in six years, and I don't plan on going back to those methods to sort things. I'm checking you're all right, that's all.'

Alice raised her eyebrows. 'This is me you're talking to. I know what you're capable of.'

He lifted her scarf so it was snuggled to her chin. 'I won't hit him. You have my word.'

'Can we get back to enjoying our night now?'

'We can.' He gestured at the square. 'Ready for some wreath making?'

'Yes, let's make our front door look really Christmassy. Councillor Seabridge has a competition this year for best door wreath, so we can enter. Winner receives a cheese platter.'

Jamie chuckled. 'Just what I've always wanted.'

'It'll go down well in the dining room.'

'In that case, let's crack on. We're going to need lots of pine cones and ribbons to stand a chance of winning.'

Alice laughed. 'Why does it sound like this isn't your first rodeo?'

Jamie raised a palm. 'Hey, I've hidden skills.'

They continued to joke as they made their way to Lottie's stall, where long tables were set out for anyone wanting to participate.

Alice and Jamie snagged seats next to each other as Lottie told them what to do.

The Berry Buoys choir started to sing sea shanties close by while rattling collection buckets, so everyone stopped what they were doing to watch for a while.

'Will's had about three honey and lemon drinks in the last hour,' said Lottie, grinning at Alice. 'Bless him. If he's not miming, he'll feel it tomorrow.'

Alice felt Jamie lean closer, almost cuddling her, and she just knew he had gone into protective mode, but before she could assure him she was just fine, Benny came over, munching on a burger.

'Oh, so that's your dinner sorted then,' said Alice.

Benny licked ketchup off his lips. 'Yep. Nan bought it. Have you eaten yet?'

'We'll grab something in a minute.' She turned to Jamie for confirmation.

He nodded. 'Burger sounds great.'

Benny went back to his group of friends, and Alice continued to watch Will sing, or mime, she couldn't tell.

Jamie nudged her elbow. 'I'll just grab us some food now. Won't be a sec.'

'All right.' She smiled his way, then stopped when Beth plopped herself into Jamie's seat, grinning. 'What?'

'You two.'

'What about us?'

'Are you a couple now?'

Alice shook her head. 'No.'

Beth raised her brow. 'Looks that way.'

'Oh, we're just hanging out.'

Lottie nodded. 'Best friends since childhood. Never could stay too far from each other for long.'

Alice snorted as she laughed. 'Slight exaggeration.'

Lottie scoffed. 'Please, you two always looked like a couple.'

Beth smiled. 'As long as you're happy, Alice. That's all that matters.'

'I am. Thank you, Beth.'

The Berry Buoys finished their last song, and everyone clapped and cheered, many popping money into their buckets.

Alice got on with her Christmas wreath, smiling widely when Jamie returned with burger and chips for them. She asked Lottie to keep their wreath to one side, then went for a walk with Jamie to eat their dinner.

'I've never had a snow burger before,' he said, grinning at the flakes falling on his food.

Alice had something else on her mind. 'Hey, Jamie, has anyone ever asked you if I'm your girlfriend?'

He snaffled a chip as he nodded. 'Loads of times. Why?'

'Beth thought we were together, so it just made me wonder.'

'Did it bother you?'

She shook her head. 'No. But what if you wanted to have a girlfriend to go with your new life? Me hanging around won't make you look available.'

He stopped chewing and stared at her. 'I'm not looking for a girlfriend, and as far as I'm concerned, you and me, we're like family. We are what we are, and I'm not about to change that. I don't need anything else in my life anyway.'

It warmed her to hear him calling her his family, and they shared a look, an understanding of something only they knew, then went back to eating before heading to the Christmas tree as the lighting ceremony was about to begin.

Alice smiled on the inside as she glanced at Jamie. The public would see them and make assumptions. It didn't matter. Over the years, they had shared so much, given each other parts of themselves they hadn't to anyone else, and lived with a bond that couldn't be broken.

She had tried once to forget him, move her life in a different direction, but all she got in return was nasty Alan. Was that her punishment for going against her heart? For trying to have a normal life? She owed Jamie nothing. It was right of her to live her own life, but what a mess it had been, the gaslighting Alan would do, all the blame he would place on her for anything going wrong that was his own doing.

Councillor Seabridge stepped up to a lectern and made a speech about Christmas, Port Berry, and how wonderful the community was, then he had the children join in with the countdown for the lights.

Everyone cheered as the tree twinkled with multicoloured bulbs. Music came from the church choir once more, and people started to hang wishes on the branches.

'Come on,' said Alice. 'Let's make a wish.'

They wrote something on a star, then sealed it in a plastic bauble and went to the tree.

'What did you wish for?' she asked Jamie.

'Same wish I always have.'

That intrigued Alice. She reached up to a high branch and attached her own wish. 'I guess we're not supposed to tell.'

Jamie shrugged. 'I don't believe in superstition.'

'But you just made a wish.'

He grinned. 'Yeah, but that's for you. Whenever I have to make a wish, I do it for you.'

Alice tilted her head to one side as she watched him place his wish. 'What do you always wish for me?'

He gazed into her eyes. 'Happiness.'

Alice was quite sure her heart just melted into a pool of slush. Something definitely fizzed in her stomach, and her cheeks were starting to ache from smiling. 'You don't believe in such things, yet you make wishes for me?'

'You're my angel. You deserve all the wishes.'

Alice was so glad she had made a wish for his happiness now that she knew he wasn't using wishes on himself. 'You deserve good things too.'

His smile was small. 'I have all I need.'

She went to tell him she had all she needed as well now but closed her mouth on seeing his glare directed over her shoulder. Her immediate thought went to Alan. Jamie must have spotted him for sure, but as she turned, she saw his twin, Shannon, marching their way.

'Oh, there you are.' Shannon's dark hair and blue eyes were so like Jamie's, but she had a natural sneer to her features that he didn't. 'You weren't at Seaview.'

'What are you doing here?' he asked, making no attempt to greet her.

'Hello, Shannon.' Unlike Jamie, Alice opted for polite.

Shannon rolled her eyes up and down Alice's coat. 'Thought you'd got away with it, didn't you?'

Alice had no idea what she was talking about. 'Away with what?'

'Taking my nan's B&B.'

Before Alice could respond, Shannon closed in on her face.

'Well, think again, Dipple. I'll be seeing you tomorrow morning. Make sure you're around at ten.' And with that, Shannon stormed off, disappearing into the crowd.

Alice looked at Jamie. 'What just happened?'

CHAPTER 14

Jamie

Jamie made sure he didn't have work at the café, as he wanted
to be at the B&B for when his sister showed up to talk to
Alice. Not once had she contacted him in eight years, and
according to Alice, Shannon hadn't bothered with Mabel
either. He knew his twin had moved to Australia, but that
didn't mean she had to cut their grandmother off all together.

He paced the foyer, checking the clock behind the desk
every two minutes, wishing Shannon would arrive earlier than
arranged, as he wanted to know what her plan was.

She always had an agenda, but he hoped she had changed
over the years, and he wanted to give her the benefit of the
doubt. After all, the people around him were giving him a
second chance.

His instincts told him trouble was brewing. Shannon had
rage in her eyes the night before at the tree lighting. Why on
earth she had it in her head that Alice had taken their grandmother's business was beyond him.

'She didn't even come to Mabel's funeral or send flowers,'
said Alice, coming out from the dining room.

'Whatever she wants, I'll sort it.' He could see Alice was concerned.

'I would have spoken to her last night if she hadn't walked off.'

'Best to do it here in private. Take her out back. Give her a cup of tea or something.'

Alice nodded. 'Oh, I'll be polite about things. I just wish I knew what things I'm dealing with.'

So did he. He went to respond but closed his mouth as Shannon walked in, head high and lips pursed.

'Come and sit in Alice's living room,' was his greeting.

Shannon smirked at Alice as she followed her brother.

Alice glanced at Jamie, but he just went straight to the sofa and sat down.

'Spit it out, Shannon. You've come a long way to be here, so let's not beat around the bush.'

She raised a perfectly groomed eyebrow. 'Trying to get rid of me already, Jamie? I wonder why.' She glared at Alice.

Alice cleared her throat. 'Last night you said I'd taken your nan's B&B, but I did no such thing, just so you know.'

Shannon sighed. 'You're the owner, so how about you tell me why my grandmother left this place to you?'

'She didn't,' replied Alice. 'I bought it from her before she died.'

'Perhaps if you'd bothered to keep in touch with Nan, you might have known that,' said Jamie.

Shannon pointed towards the door. 'In case you haven't noticed, I don't live round here anymore.'

Jamie rolled his eyes. 'Little invention called the phone.'

'I lead a busy life. We recently moved to New Zealand. Plus, we've been travelling a lot. My husband likes to take me places. I can't be expected to drop everything just to make phone calls.'

'She was your nan,' said Alice.

'Oh, mind your own business.' Shannon splayed a hand to the room. 'And this business you think you own is my inheritance — I'm here to get it back.'

Jamie huffed. 'Don't be daft. You can't take something someone bought from our nan.'

'But it doesn't belong to her.' Shannon scoffed, flicking her hair back. 'Typical of you to be on *her* side.'

'There are no sides. This is Alice's now.'

'And how do we know she didn't trick Nan into selling? How do we know Nan was in her right mind? Little Miss Goody Two Shoes here could have taken advantage.'

'I did not,' snapped Alice, jumping to her feet.

Shannon crossed her legs. 'Got proof of that, have you?'

Alice gave a sharp nod. 'Yeah. How about you ask around? Everyone who knew Mabel knew she wasn't vulnerable. She was moving to Jersey to start a new life with her girlfriend.'

That snippet of information seemed to stun Shannon for a moment.

'What girlfriend?'

Alice sat back down. 'I guess that's none of your business.'

Shannon patted her chest. 'My nan's money is my business. So where is it, eh? Did she leave it to you?' She turned to Jamie. 'Or you? Because I haven't heard a thing all this time. All I got was one short letter telling me she'd died.'

'She didn't leave her money to me,' said Jamie, wishing his greedy sister would just go away. It was all a bit much sitting there listening to her waffle on about inheritance and what she deserved. He was glad his grandmother left her out of the will.

'She didn't leave her money to me either,' said Alice. 'And if she didn't leave any to you, then I guess she didn't want you to have any.'

'One of you had better tell me where her money went, because if she sold this place, then that's a lot of cash floating around.'

Jamie took a calming breath. Shannon had always been quite blunt with her words, but the conversation was a touch too cold for his liking. 'Don't you even care that she's dead?' Judging by her expression, it didn't look as though she did.

'So, you're only here for money?' asked Alice.

'I'm here for what's rightfully mine.'

'Why have you waited so long? Mabel passed away in August. It's December now.' Alice shook her head.

'I do know, and as I've already explained — I travel a lot.' Shannon huffed. 'I really don't have time for this. Just give me my share, and I'll be on my way.'

Jamie looked at Alice before turning back to his twin. 'We don't have your share. There is no share. I don't even know what Nan did with her money. Probably left it to her partner.'

'She did,' said Alice. 'And charity.'

Shannon's cheeks went a shade of purple. 'Are you telling me that my inheritance went to some local cats' home?'

Alice bobbed her head. 'Something like that.'

'I'll see about that.' Shannon stood. 'I'm going to get a solicitor involved.'

'Well, you do that,' said Jamie, fed up with her attitude. 'And good luck to you, but it's got nothing to do with us, so no need to come back here again.'

Shannon's eyes widened. 'Could you be any ruder?'

He didn't want to argue with her. Whenever he had in the past, it had always drained him, as half of what she said never made sense. She was always right, and either the victim or the hero of the story, never able to see the villain in her ways.

Alice stood, gesturing towards the door. 'At least you now know what's been happening here. Perhaps if you'd called, you'd have saved yourself the long trip.'

'We're here visiting my husband's family.'

Jamie blew out a sarcastic laugh. 'Yeah, good to see you too, sis.'

She made for the door. 'You haven't exactly made me feel welcome, Jamie. You didn't even bother to contact me to let me know you'd been released.'

'Why would I? You didn't write to me when I was inside.'

'I moved away.'

'Does that affect your hands then?'

Shannon shook her head. 'Don't make this my fault. I was staying away from trouble. I had a new life.'

And now he had one too, and it didn't include her. There was no malice inside him, no anger or remorse connected to her. He just felt it was a shame they weren't close like some siblings he knew. She'd always been distant even when home, and as he grew he figured perhaps that was her way of protecting her mental health from all the trauma.

Shannon turned to Alice and held out a hand. 'May I have the contact details of my nan's partner?'

'Nope,' said Alice flatly. 'She's an elderly woman, and she doesn't need the stress.'

'If she gives me my money, she won't get any stress.'

Alice shook her head. 'You won't get anything from her. Mabel hardly left her a thing. Their chosen charities gained the most.'

'Fine, then tell me which charities she gave to.'

'Nope. I loved Mabel,' said Alice. 'I won't betray her.'

Shannon snarled. 'Oh, you've always been so stupid.'

'She's not stupid.' Jamie rose from the sofa.

'You would say that. Got your feet well and truly under the table here, I see. She doesn't even realize you're using her, does she? You've always been able to con this one.'

'You don't know what you're talking about,' snapped Alice, moving to Jamie's side.

He hoped Alice wasn't buying into his sister's spiteful words. 'I think we both know you've always been jealous of Alice. I wonder why. Oh, that's right, it's because people like her.'

Shannon scoffed. 'Oh, please. You know she's a soft touch, that's why you keep her around. I bet you've already found a way to get your claws into this place.' She smirked at Alice. 'Has he got you to sign anything yet? Put something in his name perhaps?'

'No, he hasn't, because he's not devious like you. There is no agenda here, just friendship. You just don't recognize that because you never had any mates.'

Shannon stormed off to the foyer. 'I keep my circle small, and I know exactly who is inside, but you, Dipple, think you know my brother. I'm telling you now, he's using you. Laughs behind your back. I bet he's in your bed every night declaring his love while thinking up ways to take Seaview from you. Wake up, you fool.'

'That's enough.' Jamie pointed at the door. 'Go away, leave us alone, and don't come back. You're no family to me. You're just poison.'

Shannon smirked over her shoulder as she went to step over the threshold. 'You'll see his true colours one day, love. When all this disappears from your grasp.' And with that, she moved to the Christmas tree and pushed it over before marching off.

Alice stared wide-eyed at the baubles and tree ornaments rolling her way. 'Really?'

Jamie pinched the bridge of his nose as a headache loomed. He was used to Shannon's nastiness so not much surprised him when it came to her. But trying to plant seeds in Alice's mind was the last straw. He swore to himself there and then that his twin was now dead to him. He never wanted to see or hear from her again.

'Spiteful cow,' muttered Alice, crouching to pick up the tree.

Jamie rushed to help. 'What she said about me, I—'

'Hey, I know that's not true. What, you think I'd believe her? I grew up with her too you know, and obviously, she hasn't changed much.'

They straightened the tree, then set about gathering the decorations sprawled all over the floor, a couple broken.

Jamie went to fetch the dustpan and brush from the cupboard by the stairs. 'I just don't know what to say.' He was now wondering if anyone else thought he was using Alice. 'I get paid soon. I'll be able to start paying my way here. You'll see I'm not using you.'

Alice stopped tucking the fairy lights back in place. 'I know you're not doing that. Don't let her get inside your head. She sure as hell isn't in mine.' She approached him and took his hands in hers. 'What have we always said about ourselves, eh?' Before he could reply, she added, 'No one understands our friendship but us.'

He nodded, dipping his head, fed up that his sister had stirred the pot. It was reassuring to hear that Alice didn't believe her, but he still felt like crap.

'Everything's okay, Jamie. Just stay focused on your goals. Don't let her ruin anything for you.'

He met the sincerity in her eyes, knowing she really was such a kind person. 'I still want to start paying my way.'

Alice gave his hands a gentle squeeze. 'Sure, that's fine. You can help out around here as well, if you like. Some housekeeping on your days off. Bit of handyman work.' She stepped back to continue picking up baubles. 'I've never seen you as a user, just my friend. And if you want to be part of the team here, then chip in when you can.'

Jamie felt a little less rattled. 'I want you to know I'd never try to take this place from you. You're the only person I know who loves Seaview as much as Nan did.'

Alice glanced his way. 'I know you wouldn't.'

'I can sign some documents to prove that if you want. You know because—'

'There's no need for anything like that. I don't even need your word. I know you'd never do anything to hurt me.'

He lowered his eyes. 'I did hurt you though, didn't I? Being stupid and getting arrested the year your sister died. You needed me, and I wasn't around.'

'I don't want to talk about that time.'

Jamie stepped closer. 'That's because it angers you. Perhaps it's for the best if you let it out. Shout at me or something.'

'I don't want to fight with you, Jamie.' She gestured at the dishevelled tree. 'Don't you think we've had a bad enough morning as it is? Let's just tidy up and get on with our day.'

'Sometimes I want you to yell at me.'

'Will it make you feel better?'

Jamie shrugged. 'I put you through a lot.'

'No, you put yourself through a lot. I just tried to be there for you. How you choose to live your life is none of my business, and how I choose to live mine is on me. Yes, it would have been nice to have had your help when Lisa died and I had to take care of Benny, but it wasn't to be, so what's the point of bringing it up? I don't want to remember things that make me angry. I have a nice life. I'm happy.' She shoved an ornament into the tree. 'And yeah, you should have been there, but it's done. I need you to let it go.'

Jamie inhaled deeply, feeling all of her pain. 'I'm sorry, Angel.'

'So am I, so forget it now. I'll not be dragged back to that time.'

'I understand.'

'No, I don't think you do. It was the worst year of my life. My family was broken, you were in prison, and I could barely breathe most days. All I wanted was to run away to your room and bury my head beneath your quilt with you holding me.'

For so long Jamie had wanted her to release that pent-up anger, as he always knew it was there. It wasn't his place to force it from her, but at the same time, he needed her to be free of the hold it had on them both. It was the unspoken issue that bugged the life out of him. He could only guess what it did to her.

'Happy now,' she said, her shoulders drooping. 'I raised my voice, and I only did that because my guests are out, and you seem to think I need to get things off my chest by blaming you.'

'I don't want anything bad between us, and Shannon just made me—'

'Feel bad about yourself again. Yes, I know what she does to you. But I'm not having her ruin what you're building here. So now can we move forward. Please?'

99

Jamie nodded slightly. 'I'm scared things might come back to bite us if we don't deal with them now.'

Alice sighed and stepped closer. 'Nothing bad is going to happen. You're all right, Jamie.'

'It just feels too good to be true sometimes.'

'It's good because you're making it so. Look at me, Jamie.' She tilted his chin so they were face to face, and he smiled into her warm gaze. 'The past is gone. You're here now and on the right track and your future looks bright. It's time for you to enjoy life.'

With her by his side, he was starting to believe happiness and peace was possible.

CHAPTER 15

Alice

Alice caught a snowflake on her tongue before heading into her mum's shop, feeling the need to do something to make herself laugh. After the morning she'd had with Shannon's nastiness, then Jamie living in the past, she thought it the best time to talk to her mum about things. There was no way she wanted any more of her days to be tarnished. She may as well deal with all the crap on the same day. It was Christmas soon, and Sophie's wedding. Alice wanted to be enjoying the time, not having arguments.

Jed was behind the counter reading a newspaper while Luna was serving someone. They both smiled as Alice approached.

'Still snowing, I see?' Jed gestured at Alice's hair.

Alice looked up, wiping her locks, feeling some dampness. 'It's only light.'

'With a bit of luck, we'll have a white Christmas.' Luna placed some money in the till, then said goodbye to the young man she'd just sold a fizzy drink to.

'Is Mum upstairs?'

'Yep, but she's not in the best of moods.'

Alice went to the stairs out the back. 'Oh?'

'She had a date, but he cancelled.'

'I didn't know she was dating again.' Alice remembered her mother trying speed dating not too long ago. She went to a single's night at a local pub, but not much came of anything.

Plodding up the stairs, she hoped her mum would at least listen to what she had to say about Jamie.

'Is that you, Alice?' called Lizzie from the kitchen.

Alice smiled to herself. Her mother knew everyone's footsteps. 'Yeah.'

'In here.'

Alice entered the kitchen to see her mum had a tarot spread laid out on the table. 'Who you doing a reading for?'

'No one. I'm just wondering why I've got a card missing.' Lizzie glanced up. 'What you after?'

'I'm here to talk because I don't like the tension.'

Lizzie patted the chair to her side. 'I've not got a problem with you, girlie.'

'Yeah, I know, just Jamie, and you're worried he'll lead our Benny astray or something.'

'Oh, Alice, he was just such a rotten egg. Stealing cars, and shoplifting. I don't know what else. You can't find me a mother out there who would want their daughter around someone like that.'

Alice started fiddling with the black crushed-velvet bag on the table. 'Mum, he changed in prison. He doesn't like that person he was, and I need you to give him a chance so I can have a peaceful life.'

'It's not as though he's your partner, love. So what does it matter what I think of him? He's not part of our family. Right now, he's just one of your guests, and if he keeps his nose clean, stays to his room, and hurries and saves some money to move on, then I'm okay with that.'

It wasn't exactly what Alice wanted from her mother. She was hoping for a bit more forgiveness. It wasn't like her mum to be so cold towards anyone.

'Okay, Mum, spill the beans.'

Lizzie looked up from her cards. 'What do you mean?'

'There's more to this. You're one of life's helpers. Always have been. You're a huge fan of reform, and you don't believe in back shaming, so why are you so different when it comes to Jamie?'

'Because you're too close to him, that's why.'

'He's my best friend.'

'I know what you're like with that lad, and I worry about just how far you'd go for him.'

Alice chuckled. 'I promise we won't turn into Bonnie and Clyde.'

Lizzie huffed. 'I just want someone trouble-free for you.'

'Mum, he wasn't all bad. He just got in with the wrong crowd.'

'See, there you go again, making excuses for him. Can't you see yourself when it comes to him? You're giddy, love. Giddy.'

Alice snorted a laugh. 'I'm not giddy. We just have a really strong connection.'

'Yeah, it's called soulmate, love.'

'Oh really? Well, if you think he's my soulmate, you would want me to be with him, wouldn't you?'

'It's because I know he's your soulmate that scares me.' Lizzie waggled a hand towards the door. 'Your nan isn't the only one around here with psychic abilities. We've all got it in us. Don't you pick up on anything when you're with him?'

Alice shrugged. 'Just our bond.'

'You love him, girlie. About time you dropped your walls and started admitting that to yourself. That way, you might be able to save your heart from a thrashing.'

'Soulmates don't beat up each other's hearts.'

'No, but if he ends up back in the slammer, your heart will shatter.' Lizzie folded her arms as she sat back. 'Be honest. Tell me how hard it was for you knowing he was locked up?'

It wasn't something Alice liked to think about. The first couple of years had been a nightmare. Not only was she trying to live a life that didn't include Lisa, she had struggled to cope with Benny's grief, not knowing what was best for him. Hiding the fact she was in contact with an inmate made things difficult, and each time she went home after a prison visit, she had cried.

'It was tough until I got used to it,' she muttered.

'I don't want anyone to hurt my baby,' Lizzie said quietly, taking Alice's hand.

'He's never done anything bad to me.'

'You need someone who is solid, Alice. Reliable.'

'He's that way now, and he's going to stay that way. Look, I can prove it.' She tapped the Four of Swords. 'Do a reading on him. Go on. Check out his future for yourself.'

'Maybe I would if I knew where my missing card was.'

Alice scanned the floor, noticing it poking out from under the fridge. 'There it is.' She grinned as she picked it up. 'The Lovers.'

'Hmm,' muttered Lizzie, shuffling her deck.

'Three-card spread. Past, present, future.'

Lizzie tutted. 'Let me just do my own thing. Anyway, we all know his past.' She turned over four cards and simply stared at them.

Alice tilted her head to have a read, knowing the meanings, having been taught at a young age, just like Luna had taught Lizzie. 'Ooh, Wheel of Fortune. Seems to be turning in his favour.'

'My attention is more on the Two of Cups.'

Alice had already spotted that card too. 'If it is a deepening connection between him and me, at least it shows a positive outcome.'

Lizzie sighed loudly. 'All right, love. You win. I'll give him a chance.'

'You will?'

Lizzie bobbed her head. 'I won't lie. I will be wary for a while, but if he's changed, I guess we'll all see in the end.'

'Benny vouched for him, didn't he?'

'Well, there is that, as well.'

'Thought so.'

Lizzie put her cards away in the black bag. 'I only want good things for you, love.'

'I want good things for me too, and I have that in my life. Jamie is just finding his feet and could do with a mate or two for support. That's all I'm being.'

'What's he up to now?'

'Putting our Christmas wreath on the door. The competition winner will be announced in a few days. Why don't you put one on the shop? It'll look nice with the fairy lights.'

'I'll pop to Berry Blooms later. See what they've got.'

'You're supposed to make your own.'

'Yes, I know. I'll have Lottie teach me, but right now, I need to get back behind the counter and give your nan a rest.'

'Okay. I'll be off. And, Mum, thanks.' Alice kissed her cheek. She practically skipped down the stairs, giving her nan a kiss as well at the bottom before heading home.

With the tarot revealing good vibes for Jamie, Shannon hopefully gone for good, and the past off of everyone's chest, Alice felt she could get on with Christmas now. She smiled widely on seeing Jamie faffing about with the door wreath while quietly singing a festive tune.

'What you grinning about?' he asked as she spun in a circle on the pathway.

Alice put her palms out to catch the light snow flurry. 'Sorted things with Mum. Oh, and Benny put in a good word for you, so now no one's judging you on your old self and we can move forward.'

'Speaking of which, I just saw Will a minute ago. I'm going to help out at the café tonight.'

'The free meals evening?'

'Yeah, it's normally two nights a week, but he's opening for three just for winter.'

Alice smiled. 'Well done for helping.'

'I want to give something back. Be a friend not foe.'

'Well, that's one way to make a start.' She came to the door to inspect his work. 'Have you had anyone say anything to you while you've been working?'

Jamie picked up a fallen pine cone. 'No, not yet. So far, people have been quite kind.'

'I think we should celebrate.'

He laughed as she grabbed his hands, spinning him into a dance. 'What exactly are we celebrating?'

Alice twirled under his arm. 'Kindness.'

CHAPTER 16

Jamie

Jamie had no idea what to expect as he started his evening shift at Harbour Light Café. Will was there, helping the cooks in the kitchen set up, and two women were ready to serve anyone that came through the door.

'Hi, I'm Kaz,' said a young woman with red curls. 'I've been volunteering like this for a good while now, so feel free to ask me for any help. I know how nerve-wracking it can be when you're new.'

Jamie smiled. 'Thanks. To be honest, I don't feel nervous, more inexperienced. I know I'll be clearing up and serving food, but I'm not sure what else happens on these evenings.'

Kaz pointed at the door. 'Basically, people on low incomes, or even homeless, come in for a free meal and a chat. We don't just feed them. Some people like a bit of company, so just greet them when they come in, and see if you can pick up on whether they want to be left alone or not.'

'And the one's that want a chat?'

'Sit with them. As long as we're not rushed off our feet, which we never are around here, you'll have time to keep them company.'

Jamie was only just starting to get used to the quiet life he now had, but knew from other inmates that some people needed others around them. He used to be that way too but, as the years passed, he found he enjoyed time to himself.

The door opened and a man in his early twenties entered, giving a small wave to Kaz.

'Hey, Henry. How you getting on?' asked Kaz.

Henry's gaunt face showed how worn through he was. 'Doing okay, but Mum's in hospital again.'

'Oh no. Hopefully she won't be in too long this time.' Kaz gestured at Jamie. 'Henry, this is Jamie. He's new to the scheme.'

Once again, Henry offered a small wave, and Jamie figured the young man didn't want to shake hands so didn't bother to try.

'Hello,' said Henry. 'You can sit with me for a bit, if you like. I'll help you get settled.'

Jamie smiled. 'Thanks. Very kind of you.'

'What can I get you to eat, Henry?' asked Kaz. 'I happen to know chicken and chips is on the menu.'

Henry looked at Jamie. 'She knows that's my favourite.' He glanced up at Kaz as he sat. 'I'll take that, please.'

Kaz smiled. 'Coming right up.'

Jamie sat opposite him. 'The chicken does smell nice.' He sniffed the air as if to prove his point.

'They have lovely food in here. I'm glad they started offering this kind of help. I get some bits from the food bank at the Hub, but there's nothing quite like a home-cooked meal. I'm not very good at coping by myself when Mum is away.'

'When will she be home from hospital?'

Henry started to unravel his knife and fork from a white paper napkin. 'Next week, which is good. I wished so hard for her to be home for Christmas. I've never spent that day alone before, so I've been stressed in case it happened.'

Jamie had spent many a Christmas without family. He knew how hard it was. Some of the men in his wing were really run down on the day, as no visits were allowed due to staff shortages. He'd often sit with someone, trying to keep their spirits up, speaking of better times to come, especially Boxing Day, when the families were allowed to visit.

It was hard for Alice to find an excuse to visit him on that day, only managing it once by pretending she was helping a poorly friend for a couple of days. That was the best Boxing Day ever, and when it was over, he'd gone back to his cell, cuddled the Christmas card she'd sent him, and quietly shed a few tears.

Some men were okay about being inside, but Jamie hated that life, and after he'd got his head straight, all he focused on was making a better future for himself. And every interaction with Alice fed him strength and hope.

Jamie sat and chatted with Henry for a while, mostly talking about basketball, which Jamie knew little about, but Henry loved.

More and more blessings were counted as the evening went on. Talking to people in need of food took Jamie back to his prison life, where many a story of hardship floated around. He was so grateful he had a roof over his head and a full stomach.

Matt entered and called Jamie over to a table by the door, on which he started to place pamphlets. 'See if you can get anyone to have a nosey at these.'

Jamie spotted one for The Butterfly Company.

'They're places people can go for guidance, respite, advice, that sort of thing,' added Matt. 'Brought them in from the Hub. Thought they might be of use to someone.'

'Good idea.' Jamie browsed the information about the Sunshine Centre, liking the look of their art classes.

'What are these?' asked Henry, peering around Jamie. He picked one up. 'Oh, my mum goes to Sunshine sometimes. The centre helps her mental health. She's in hospital having treatment for her mind now,' he told Matt.

Jamie didn't know Henry's mother was away because of something like that. He'd assumed she was having an operation. 'You could join too. I'm thinking of checking it out.'

Henry smiled. 'I normally just drop Mum off.'

'They have lots of different things there,' said Matt. 'My friend Demi hosts cookery classes, and I know someone else who likes to go just to draw.'

Henry's eyes sparkled a touch. 'Mum never said they cook there.'

Matt shrugged. 'It's pretty new. Demi was helping women build confidence through gaining a new skill, but now she's giving classes to anyone. Worth a look, I say. I know she's hosting a class next week where they're going to learn how to cook a chicken and make stuffing for Christmas. You could pop along beforehand and ask to join in with the fun.'

Jamie nodded. 'That sounds great, Henry. Would you like to learn how to cook?'

Henry nodded. 'Yes, I would love that. And Mum would be so surprised if I made stuffing.'

'Would you like me to come with you at all?' asked Jamie.

'That's okay. I know Debra who runs things there. I can see her by myself, but thank you.' Henry pointed his pamphlet towards the door. 'I'm going to go home now and make plans.'

Jamie felt so happy for the young man, and Henry had a real skip in his step as he walked away, only stopping for a moment to take the blueberry muffin Kaz was offering.

'Makes you feel good, doesn't it?' said Matt.

For so long, Jamie had only felt empty. Giving back to his community by helping in any way he could had sparked joy.

'Do a shift at the Hub, Jamie.'

Jamie glanced at the table, then Matt. 'What would I be expected to do?'

'Pretty much the same thing you're doing now. Talk to people. See what they need. Make up food parcels. I can put your name down to work a couple of hours with me, then I can show you the ropes if you like.'

It didn't take a lot of thought. Jamie already knew he wanted to be part of the Hub. It was one of Alice's favourite subjects, so he knew some things about the role. He just wasn't sure if he'd be the right fit.

As if reading his mind, Matt offered a sympathetic smile. 'Are you worried someone might come in and tell you you're not welcome or something?'

'I guess I'm just finding my feet around here, and even though so far no one has had a go at me, I'm still expecting someone to say something at some point.' He didn't include Lizzie, as he understood she was just concerned about her daughter.

Matt patted his arm. 'Look, if someone comes into the Hub with something to say, that's your chance to tell them you've changed and you're now someone who volunteers and helps. It's up to them what they do with that info, but at least they can see the man you are now.'

'I suppose.'

'So, should I put your name down? We really could do with an extra set of hands this time of year. It gets busy.'

Jamie nodded. 'Okay. Oh, and, Matt — thanks.'

Matt smiled. 'No worries, mate. Don't know if you know my story, but when I arrived here, I was homeless and the Hub helped me no end. Mostly Jed, who was on a mission to give me a new life. Seriously, the man went above and beyond. A real diamond he is. Don't get me wrong, I had already reached a stage where I'd started fighting for myself, but to have that kind of support makes all the difference.'

Jamie's thoughts were with Alice. 'Port Berry has always been a friendly place.' He hated himself for being one of the few that had caused problems and trouble.

'I love it here,' said Matt.

Jamie grinned. 'Sophie have something to do with that?'

Matt laughed. 'Yep. It wasn't just the harbour I fell in love with.' He shook his head. 'When I think back to life before Sophie Moore, it's hard to believe someone as wonderful as her was in my future. It does blow my mind sometimes.'

'You just never know what's around the corner, right?'

'I never had the best life, Jamie, and I had no idea where I would end up when I started walking away from London. Even though I had goals, never in my wildest dreams did I think my life would ever be this happy. I'm not just grateful to Jed and Sophie and the people around here for their help and kindness, I'm also grateful for whatever it was inside my brain that pushed me towards change. Lord knows where I'd be today if I didn't make that decision to change my life.'

Jamie knew the feeling.

An elderly couple came in, so Jamie went over to show them to a table and see how he could assist. He carried on working through his shift with a pleasant smile for everyone and a real sense of belonging. And when Alice popped in at the end of the night to playfully ask if he wanted someone to walk him home, his joy lifted to the highest level.

CHAPTER 17

Alice

The last few days had been so lovely for Alice. Christmas songs playing, and the last of her guests departing in full festive mood, assuring her of their return again one day. The hearty lunches Demi served had people coming in from the cold for something warm and homely, and all of her aches and pains sat at a level two.

She grinned to herself as she unlocked the front door, knowing no more guests were due till New Year's Eve. She could relax a little and perhaps get some Christmas shopping done.

Wondering what she could buy for Jamie, and so pleased she could get him anything that didn't have to be approved by the authorities, she swung open the door to see the snow they were having on and off had left a thin covering on the pathway.

'Oh, how beautiful is . . .' She glanced down, spotting her door wreath on the floor.

At first, she assumed it had fallen off, but on closer inspection, she could see it had been ripped apart.

113

Alice looked around the front for signs of any other damage, but all was in order. She picked up what was left of the wreath and headed over to the desk. Jamie was making his way downstairs.

'What's happened to that?' he asked, frowning.

'I guess it fell off the door and some animal got its claws into it. Oh, what a mess, and the competition was today. We won't be entering now.'

Jamie picked up what was left of the small gold bell that had been attached. 'You sure it was an animal?'

'Well, unless someone ripped it off the door and stomped on it, then yeah.' Alice slapped a hand to her mouth. 'Oh no, you don't think that masked man is back, do you?'

'One way to find out.'

Alice went straight out back to fire up Benny's laptop.

Benny was slipping into his school blazer. 'I was going to give you my Christmas list if you're doing a bit of online shopping, but judging by your face, I'd say you're on my laptop for a different reason.'

'The door wreath has been torn apart,' she told him. 'Just checking to see if we can spot what happened.'

Benny took over, getting the footage up quickly. He sped through, stopping when the masked man came into view, tugged the wreath off the door, and placed it on the ground. They couldn't see if he ripped it apart, as his back was to the camera at that point.

'Who is that?' snapped Alice. 'And why is he picking on me?'

'Another one for the file for the police.' Benny tapped on the keys, getting everything ready.

'I'm not sure they're going to bother arresting someone for this kind of behaviour.' Alice flopped to a seat and sighed. 'If they catch him, he'll just say he was pranking me or something.' She turned to Benny. 'Do you think it's one of your mates thinking they're funny?'

Benny crinkled his nose. 'No, I don't. My friends aren't idiots, and this man definitely is, going by the stuff he does.'

'This is classed as harassment. If he does think he's being funny, he's got a bit of a shock coming to him when the police nab him,' said Jamie who had joined them.

Alice looked up to see Jamie studying the screen. 'You don't think this has anything to do with Shannon, do you?'

'Not really her style.'

'Would she pay someone to annoy me?'

He shook his head. 'My sister's too wrapped up in herself to spend that kind of energy on someone else.'

Alice waved a hand at the screen. 'So, who the bloody hell is doing this?'

'We need to lay a trap,' said Jamie, eyes still on the footage.

Benny chuckled. 'Ooh, booby trap.'

Alice gestured at the door. 'You can get to school before you're late.'

'But I want to help trap the idiot,' Benny moaned.

'No one's trapping anyone. We're not getting into trouble with the police for snaring someone.'

Jamie glanced her way. 'I wasn't about to put down a bear trap.'

'What were you thinking?' asked Benny, looking keen to join in whatever it was.

'School, Benny,' said Alice.

Benny grabbed his bag. 'Fine, but I want to know everything when I get home.' He kissed Alice's cheek, then headed off.

Alice turned to Jamie. 'What have you got in mind?'

'I'm thinking we could put up a new decoration out front, as he seems to like breaking anything cheerful out there, then I wait behind the door and pounce.'

She widened her eyes. 'That's your plan?'

Jamie shrugged, closing down the laptop. 'I'd have a word with him. Make him see the error of his ways.'

'Oh great, then you'll end up back in prison.'

'I'm not going to rough him up.'

'What if he has a weapon? I'd rather the police dealt with him.'

'Unfortunately, they won't sit outside in case he strikes again.' He grinned, then headed for the door. 'And I know just the thing that will lure this dimwit out.'

Alice followed him to the foyer. 'What?'

'I saw it at the supermarket yesterday. Won't be a sec.' And with that he was off.

Alice frowned as she went back to the destroyed wreath. All she wanted was a peaceful life. She hoped that if Jamie did somehow manage to grab the harasser, none of the trouble was connected to Shannon. She was sure it would sting Jamie, even if they weren't the best of friends.

Demi came in, losing her smile as soon as she saw the wreath. 'What happened to that?'

Alice explained the situation, including Jamie's cunning plan to capture the criminal.

Demi's mouth gaped for a moment. 'And I only popped in to double-check we had no guests till after Christmas. Now I feel like I'm part of a detective ring.'

'It would make more sense if he was stealing our things, but all he seems to do is break stuff. I'm not sure what he's gaining from doing that, but it's starting to make me feel a bit ill, Demi.' She reached across the desk. 'Please don't tell anyone. I don't want my mum worrying or Jamie.'

'I won't say a word, but you need to talk to the police again. Let them know how badly this is affecting you. We can do it together now if you like?'

'Okay, let's give them a call.' Alice closed the front door, then went out back with Demi to speak to the police.

Luckily enough, the nice officer who had helped before was available to talk, and Alice gave her as much information as possible, including how the whole thing was starting to rattle her nerves.

After the conversation, Demi suggested a coffee in Ginny's Tearoom as a little treat, which was nice, as Ginny was inside working a shift.

The three women happily chatted away about Sophie's wedding and how much they were looking forward to the big day, and Alice started to relax, forgetting about her worries for a while.

Demi stayed behind in the tea shop to help Ginny because a staff member had just called in sick, so Alice headed back to the B&B alone. She came to an abrupt halt when she saw the new Christmas decoration Jamie had purchased for the front.

'Who's your friend?' she quipped, pointing at the six-foot inflatable snowman swaying in the cool breeze.

Jamie grinned. 'I'm calling him Buffy.'

Alice laughed. 'A vampire slayer?'

'I reckon he'll do the job.'

She walked up the pathway to stand by its side. 'Its face looks a bit creepy.'

'I thought that, but I still think this dude will be like a flame for our moth boy.'

Alice wasn't so sure. 'Can't see him legging it down the road with this under his arm.'

Jamie raised an index finger. 'Let's think about this logically. We know he doesn't steal, just wreck, and we know he waits till dark, and if you check the footage, he only strikes between the hours of four and ten in the evening. He's given us a time slot. We haven't got any guests to think about, so we can keep the front door closed, and I'll sit behind it on stake-out with the laptop.'

'You make it sound so simple.'

'It is.'

'A million things could go wrong, Jamie.'

Jamie headed back inside. 'Nothing will go wrong. I'll have the element of surprise on my side, and he'll get a stern warning when I unmask him.'

'This isn't Scooby Doo. Someone could get hurt.'

'Well, it won't be you, because you'll be safe and snug back there.' He gestured to her quarters.

'I spoke to the police earlier, so if you do catch him, I want you to just try and get a picture of his face. I want them to be the one to give him a warning, if they don't arrest him that is. Just getting caught might scare him enough to stop him being stupid.'

'Okay. I'll do it your way.'

She wasn't sure whether to believe him. One thing she knew about Jamie was how protective he was of her. She just prayed he didn't fight the man.

'It'll be over soon, Angel. Don't you worry.'

Easy for him to say. She was worried and annoyed. It was all a bit too much and ridiculous in her opinion.

'With a bit of luck, he won't come back.' She hoped.

'If he does, it'll be within the next few days, for sure. It won't take him long to notice Buffy out there.'

Alice raised her brow. 'It won't take anyone long to notice that thing out there.'

'We could use it for Halloween as well.'

'If it lasts that long. I kind of get the feeling that Buffy's nemesis will come armed with a pair of scissors.' And she'd just had the most awful thought! She shot her now terrified gaze Jamie's way. 'What if he brings a knife?'

'Let's not overthink things. So far the only aggression he's shown is towards the front garden.'

Alice's stress levels were sky high again.

CHAPTER 18

Jamie

Lottie had invited Jamie up to her house to work on the Hub's website after lunch, Will having mentioned that Jamie wanted to get into web design.

Jamie had jumped at the chance, not only because of his interest, but because he really wanted to be good friends with Lottie again.

Nothing much had happened with Buffy the snowman in the last three days, which was a relief for Alice, but frustrating for Jamie. He was determined to catch the delinquent, thinking him probably young and, like Jamie years ago, doing stupid dares with his gang.

Whistling a merry tune as he strolled up Berry Hill, Jamie took in the spectacular view of the harbour. Every so often, he would simply stare out to sea, amazed it was his view once more.

He knocked on the large coastal home, then presented Lottie with a poinsettia as soon as she opened the door.

Lottie grinned. 'Did you buy that from my shop?'

'Nope. Supermarket.'

'Well, thank you anyway. Come in.'

Jamie perused her home. 'I don't remember these houses being so big inside.'

'I inherited George's house, and Sam bought Ginny's so, with mine in the middle we knocked three into one.'

'Oh, yeah, I can see that now.' He followed her into an office on the ground level. Large patio doors revealed a neat garden and a greenhouse at the back. 'Not much used to change around here.'

'Not much has changed since you were last here. A couple of shops along the front, oh, and the mini supermarket up the road.'

'I like that it's the same.'

Lottie smiled and offered tea, which he declined. 'Before we get into some Christmas designs for the website,' she said, 'I wanted to ask you if you'd be willing to be one of the guests on there.' She tapped a microphone set up on the desk that he hadn't noticed on entering.

'What do you mean?'

'I interview people and post their stories on our website. You can listen to some of the others here first to get the gist of things, but basically, they talk about social issues, life changes, reform, trauma, that sort of thing. It can help others in similar boats, and it can stop them feeling so alone. I thought your story might be of some use. What do you think?'

Jamie wasn't sure if talking about his past would stop someone else from committing crimes. What could he tell them about prison other than it was one of the worst experiences of his life?

'You can think about it and get back to me,' added Lottie softly.

'I don't mind answering your questions, but I'm not sure how helpful my story can be. I'm just someone who got into trouble and paid a hefty price.'

Lottie moved her wheelchair closer to the desk, placing her hands by the keyboard. 'Actually, I was thinking more along the lines of you talking about having cancer as a child.'

'Oh.' It wasn't something he spoke about much. 'I don't know what to say.'

'Like I said, you can think about it. This interview wouldn't go out till February. And if it makes things easier for you, I can give you a list of questions. You can write down your answers, ready for the time.'

He wrinkled his nose as he glanced up from fiddling with his hands. 'Do you think people would want to listen to me saying how lonely I felt? How much I missed school? How I just wanted to be like the other kids?'

Lottie gave a small shrug. 'That's the thing with these interviews — my guests talk about hard subjects. Afterwards, there are always comments left by listeners saying they could relate. There could be a parent out there who hears your story, then understands the kind of things their child might be keeping to themselves.'

It certainly was something to think about, but it was also like rubbing salt in a wound. He tried to quickly weigh up which part of his life was the hardest to talk about and realized he held quite a lot of baggage.

'I guess it would be like a therapy session,' he questioned, more so to himself.

'A lot have said that.'

Jamie couldn't decide on the spot what would be best for him, so he agreed to take a list of questions home and mull it over. He figured he'd listen to what the others had to say during their interviews as well. He was sure Benny would let him use the laptop to check out the Hub's website.

Lottie smiled. 'I think that would be for the best, too. I'm sorry if I come across a little pushy. I just get excited for the Hub because I know the interviews help.'

'That's okay. I can see how passionate you are about this.'

'I love the Hub. There are times when someone walks in looking so lost and sad, then after they've had a chat and a cuppa with one of us, they've perked right up and show signs of hope in their eyes. It's a marvellous thing to experience.'

121

'I'm booked in for my first shift with Matt the day after tomorrow. He told me to be prepared for a bit of a Christmas rush. Why does it get busier this time of year?'

Lottie shrugged slightly. 'To be honest, I'm not entirely sure. We have more food parcels to hand out. We get more donations come in, and we add extras like chocolate selection boxes for the kids. It's not always a fun time for people. Some are at their lowest for whatever reason, so we get more coming in just for company. When we started, we thought we'd only get one or two walk through the door, perhaps looking for help filling out applications or wanting advice or a job.'

'I remember Alice telling me you were set up to help the homeless.'

'We were, then we just expanded in all sorts of areas because people were coming in asking for the kind of help we weren't expecting.'

Jamie was looking forward to helping out. He continued to chat about the Happy to Help Hub for a while before making a start on the website with Lottie, happy to listen to all her handy hints and tips.

It was nice not having any animosity between them, and he was so thankful she was making him feel comfortable and welcome, giving him and their friendship this second chance.

They spent a couple of hours together, then he headed home, whistling the same tune he'd arrived with. Things were definitely looking up.

It was just past four, and the sky was already dark, but the twinkling Christmas lights on all the shops along the harbour cheered the evening no end.

Some of the volunteers for the local charity shop were gathering outside their premises, dressed as characters from *The Wizard of Oz*, and Jamie recognized Henry, wrapped in silver material, blusher on his cheeks.

'Hello, Henry. What's going on here?'

Henry beamed. 'I'm the Tin Man, and we're going to sing carols as we walk along the harbour to cheer everyone up and raise awareness for the shop.' He held up a battery-operated lamp. 'Look, I have a lantern I can swing.'

'That's brilliant, and you look great.'

'I come in here a lot, so Mary said I can join in with the songs.'

The woman called Mary stepped forward. 'Who's your friend, Henry?'

'This is Jamie. He's new at being a volunteer.'

Jamie smiled at Mary, dressed as Dorothy.

'Fancy joining in, love?' she asked Jamie. 'Only our scarecrow just pulled out at the last minute. Stage fright, apparently.' She rolled her pale eyes. 'It's just a bit of "Jingle Bells" as we stroll around the harbour. You up for that? Come on, you know you want to.'

Jamie had to laugh. It was the last thing he was expecting on his way home. 'Oh, go on then. I can get my holly jolly on and wave a lamp.'

'Better than that,' said Mary, shoving a straw hat on his head. 'Here you go. And . . .' She whipped out some blusher and reddened his cheeks, creating round circles. 'We have ourselves a scarecrow. Right, let's get this show on the road,' she said to the women behind her.

Jamie chuckled, then joined in with the song, holding his lantern high while walking beside a happy Henry.

They were just getting into their swing, belting out "We Wish You a Merry Christmas", when a scuffle on the pavement outside the B&B had them all gasp in fright.

It took a moment for the scene Jamie was witnessing to register in his brain.

Buffy the snowman was bouncing on top of Lizzie who was splayed on the ground, a masked man beneath her. Benny was frantically trying to tackle the inflatable while Alice was screaming for help.

The streetlamps shone down like a spotlight on the commotion, and noise from the beer garden at the pub flooded out towards the conflict as customers ran out to see who had cried out.

Within seconds, Jamie took out the snowman with a rugby tackle, slid between Lizzie and the intruder, avoided flailing fists, and pinned the masked man, pressing his head deep into the gutter.

'Jamie!' Alice yelled.

Flashbacks of fighting in prison entered Jamie's mind, temporarily blinding him, telling him to hit first. Hit hard. He pulled his arm back, ready to punch, but something snagged him. Suddenly he could see clearly again. Alice was clenching his hand.

'Jamie!' she shouted, and he met fear in her eyes.

He took a calming breath before looking back at the man unable to move beneath him.

A siren sounded in the near distance as a circle of men from the pub surrounded Jamie and Alice.

Jamie quickly tugged off the balaclava to see who he was dealing with.

'Alan?' Alice gasped.

'This isn't what it looks like,' said Alan, tears in his eyes and nerves in his tone.

'You!' yelled Lizzie, waggling a shaky hand. 'I'm going to get you arrested for this. We've got security cameras.'

'I'm sorry, Alice.' Alan sobbed. 'I did it for you.'

Jamie pushed Alan's sweaty head further into the damp road. 'Scared her, destroyed her things — you did that for her, did you?' Jamie pressed his finger into Alan's cheekbone. 'Did you set fire to her carpet?'

Alan looked up at Alice. 'I'm sorry. I thought it would make you need me.'

'She doesn't need you,' spat Jamie, glaring in his face.

'Jamie, get off him.' Alice tugged his arm as the sirens got louder.

Knowing there was nowhere for Alan to run, Jamie sat back, keeping his eyes firmly on Alice's ex-boyfriend, blaming himself for her going out with the idiot in the first place.

Jamie couldn't sit there stressing over Alice's life choices. She had every right to find a partner and settle down. He was lucky she gave him her time at all, being under no obligation to visit him in prison or write. But he couldn't help but feel disappointed that not only had she hidden Alan from him, but she'd had a relationship with the man in the first place. He truly believed she wouldn't have found a boyfriend if he was by her side.

Pushing Alan away, Jamie stood, listening to some of the men from the pub jeer at Alan. A police car pulled up, and Lizzie rushed straight to the first officer on the scene to explain what had happened while Jamie watched Alice shield him as though trying to hide him from the police.

'This creep,' said Lizzie, pointing at a dishevelled Alan, 'has been harassing my daughter. He just tried to cut Buffy.'

The police officer frowned, so Benny stepped forward to let him know who Buffy was and what had been happening lately.

'And she bloody attacked me,' Alan told the officer as he was brought to a stand. 'Arrest her, not me. Look.' He pointed at the B&B. 'They said they've got security cameras. Check them. You'll see what she did to me. It'll all be on there. She drew first blood.'

'I'll give you first blood in a minute,' snapped Lizzie.

Jamie felt Alice's hands reach back for his, so he leaned closer to cradle her in his arms. 'You all right, Angel?' he whispered close to her ear.

Alice turned, showing puffy eyes and a quivering lip, and suddenly she flopped into him and cried.

He held her close, rubbing her back and telling her everything was going to be okay, but it wasn't okay. Because the police didn't just take Alan away, they took Lizzie as well.

CHAPTER 19

Alice

Alice walked into the B&B to see Jamie, Benny and Luna huddled by the desk. It was obvious they were all waiting on news about Lizzie.

Luna was the first to rush forward. 'Where's your mum?'

Alice thumbed behind her towards the door. 'I've just settled her indoors. She's a bit worn through.'

'She's not the only one.' Luna grabbed her coat from the chair where Benny was sitting. 'And how are you?'

'I'm fine, Nan. Just tired. It's been a long night.'

Luna nodded. 'Right. I'm off home to see Lizzie.'

Alice kissed her grandmother's cheek, then followed her to the door to wave her off.

'Thanks for ringing with the update,' said Benny, getting up. 'Granny's been worried sick.'

'Everything's sorted now, so you can go to bed as well.' Alice yawned. 'I think we all need a good night's sleep.'

Benny frowned. 'I still don't think it's fair Alan got off with a warning.'

Jamie agreed. 'What exactly did he tell the police?'

Alice took a calming breath before replying. 'He said he thought if it looked like someone was messing with me, and he showed up, I might ask him to stick around and help.' She shook her head and sighed once more. 'Honestly, even the police were baffled by his logic.'

'He created trouble for you hoping he could come along and be your hero.' Jamie shook his head. 'That was his logic?'

'Pretty much, but it's just so weird.' Alice didn't have much energy to dissect Alan's mind. 'Anyway, he has been well and truly warned to stay away from me, and he was scared enough to listen. He didn't like being locked in a cell.'

'They should have thrown away the key,' spat Benny.

As long as Alan kept his word and stayed away, she really didn't care. She was simply glad his nonsense was over. 'They said he kept apologizing. Reckons he only meant to scare me a little bit.'

Benny huffed. 'What a loser.'

'Yeah, he's definitely that,' said Alice. 'And now he's on the police radar, I can't see him messing with anyone ever again.'

'Doesn't he have to pay for the damages?' asked Benny.

Alice shook her head. 'Nope, because he said he didn't do any of the things he was being accused of. It was just the snowman he was going to tamper with, but Mum jumped on him first.'

Benny flung a hand to the back room. 'But we have footage.'

Alice nodded. 'Of a masked man removing lights from the tree, putting the gnome back, and placing the wreath on the doorstep. It doesn't show who it is.'

'And they can't arrest him for harassment?' asked Jamie.

'They told him they will if he comes near me again.' Alice yawned once more. 'Oh, I'm so tired. Let's lock up and forget this night happened.'

Benny headed off to his room. 'I'll go see Nan in the morning.'

Jamie went with Alice to the front door. 'How is your mum really?'

'As tired as me, but okay. I'm just glad all she got was a warning as well. And Alan told the police he wasn't going to press charges against her for jumping on him.'

'That was big of him.' Jamie shook his head.

'At least things can get back to normal around here now.' Alice turned to face him. 'And thank you for not hitting him. You wouldn't have got a warning. We both know that.'

Jamie shrugged. 'Who knows. Just because I'm ex-crim, doesn't mean I don't get to defend my family.'

Alice rested her head on his shoulder. 'What a nightmare that man is.'

'Yeah, well, he's gone now. He won't come back.'

She glanced up, trying to read his expression. 'The police really scared him, so I don't want you doing anything to add to that.'

Jamie held a small smile. 'I won't go after him, I promise. But if he does show his face round here—'

'I'll call the police.'

'Fine.'

'Honestly, Jamie, he was so scared. And he knows he's been caught out now. Let's just leave it be and move forward. He's a sad little man who has proven himself to bully women, and one day he probably will end up in prison if these are the stunts he pulls on his ex-girlfriends. Who knows? I really don't want to waste any more of my time thinking about him.'

Jamie tipped her chin as she went to flop on him again. 'All right. When we wake in the morning, all this will be behind us, and we'll be okay.'

Alice smiled softly. 'That's what Mum said.' She pointed at his cheek. 'I see you washed off your blusher.'

Jamie grinned. 'I lost my scarecrow hat as well.'

'I don't know what was more surreal, Mum scrambling with Alan and Buffy the snowman, or you looking like a scarecrow, diving in.' She walked with him over to the stairs. 'This has been one really bizarre night. I'm not sure I'll get much sleep.'

'I can see you're exhausted. I can sit with you for a while, if you want. Help you settle?'

Alice gave a small smile. 'That would be nice.'

'Give me two secs to get my PJs, and I'll be right with you.'

She watched him go upstairs, then headed for her bedroom. Benny had gone to bed, so she got changed into her nightclothes and snuggled beneath the covers, waiting for Jamie to join her.

Regrets about giving Alan a chance hit hard. She wished so badly she could go back in time and unmeet him. She'd never felt that way about anyone before. A shiver went down her spine at the memory of being with such a creep. She was so glad the police had scared him.

Alice sat up. 'Right, that's it. He no longer exists. I'm at the church hall tomorrow, helping with Christmas toys for the kids in hospital, and that's all I'm going to focus on.'

'Good to know,' said Jamie, entering her room.

'Oh. I was giving myself a positive push.'

'So I heard.' He sat on her bed. 'I double-checked the door was locked.'

'Thank you. And thanks for being here tonight.'

'I would have liked to have gone to the police station with you.'

'No, you were right where I needed you. Here with Benny.' She nudged his side as he rested against the headboard. 'Anyway, we're not talking about that anymore, remember?'

'Yep, sorry. So, tomorrow, Christmas toys, church hall. You need another pair of hands?'

'Ooh, yes please.'

'Count me in then.'

Alice felt so much better already. She just hoped all the gossips wouldn't question her about Alan as soon as they saw her. 'Jamie,' she said quietly.

'Hmm?'

'I'm so glad you're here.' She closed her eyes, smiling as his arm leaned into hers.

'Me too,' he whispered.

Alice relaxed. Being with Jamie had always been where she felt safe.

CHAPTER 20

Jamie

After all the stress of yesterday, Jamie was pleased to see Alice looking relaxed and happy. Sat in the church hall, making gift boxes for toys, she hummed along to the festive music playing quietly from the radio in the corner.

He glanced over at the row of windows in the bland wall, then peered at the high ceiling as he yawned. He hadn't got much sleep last night, worrying about Alice, the B&B. Whether stupid Alan would return. He looked at the walking stick leaning against Alice's chair, and she caught him staring.

'That's about the fifth time I've seen you peering at my walking stick.'

He smiled softly, reaching for a small cardboard box and some festive wrapping paper. 'I'm just worried about you.'

'I'm okay. It's just a flare-up. My knee will be back to normal in a couple of days. It normally works like that with me.'

'Fibromyalgia is weird, coming and going like that.'

Alice nodded. 'Yep. I just count my blessings I'm not in major pain every day like some.'

'Do you use the walking aid often?'

'Nope. So stop worrying.'

He gently nudged her arm. 'Let me know if you ever need me to carry you.'

Alice grinned. 'I might make you do it just for the exercise.'

'Hey, what you trying to say?' He patted his flat stomach and chuckled.

Spencer stood up at the other end of the table. 'Right, I'm going to start loading the boxes onto the minibus, then we'll set off to the hospital.' He waggled a hand at the remaining toys. 'We've got about half an hour left before we need to set off, so get a wriggle on, and whoever is getting changed into an elf costume, can you sort that now, please?'

Needing to get changed, Jamie sped up his wrapping duties, covering the last two boxes assigned to him in reindeer paper.

'You don't have to come to the hospital,' said Alice quietly, leaning his way.

He knew why she'd said that. The last time he was in a children's ward was as a patient. He guessed Alice was thinking it might be triggering for him. If he was honest with himself, he wasn't entirely sure how it would make him feel — he just knew it was something he wanted to do.

Jamie packed some Christmas gifts, then helped Alice with hers. 'I'll come to the hospital.'

Her smile was warm and encouraging as she reached for her walking aid to stand.

Jamie went to help but lowered his arms after she blew out a small laugh at his flapping hands around her. 'Sorry. I'm fussing, I know.'

'Thank you for fussing, but I'll let you know if I need any help, okay?'

He gave a brief nod. 'Okay.'

'Come on, let's get our costumes on, then get in the minibus.'

The December air was fresh and not as cold as it had been lately but still held a bit of a chill in each breeze. Jamie was glad of the warmth in the vehicle, especially as their red-and-green elf outfits were quite thin.

It wasn't long before they were at the hospital, and entering the building brought back so many memories. Jamie had spent a big part of his childhood going in and out of hospital. One time, he'd even spent Christmas Day in a ward. Alice came to visit that day. That memory had him lean a little closer to her.

'You okay?' she asked softly.

'Yeah, I'm good.'

Spencer got them carrying the gifts up to the children's ward. Only Alice and an elderly woman called Marisa, who loved talking about her cats, didn't have to lift anything.

There used to be a disinfectant smell that Jamie associated with hospitals, but the children's ward no longer had that scent.

The children and nurses lit up as a bunch of elves entered with Christmas presents. Spencer sang a little of "Jingle Bells", then had the kids join in before handing out the gifts.

Jamie went over to a blond boy, around the age of ten, and sat in the chair to his side, introducing himself.

'I know you're not a real elf,' said the boy. 'But it's okay, I won't tell the little kids.'

Jamie thanked him for being thoughtful. 'So, tell me, what's your name?'

'Kyle.'

'You in for Christmas?'

Kyle shrugged. 'They said I can go home Christmas Eve. I've got my fingers crossed because I don't want to be here on Christmas Day. All my friends will be home with their families.'

Jamie knew how he felt. He also wasn't about to ask what was wrong with the child, remembering how he hated people asking questions about his illness when he was going through treatment. All he wanted was to be like everyone else.

'Have you ever been in hospital?' asked Kyle, looking over the wrapped present Jamie gave him.

'Yep. A few times.' He pointed at the gift. 'You're allowed to open that today if you like.'

Kyle smiled and unwrapped the box to find a book about a wizard boy. 'Thank you, but I don't read.'

Jamie loved books at his age, especially when Alice read to him. Perhaps Kyle might like to listen rather than read. 'Hmm, let's check it out together. See what we think of the first chapter.'

Kyle nodded. 'Okay.'

Jamie scraped his chair closer, then leaned towards the bed as Kyle got comfortable. He opened the book to chapter one and started to read while Kyle kept his eyes on each page.

Before long, they had gone through the first three chapters and Kyle was eager to hear more, but the nurses told the children it was time for the elves to head back to Santa's Grotto. Jamie folded a piece of the wrapping paper and used it as a bookmark.

'Do you think you'll read the rest, Kyle? Have I got you interested in books now?'

The boy nodded. 'Yes, I like it, and at least now I won't be bored tonight.'

'And if you do end up in here on Christmas Day, just know it won't be so bad. I had a good Christmas here once. My nan brought me chocolate, and my best friend played games with both me and the doctors. We had Christmas dinner, watched a film about a snowman, and we wore paper hats. It wasn't so bad in the end.' It was far worse in prison, what with so many missing their loved ones, but he wasn't about to add that to the conversation.

Kyle looked a lot brighter by the time Jamie said goodbye, which made Jamie feel a lot better too.

The atmosphere in the ward was joyous, and the children were showing each other their presents as the volunteers headed back to the minibus.

Jamie stared out the window, watching the world go by. He hoped Kyle would be okay. He mentally thanked the doctors who helped save his own life as a child.

The thought of wasting so many precious years had him chastise himself as rolling hills came into view. Why did he have to go down such destructive roads? He should have just stayed by Alice's side all day every day, then his life would have been very different.

He glanced her way for a moment, watching her chat to Marisa, across the aisle.

You've always been by my side.

As if knowing he was having negative thoughts about himself, Alice's hand slipped into his while she continued talking to Marisa.

Warming, he smiled softly as the coastline of Port Berry came into sight. There was nothing he could do about the past, but he and Alice would have the best future. The life he felt they should have had. He was going to do everything he could to make sure happiness took centre stage. Just looking at her walking stick, knowing her flare-up had come from stress, made him even more determined to bring peace to the table.

CHAPTER 21

Alice

The lunch trade at the B&B was closed for the Christmas holiday and Alice and Demi were helping Ginny make festive cupcakes in Ginny's Tearoom. Not only were they going to hand them out for free at the Hub, they were going to take a large batch over to the Sunshine Centre for the workers and volunteers there as a thank you for all their help with the Hub over the year.

Green, red, and white icing covered Alice more than the cakes, and the silver and gold sprinkles were strewn across her table, seemingly having a life of their own.

'I hear Jamie's doing his first shift in the Hub this morning with Matt,' said Ginny, icing her cupcake perfectly.

Alice glanced at the blob she'd created on her one. 'Yeah. They've got loads of food parcels to make up, so that should keep them busy.'

Demi was packing some of the sweet treats into boxes, ready to transport. 'How did it go at the hospital yesterday, Al?'

'Aww, the kids loved their presents. It was so good of the church to get the locals to donate.'

Ginny started icing another cupcake while Alice tried to tidy her own one. 'And how's your knee today?'

Alice glanced down at her lap. 'Much better, thank you. Jamie made me a lovely hot bath last night, and that helped soothe the old bones.'

Demi laughed. 'And did he stay in the bathroom with you?'

Alice felt her cheeks flush. 'No, he did not. He was just being thoughtful.'

Handing over a fresh cupcake to Alice to ice, Ginny grinned. 'Any developments to talk about, chick?'

'What do you mean, developments?'

Ginny scoffed. 'Erm, you know exactly what I mean.'

'There is nothing to report. We're just friends.'

'You've never been *just friends*.' Ginny looked at Demi. 'Seriously, I've never known friends to act the way they do.'

Alice reached for the red icing bag. 'It's not a big deal to us how we act. It's just the way we are, and nothing has developed.' She eyed Ginny when she said the last word.

The door to the tea shop flew open, and in rushed Benny, all rosy cheeks and big smile. 'Mum, you'll never guess what's happened!'

Alice frowned. 'Why aren't you in school?'

Benny shrugged, closing the door to keep the chill out. 'We break up next week for Christmas. There's not much going on right now, so we had a free lesson.'

'I'm pretty sure you're still supposed to stay in school when that happens.'

Ginny looked up. 'We used to go over the park whenever we got a free lesson.'

Alice frowned at Ginny. 'Yes, well, I'd prefer Benny to stay in school.'

'But I have big news,' Benny cried.

'Ooh, let's hear it, chick.' Ginny lowered her hands and sat up straight.

'Trey said Alan got arrested last night and is going to prison.'

All three women gasped in surprise.

'What does Trey Seabridge know about Alan?' asked Alice.

Benny shrugged. 'Nothing. His mum told him.'

Ginny turned to Alice. 'Wouldn't the police let you know if they were charging him, chick?'

Benny shook his head. 'It's not about us. Trey's mum said he's been harassing another ex-girlfriend as well, and she had loads of evidence, even stuff showing his face. He's in serious trouble this time.'

'And this ex of his has only just come forward with her proof?' questioned Alice.

Benny nodded. 'Trey's mum said the woman heard about what happened with us, and that's why she decided to tell the police what had been happening to her.'

Demi raised her brow. 'Trey's mum says a lot.'

Ginny agreed. 'She's that type. Got her nose in everything.'

Demi smiled softly at Alice. 'At least he's off the streets now. A win for all women.'

Alice wasn't sure how to feel.

Benny sat close to her. 'He's getting what he deserves, Mum. Don't think about him anymore.'

Alice faced him, blinking back tears. 'I'm sorry I brought him into our lives.'

He leaned into her arm, giving her a cuddle. 'It's not your fault.'

'He's right,' said Ginny. 'All you did was try to find love. How's anyone to know who the weirdo narcissists are at first? They're skilled manipulators. I'm just glad he's been arrested.'

Alice composed herself and nodded. 'Yes, so am I. It sounds like that poor woman had it far worse than me.'

'I better get back.' Benny kissed Alice on the cheek. 'But I had to see you as soon as I heard. You feel better now, don't you?'

'A little. People like him should be behind bars.' Alice saw Benny to the door, giving him a cupcake to take with him.

'Well, what a turn up for the books, eh, chick?'

Alice smiled at Ginny, feeling slightly lighter. 'It's good news Alan is off the streets.'

Ginny waggled a hand towards the door. 'Go on then.'

'Go on then what?'

'You know you're dying to go to the Hub to tell Jamie.' Ginny winked. Alice grabbed her coat and scarf.

'I'll be right back.'

A gust of salty sea air hit Alice straight in the face as she made her way along Harbour End Road to the Hub. Not even the harsh weather at the harbour could dampen her mood.

What a relief it was to know Alan wouldn't be popping up anymore. She figured he wouldn't come near her again anyway, especially after his encounter with Jamie, but she was certain now, thanks to the bravery of his other ex, whoever she was.

Alice passed her family's shop first, so went inside to tell her mum and nan the news.

Lizzie raised a hand from behind the counter. 'Benny just told me. Bloody brilliant, eh, love?'

'Yes. Have you told Nan?'

'Yep, but I think she's still finding ways to hex him.'

Alice breathed out a laugh. 'Between Nan and the woman who got him arrested, he doesn't stand a chance.'

'Good riddance to bad rubbish.'

Alice waved. 'Got to go. Speak later.' She laughed as she heard her mother let out a squeal of delight.

Jamie was at the front of the Hub, handing over a food parcel to a young man as she approached. He said goodbye to the man, then flashed Alice a warm smile. 'Hello, Angel. You here to see me?'

'Yes.'

'Come inside, it's cold.'

Alice went straight to the big blue comfy chair and sat down.

'Matt's just out the back, packing more food parcels.'

Alice wiggled her index finger, beckoning Jamie closer.

He grinned as he leaned to her cheek.

Alice told him the good news about Alan, then bit her lip and waited for his reaction.

'I want to shake that woman's hand.' He pulled up a chair to her side. 'How are you feeling?'

'Relieved.'

'He wouldn't have come near you again, Alice. Just know that.'

She raised an eyebrow. 'Well, you never can be too sure with people like him, but I do know he would have been afraid of you, so that would have stopped him. He's a bully who only picks on women. He'd never take on a man.'

Jamie sat closer. 'I'm so sorry for whatever he put you through. I know you've never gone into details about your time with him, but whatever happened, it wasn't good, and I'm just glad you got yourself away from him.'

'Yeah, well, I've had enough misery in my life without him adding to it.' She stared into his eyes. 'And I don't want you blaming yourself.'

'We're all about moving forward now, right?'

She nodded. 'Definitely.'

'Good. Now, how about fish and chips for dinner tonight, on me, and a Christmas film? Something funny.'

'Sounds perfect.'

'You want to stay in here with me for the rest of the day?'

Alice stood. 'I can't. I'm in the tea shop, making the cupcakes, then I'm off to the Sunshine Centre with Ginny and Demi to drop some off. We'll be back in here later with some of the cakes, so I'll see you then.'

Jamie followed her to the door. 'Okay. Look forward to it.'

She turned, grinning. 'What, seeing me?'

'Nah, scoffing one of the cupcakes.'

Alice burst out laughing. 'Life's good, isn't it, Jamie?'

'Yep. And it's going to stay that way, Angel.'

Alice practically skipped all the way back to the tearoom.

CHAPTER 22

Jamie

The next few days were like heaven. Jamie couldn't stop smiling about how wonderful everything was. His new life was going in the direction he wanted. Peace was in his heart, along with Alice, but that was nothing new. She always had a place there. He figured he should talk to her at some point about their future, but with Christmas and Sophie's wedding on top of them, Alice was preoccupied. Besides, he wasn't sure about building on what they had for fear of ruining anything.

Jamie was up the stepladder, changing a light bulb in the dining room, when his sister walked in, deflating his cheery mood immediately.

'I see she's got you working.' Shannon slid onto a table and stared up at him.

'Can you not sit on the table?'

'I'm comfy. How about you?'

He glanced at the ceiling. 'I'm busy.'

'I've only come in to say goodbye. I'm off home tomorrow.'

Jamie remembered when the B&B used to be their home. It felt strange all of a sudden, even though not much had changed since his grandmother owned the place. Even the Christmas decorations were the same.

'I can't believe you want to hang around here,' she added, examining her fingernail.

'Not all the memories are bad.' He thought of Alice. His nan.

Shannon wrinkled her nose as she scoffed. 'Not sure what you remember, but I only have to set foot in this place and I smell Dad, reeking of stale booze.' She shuddered, touching her chest. 'Seriously, Jamie, leave it behind. Don't you think you've been through enough?'

'It's different here now.'

'What, because of Miss Goody-goody?'

He ignored her, hoping she would leave, but no such luck.

'I know I can't do anything about getting the B&B back. But I did wonder if Dipple would feel sorry for me and toss a few quid my way if I laid it on thick.'

Jamie shook his head, not surprised at all. 'Guess she's not as soft as you think.'

Shannon gazed at the floor. 'I still wish Nan had left this place to me.'

'You hate it here.'

'I would have sold to property developers. Made sure it was turned into flats or something. Anything but this.'

Jamie climbed down the ladder and pointed at the doorway. 'You live on the other side of the world, Shan. Don't let it bother you what happens here. It's not as though you have to pass by every day.'

'Just knowing it stands irritates me.'

'Yeah, well, that's probably why Nan sold it to Alice. She sure as hell wasn't about to leave any of it to you in her will.'

Shannon scowled. 'She was being spiteful to us, hope you know.'

'I don't believe that. Nan was just moving on with her life. You should try taking a leaf out of her book.'

'In case you haven't noticed, I am the one who moved on. Look at you, little bro. How far have you gone?'

He hated when she called him that, like she was somehow wiser and held more authority because she was a few minutes older. 'Change isn't just about scenery. I've gone through many personalities to find me, and I now like myself. So, to answer your question, I've come a long way.'

Shannon sighed as she stood. 'Good for you.' She scanned the room, and he couldn't tell if she was reminiscing or perhaps saying a silent final farewell. 'If you ever want to come over to see me, you can.'

Jamie quirked an eyebrow at her casual offer. 'Thanks.'

'I won't be back,' she told him bluntly.

'I figured that much.'

Shannon stopped in the foyer. 'And it's not because I couldn't get any of Nan's money.' She checked the time on her phone, then slipped it into her pink handbag. 'This was no home, just someone's business, a place for our father to sleep, and somewhere our mum left us.'

'Mum died, Shan. You can hardly hold a grudge for that.'

'Can't I?'

He had no argument for her. She felt how she felt and there was nothing he could do about that. 'Hope you have a nice Christmas, Shannon,' he said, following her to the front door.

'I think you're an idiot staying here, Jamie, but if that's what you want, then I hope you have a nice life.' She reached out and touched his arm; her way of affection. 'Stay out of trouble.'

He watched her walk away, knowing that was probably the last time he'd see his twin.

'Everything okay?' asked Alice, coming out the back room.

Jamie turned to smile. 'Shannon just popped in to say goodbye.'

'Oh, and the money?'

He shook his head. 'She's walked away from that, too. She was just trying her luck while she was around.'

Alice moved around the desk. 'Jamie, do you ever want to walk away? I know we made arrangements about you living here, but do you ever have moments of regret?'

'No. I want to be here.'

She glanced over at the Christmas tree. 'Well, it was your home for so long.'

'I want to be here because of you.'

'So, if I lived somewhere else, you'd be happy to live with me there?'

Jamie breathed out a small laugh. 'I thought we only made the arrangement of me staying here because you have the room.'

Alice shrugged. 'Wherever I am, there'll always be room for you.'

Her words just blew his mind, taking away all breath and heartbeats. She really was the sweetest person he knew, and he had to wonder how he got so lucky having her as a friend.

'I just want to know if you're happy,' she added.

'I'm always happy when I'm with you, Angel,' he told her softly, taking a step closer.

'Do you want to talk about anything? Shannon, the B&B, us, anything at all?'

There was a lot he wanted to say, but he didn't know what was for the best. *Oh, just change the subject.*

'You fancy a sleigh ride?'

Alice chuckled. 'The one going around Anchorage Park?'

'Yep.'

'Right now?'

Jamie bobbed his head. 'Yep.' He watched her chew her lip for a moment before agreeing.

'I'll get my coat.'

'And scarf and hat,' he said, heading for the stairs. 'It'll be cold.' He went to his room, grabbed his outerwear, then met her back in the foyer.

They headed outside and noticed Demi drive by as Alice was locking up. He stuck out his thumb, laughing as she stopped. 'Couldn't give us a lift up to the park, could you, please?'

Demi smiled. 'Sure. Hop in.'

He let Alice sit up front, then settled on the back seat, listening to the women talk about the upcoming wedding.

It wasn't that busy in Anchorage Park, the cold day keeping the visitors away. A couple of people walked their dogs, and there were some joggers, but no queue for the horse and carriage designed to look like Santa's sleigh.

'You working, mate?' Jamie asked the man adjusting reindeer antlers on the dark horse.

'Yeah. I've got a booking in about an hour, so if you fancy a ride, now's the time to hop on board.'

Jamie nodded. 'Great.' He paid the man, then helped Alice clamber inside the red open-top carriage.

Alice unfolded the green-check blanket that was on the seat and draped it over both their legs as the driver told Rudolph to walk on.

Jamie chuckled, his breath visible in the cold air.

'What are you laughing about?'

'Just my unexpected day.'

Alice snuggled into the blanket. 'I like this day.'

He leaned closer. 'It's definitely improved.'

Alice pulled out her phone and started taking pictures of them, Jamie smiling widely in each one. 'We don't take enough photos,' she remarked, showing him the screen.

'Do you still have the ones you used to take when we were kids?'

'I do. Do you want me to show you later?'

'Just the ones where I look healthy.'

Alice nodded, then put her phone away. 'Do you want to go ice-skating tonight? Benny's been asking for ages. There's one of those pop-up rinks over the back.' She gestured forward. 'It'll be cold, but all lit up, and they serve hot chocolate. What do you think?'

'I think I'm worried about you skating with all your aches and pains.'

'I try not to let these things stop me. Anyway, I'm only at level two today.'

'That's great. All right then, let's go ice-skating.'

Alice rested her head on his shoulder for all but a second. 'Yay, we're going skating!'

'I don't know why you're cheering. You could still go even if I didn't want to.'

'I don't want to go without you. I've been looking forward to the day I get to do things like this with you, so that's why I'm cheering.'

Jamie's heart warmed. 'I've been looking forward to doing things like this with you too. And in all honesty, sometimes I have to pinch myself that we're actually doing anything together.'

'We used to talk about all sorts, didn't we?'

'Yeah, but it was just a dream back then.'

Alice looked up. 'Not to me. I saw them as goals. I knew you would get out one day, you would come home, and we'd be happy.'

'Seeing as you come from a family of psychics, I'll take that as a premonition.'

Alice giggled. 'Take it any way you like, Mr Stark. It's all about belief.'

He looked up at the cloudy sky. 'Yeah, you certainly believe in the magic of the universe or something.'

Alice smiled. 'No. I just believe in you.'

Once more, her sweet tone warmed his heart.

CHAPTER 23

Alice

The far end of Anchorage Park was filled with multicoloured twinkling lights surrounding a rectangular ice rink and two wooden alpine cabins. Large animatronic reindeer bobbed their heads as a mechanical Father Christmas waved over by the entrance, where lively festive music played.

Alice, Jamie, and Benny went straight to the skate-hire lodge and paid for an hour on the ice.

With how illuminated everything was, there was no telling just how dark the sky was, and there were so many happy skaters around, their combined warmth seemed to take the edge off the night-time chill.

Benny pointed out some of his friends as they plodded over to the rink.

'Off you go then,' said Alice. 'Have fun.' She turned to Jamie. 'You ready?'

He laughed, carefully stepping onto the slippery ice. 'Not sure I know how to do this anymore. We were teenagers the last time I went skating.'

Alice grabbed the rail to help steady herself as she joined his side. 'The last time I did this was with you, so we're in this together.'

He laughed and took her free hand. 'We'll go slow.'

Robson came whizzing by, bringing himself to a halt in front of them. 'Hello, you two need some help from a pro?'

Alice grinned. 'No one likes a show-off.'

Demi stumbled into Robson's side. 'He makes it look easy.' She pointed behind her. 'I've been round twice already, and so far so good. Come on, Al, let go of the rail and give it your best shot.'

Alice let go of her strong grip and shuffled forward with Jamie holding her hand tightly. 'We'll see you round the other side.' Laughing, she watched Robson swirl off like he skated for a living, and Demi do her best to slide across the ice with grace.

'I think we're doing great,' said Jamie, holding his posture well.

Alice wasn't too sure but no longer cared. It was a lovely night, and she was out enjoying herself, even if she was praying every five seconds to not fall over, or worse, take Jamie with her.

They came to a stop in front of Benny, who was helping a girl around his age get back up from a fall.

'All okay?' asked Alice, watching the girl tidy her blonde hair, then wipe along the dampness of her jeans.

Benny nodded. 'Yeah. Oh, hey, Mum, this is Ellie.' He turned to the rosy-cheeked girl, who looked slightly nervous. 'This is my mum, Alice. And that's Jamie.'

Jamie said hello first, as Alice was too busy wondering if Ellie was more than just a friend, seeing how Benny was holding the girl's hand even though she was back on her feet and in no need of further assistance.

'We'll see you later for hot chocolate,' said Benny, skating off with ease, still holding Ellie's hand.

'Huh!' Alice looked at Jamie. 'Did I just get introduced to his girlfriend?'

Jamie grinned. 'It did look that way.'

'Well, it's the first I've heard.'

'Did you tell your mum about all your boyfriends straight away?'

Alice scratched beneath her red woolly hat as she raised her brow. 'And just exactly how many boyfriends did you see me with?'

'I said that without thinking, didn't I?'

'Hmm.'

'Well, perhaps if you didn't spend all your time hanging out with me, you would have had some.'

Alice slipped her hand from his. 'I was happy doing what I was doing, thanks.'

'You don't feel you missed out? Especially as we got older and I'd go off a lot with Gregg and that.'

'I won't lie, when you weren't around as much, I did miss your company, but I never felt I missed out on having boy-friends because of being around you.' She gave a half-shrug. 'I was happy enough.' She met his eyes, seeing curiosity and something else she couldn't make out. 'I used to hear whispers about you, but I never saw you with a girlfriend. Did you have any?'

'Not one.' His eyes remained locked with hers, his tone blunt, certain.

'I was never sure,' she said quietly. 'So many years, and no one?'

He leaned forward and placed the lightest of kisses on her cool cheek. 'I've got my angel. I don't need anyone else. Never have.'

Alice was quite sure it wouldn't be the ice that tipped her over — her legs had turned to jelly while her butterflies somersaulted all over the place. She simply gazed at him, not knowing how to respond.

Jamie looked down at his skates.

'Jamie, do you ever want to do anything about us?'

His gaze shot up. 'Always.'

'What stops you?'

'Everything.' He gently squeezed her gloved hand. 'I'm scared, Alice. I feel like I've spent my whole life in a state of fear.'

Alice stared at him for a moment, wishing they weren't on such a slippery surface because she wanted to tug him in close, but she was sure if she attempted the move, they'd both end up flat on their faces. 'Let's just carry on being us. There's no rush. I'm not going anywhere.'

A hint of a smile hit his eyes. 'I'm not going anywhere either.'

'In that case, all we have to focus on is getting around this rink at least once.'

They shared a laugh, then started shuffling along again, picking up a little speed as they got used to the ice. Not letting go of each other, they managed to go around twice, passing Demi and Robson having a cuddle, Benny showing off his twirl to Ellie, and spotting Sophie and Matt entering the hot drinks cabin.

'Hot choccy time?' asked Jamie, gesturing towards the edge of the rink.

'Yes, I think we've earned one.'

'With marshmallows and cream.'

'And cinnamon.' She smiled as they waddled over to the counter to swap their skates for their boots.

'I feel so much better on solid ground.'

Alice giggled. 'It was fun though, wasn't it?'

'Yep. And we didn't fall once.'

'I know. How lucky were we?'

'It's called skill.'

Alice approached the long dark bar to gaze up at the menu of drinks at the back. 'Ooh, they've got mulled wine as well.'

'You fancy some of that?'

'Nah, hot chocolate will do me.'

Jamie ordered two, then they sat over by the windows facing the ice rink, watching Benny still skating around with his friends and Ellie.

'It's quite nice here,' she said, lifting her drink. 'I feel like we're in the Alps.'

'I'll light the wood burner when we get home, and we can continue to pretend we're high in the mountains.'

Alice glanced at the damp floor while she sipped her drink, getting cream on her nose, which Jamie wiped off while laughing. 'It's starting to feel Christmassy now,' she said.

'I don't normally look forward to the day, but it's growing on me this year.'

'It's going to be the best one ever.'

'I like your optimism.'

Alice tapped his disposable mug with her own. 'What do you want from Santa?'

'I have everything I want. So how about you tell me what's on your wish list?'

To live a normal life. With you. What I've always wanted.

Alice shrugged. 'Happiness all round.'

'I'll see what I can do.'

'You were an elf one time, and suddenly you think you can grant those kind of wishes?'

'Yes, I'm one of Santa's helpers now.'

Alice noticed Benny heading for the skate hut. 'Looks like we might be heading home soon.'

'You want to watch another Christmas film?'

'Not tonight. I feel a bit tired. A snuggle in front of the wood burner will suit me.'

'Consider it done. I'll read to you.'

Alice smiled. 'I'd like that.'

'Then what?' He tilted his head to meet her face, and Alice simply gazed at him.

'Bed,' she replied softly.

Jamie gave a small nod. 'Alone?'

'With you. To talk all night about anything and everything, like we used to.' She saw a slight smile. 'It's all right, Jamie. We're just being us again,' she added quietly.

'I did miss us, Angel,' he whispered. 'How close we were.'

'I missed us too.'

Benny came sprinting over, making Alice jump out of the daze she found herself lost in. 'I've asked Ellie to come round for lunch tomorrow, so I'd like the kitchen to myself.'

'Okay.' Alice glanced at the girl, waiting with their other friends at the bar. 'Do you want some hot chocolate before we head off?'

'Yes, please.'

Alice pulled out her purse and gave him some money. 'There's enough there to buy Ellie one as well.'

Benny kissed her hat. 'Thanks, Mum.'

Alice turned back to Jamie. 'Seeing our Benny with a girlfriend has officially made me feel old.'

Jamie laughed. 'There's life in us yet, Angel.'

She smiled to herself, happy with the life they had created so far. The past was over, and she was sure that nothing from that time could set either of them back ever again.

CHAPTER 24

Jamie

Poor Benny looked a bundle of nerves as he pottered around in the kitchen, making sandwiches.

Jamie sat at the table, having a coffee. 'Relax, mate. You've got this.'

'It's half ten, and I'm making lunch already. I don't think I have got this.'

'There's nothing wrong with being prepared. And the sarnies will stay nice and fresh in the fridge.' Jamie couldn't help but be amused as Benny stopped rushing around to take a breath. 'Did you check she hasn't got any dietary requirements? Allergies?'

The lad's face paled. 'Allergies? She's not mentioned anything about that.'

'Probably not got any then, but double-check.'

Benny pulled out his phone and sent a text to Ellie. 'I didn't realize I'd feel so stressed when I asked her to come round for lunch.' He looked up, flustered.

'It's not every day you bring a girl home, that's why.'

153

Benny sat opposite him, slumping his elbows on the table. 'What did you do?'

'What do you mean?'

'The first time you brought a girlfriend home. Did you make her lunch?'

The question made Jamie realize he'd never even made Alice dinner. Something he needed to rectify. 'Erm, well, no. I never invited anyone home. There was only Alice, and she was here all the time anyway.'

Benny smiled. 'Alice has been your only girlfriend?'

When it came to Alice, Jamie didn't always know how to explain their relationship. 'Sort of.'

Benny's blue eyes held a twinkle of interest. 'It's okay with me if you're together. I can see how happy she is with you. And I'm not stupid — I know that you've slept in her room.' He gave a small shrug. 'It's none of my business what you two do. All I care about is my mum not getting hurt.'

'We just talk, then end up falling asleep. And I'd never hurt Alice.'

'I once overheard Granny telling Nan that you broke Alice's heart.'

Jamie felt his own heart crack on hearing that information. 'It was because I was sent to prison. It hurt her. It hurt us both.'

'But you're good now?'

'I like to think so.'

Benny shifted in his seat. 'What was it like in prison?'

'It's different for everyone, but for me, it was a nightmare. A place I didn't think I would survive at first. You go in as one man and come out another. Not always in a good way. But I was one of the lucky ones. I had someone on the outside who believed I could be a better person. Alice saved me in some ways, then I started fighting for myself. You have to put in the work today that gives you a better tomorrow. Make good choices, Benny. Think before you act, and be grateful for any support you receive.'

Benny smiled softly. 'Alice saved me too.'

'She's an angel, isn't she?'

154

Benny nodded. 'Granny was too old to look after me when my mum died, she just didn't have the energy, and Nan fell apart and wasn't right for a long time. It was Alice who held us all together.'

While still looking out for me.

Jamie closed his eyes for a moment, taking a silent deep breath.

'When I leave school, I want to study to become a doctor,' said Benny. 'Alice goes into schools and raises awareness about cancer screening. I want to help cancer patients. To be someone who saves lives, like she does.'

Jamie looked at the lad. 'That's a great job to have. I look forward to your graduation day.'

'You'd come?'

'I'd like to. Guess that's up to you who you want there.'

Benny offered a warm smile. 'If you're still making Alice happy by then, you can come.'

'In that case, it's a date for my calendar.'

Benny gasped, shooting out of his chair. 'Oh no, date. I forgot for a moment.' He glanced at the fridge. 'Do you think sandwiches are enough?'

Jamie tensed his brow as he gave a brief nod. 'Add some crisps to the plates, and pour some juice. That's a decent lunch.'

Benny checked his phone. 'She's got no allergies.'

'Looks like you've got no worries.'

'I said I'd take her out for a pizza tonight, so why am I so worried about this?' Benny's hand waggled towards the bread bin.

'If it makes things easier for you, how about instead of sitting at the table, you take your food in front of the telly and watch a film or play a video game. Just something to help with the conversation. When you're out and about, you have distractions, but the lunch you arranged will be quiet. Intimate. So, add some distractions around you.'

Benny glanced at the door. 'I think Alice will be distraction enough. I so know she's going to pop her head around the door every five minutes.' He clutched his stomach. 'I don't even feel hungry.'

'You leave your mum to me. I'll take her to the café, that way you'll have the place to yourself.'

'Thanks. And I think I'll put the telly on. I like that idea.'

Jamie gave him the thumbs up, then rinsed his coffee mug in the sink before leaving the ruffled boy to get on with making a fuss.

Alice was coming down the stairs. 'Hey, what you up to today?'

Jamie placed his arms behind his back so he wouldn't cuddle her into his arms. 'I'm taking you to the café for lunch, then I've got my shift there.'

'Oh, so your plan is to keep me away from Benny and Ellie.'

Jamie chuckled. 'My plan is to cook dinner for you tonight. Benny's out for pizza, so it's just the two of us.' He met her eyes and grinned. 'You want to be my date?'

Alice chuckled. 'Why not?'

'Good.' He wished so badly he could kiss her. 'Right, I just need to pop out — I'll see you at lunch.'

If anyone knew how to cook what he had in mind, Demi was the one, so he made his way to the pub to see if he could find her. He figured she might be helping in the kitchen.

Luckily enough, she was heading to the bar with a cloth.

'Hello, Jamie. The cleaner's off sick, so I said I'd muck in.' She glanced over her shoulder. 'I don't normally leave the door open, but it needed some fresh air in here. Robson likes to keep it locked until we're open.' She checked the time on her phone. 'Not long now.'

'Oh, sorry. I wasn't thinking about times. I just walked in.'

'What's on your mind?'

'I want to make dinner for Alice tonight, and I need your help. I'm only a basic cook, so was hoping you might be able to give me some instructions.'

Demi tossed the cloth on the bar. 'I'm all yours.'

Jamie smiled. Tonight was going to be special, and now he was starting to feel as nervous as Benny.

CHAPTER 25

Alice

Even though she was just having another dinner with Jamie, Alice found herself faffing about in her bedroom with her clothes. She had told herself off more than once for making a fuss. It was just dinner at home, in the kitchen.

The smell of something roasting in the oven wafted her way, making her mouth water, and seeing how she wanted to act natural about things, she wiped off the lipstick she'd just applied, leaving some blusher and mascara in place.

Alice raised her palms as she stared in the tall floor mirror. 'Just stop.' Taking a breath, she slipped into her comfy trousers and blouse, then made her way to the kitchen to see if Jamie needed any help.

Jamie was crouched in front of the oven, concentrating on the timer in his hand. He didn't even notice her enter.

Alice took a peek at the list on the worktop, recognizing Demi's handwriting, and smiled to herself. It seemed she wasn't the only one making a fuss. She dramatically cleared her throat to gain attention.

Jamie's head shot around. 'Oh, hello. Come in. Take a seat. I'm about to get everything out the oven in two minutes.'

Alice widened her eyes on seeing how the table was decorated. Christmas crackers and gold napkins, holly around a white pillar candle, and cutlery and glasses all in place with a bottle of chilled white wine.

A buzzer went off, and Jamie began draining vegetables, carving chicken, and serving up roast potatoes and pigs in blankets.

'Are we having some sort of Christmas dinner?' asked Alice, pouring a glass of wine.

'Yep.'

She sat, straightening her blouse, then poured Jamie a drink as well. 'It smells delicious.'

'I won't lie, I got help from Demi, so there should be no food poisoning. I wanted to make sure this chicken was cooked thoroughly, so if it's a little overcooked, that's why.'

Alice smiled as he put a roast dinner in front of her. 'Ooh, lovely, thank you.'

Jamie sat opposite and took an obvious breath.

'A little hot there, Jamie?'

He fanned his face with his hand. 'Just a touch.'

'You'll have to cook more often, then you'll get used to it.'

'I felt like an octopus at one point.'

'When you do it a lot, you get used to the timing of everything.'

He sipped his wine. 'That's why I asked Demi. I have no idea how she does this for a living.'

Alice chuckled. 'She loves it.'

'Next time, I'll just throw in some oven chips.'

'And I'm sure I'll enjoy that too.' She stuck her fork into a roasted slice of parsnip.

Jamie raised his glass. 'Cheers.'

Alice put her food down to clink glasses with him. 'Merry Christmas.'

'I know it's Christmas soon, but we're sharing that day with so many others — I just wanted to have a Christmas moment with you.'

Alice smiled warmly. 'I knew you had something more up your sleeve than just dinner. You looked shifty all through lunch.'

Jamie laughed. 'Shifty?'

'Yeah, you always have guilt in your eyes when you're up to something.'

'Oh, is that right?'

'Yep. Been like that since you were a kid.'

'Well, I wasn't being shifty. I just wanted dinner to be perfect.'

Alice swallowed some chicken. 'You don't have to go to all this trouble with me, but I know where you're coming from, and I appreciate you.'

Jamie grinned. 'I appreciate you — and this was important to me. Every Christmas in prison, I used to pretend I was sitting with you like this. It helped get me through the day. I knew I wouldn't always see you on Boxing Day, so my imagination was all I had. It was a hard time of year.'

'You won't ever have to have another Christmas like that again.'

'I know, but I needed one like this with you.' He picked up a small red box from the chair by his side. 'I even bought you a present for today.'

Alice's heart fluttered on seeing the affection in his eyes.

'I want you to know how much you mean to me. How my life is better because of you.' He passed her the box. 'Open it. This one can't wait till Christmas.'

Taking a silent steady breath, Alice opened the box to see a gold necklace inside with a small angel attached. 'Oh, it's lovely! Thank you.' She put it on at once. 'I feel like I should have bought you something for tonight now.'

'No, this was about me living my Christmas dream.'

Alice held her angel as she glanced at the candle. 'So, is this how you saw us, right here in this spot?'

'Mostly. Sometimes in the dining room, other times we'd be in a cottage.' He gave a small shrug. 'It didn't really matter where we were. It was about sharing the day.'

'I used to think about you a lot that day. I always hoped you were happy, that the day wasn't too bad.'

Jamie reached for her hand. 'I have so many regrets, Alice.'

She gave his fingers a gentle squeeze. 'I know you do.'

He sniffed and sat back. 'Well, I wasn't expecting this dinner to take a nosedive. Right, let's perk up.' He handed her a Christmas cracker to pull. 'We have good times now.'

Alice picked up the silver paper hat that fell out of the cracker and placed it on her head. 'We do. But it's okay to get things off your chest.'

'I don't really need to get anything off my chest. It's more the past haunting me every so often.'

'You haven't been out five minutes. Give it time. You're still adjusting.'

'I just get annoyed with myself when I think about how much we've missed out on because of me.'

Alice had him pull the other cracker so he, too, could wear a festive hat. 'If we were both thinking of each other on Christmas Day, we were kind of together.'

Jamie smiled. 'You always make everything sound better.'

Alice bit into a potato and grinned. 'It's true though,' she said, through her mouthful.

'Well, I much prefer this kind of together.' He put on a red hat and winked.

'Perfect.'

Jamie chuckled. 'You look adorable.'

'Silver hats are my thing.'

'How's the dinner going down?'

Alice made a show of rubbing her stomach. 'Mmm, lovely.' She giggled. 'I'll thank Demi tomorrow.'

'Oi, cheeky!'

'Eat up, then we can do more Christmas stuff,' she said.

'Like what?'

She watched him tuck into his food. He always seemed to eat faster than most. It was as though he was on a timer. 'Board games. Bit of a boogie.'

Jamie choked. 'Boogie?'

'We need to rock around the Christmas tree.'

Jamie shot out of his chair. 'Let's do that now. Come on.'

Before she had a chance to respond, he had her out in the foyer by the tree, slow dancing to music that wasn't playing.

Alice laughed. 'We haven't finished our dinner.'

'I want to do it all with you.'

'And you can. We've got time.' A sudden unwanted thought occurred, making Alice's stomach churn. She stopped dancing and pulled back to look into his eyes.

Jamie frowned. 'What's wrong?'

'You tell me.'

'I don't know what you're talking about.'

'Why are you rushing?'

Jamie shook his head slightly. 'I'm just mucking about.'

Alice took a steady breath. 'Jamie, are you sick again?'

His head tilted to one side as his shoulders dropped. 'Oh, Alice. Is that what you think?'

'It just hit me, that's all. You're acting like we won't have another Christmas together. Like you want to wrap it up right here and now because you know something I don't.' She blinked back tears at the thought. He reached for her hand but she pulled away.

'Hey.' Jamie's voice was hushed as he moved closer to her. 'I'm okay. I promise. I would tell you if I weren't. You have my word.'

She didn't mean for the tear to escape her eye and quickly swiped it away. 'Do you plan to leave?'

'I told you before, I'm not going anywhere.' He motioned towards the door. 'The only way I'm leaving is if you tell me to.' He reached for her hand again, and this time she let him hold her. 'I'm not ill. I'm not going anywhere. I'm just over-whelmed and a little too excited because I wanted this so badly with you.' He gave a small shake of the head. 'I didn't think this would worry you, but I can see how it has.'

Alice inhaled deeply. 'I just got scared for a moment. I'm sorry.'

He lifted her chin. 'Hey, you have nothing to be sorry for.'

'I've ruined our night now.'

'No, you haven't. We had a misunderstanding, that's all. And I'll let you into a little secret — we'll probably have loads more over the years because we're going to share a lot of years together.'

She warmed at his soft tone and kind smile. 'I want all the years, Jamie.'

He lowered his head so their lips were inches apart.

Lizzie opened the front door and stood there staring at them. 'Interrupting something, am I?'

Alice stepped back from Jamie. 'Mum. What are you doing here?'

Lizzie raised the two carrier bags she was holding. 'Bringing over some of Benny's presents to put beneath your tree out back. Perhaps you should lock the door if you're going to be intimate.'

Alice squirmed on the inside as she watched her mother glare at Jamie, and he seemed to notice as well.

'Look, Liz, I know you don't think I'm good enough for your daughter, but—'

'Oh, what gave you that idea, son?' Lizzie's tone was filled with sarcasm, and Alice didn't know what to say.

Jamie's chest rose and fell steadily. 'I just want you to know I'd never do anything to hurt Alice.'

'Oh, is that right? And your word is as good as . . . What exactly?' Lizzie lifted one bag, attempting to circle a finger. 'With all the stunts you pulled around here, your word is suddenly worth something, is it?'

'Mum, I thought you were giving Jamie a second chance.'

Lizzie's lips pursed for a moment. 'I was. I am. I just would prefer it if he . . . Well, if he . . .'

'Wasn't around your daughter,' said Jamie.

Lizzie didn't correct him.

'Mum, please. You're not being very fair. He hasn't put a foot wrong since he's been out. Doesn't that show you anything?'

Jamie sighed. 'I get that you don't trust me. It's early days, but you'll see how much I care about Alice. How I won't ruin her life.'

Lizzie scoffed. 'No, you already did that once, didn't you?'

'I was an idiot. I made mistakes and I got arrested. That wouldn't happen now.'

'And I'm just supposed to take your word for it, am I?' Lizzie's voice was a little louder.

'No,' snapped Jamie. 'But you'll see. I'm telling you, Alice is fine with me. I won't hurt her.'

Lizzie dropped one bag and slapped her chest with a thud. 'How do you expect me to believe that when I know what you're capable of?'

'I'm asking you to try and have a little faith.'

'Why did you come back here, Jamie? Why my daughter? She's nothing but a roof over your head to you, isn't she?'

'She's more than that.'

'No, she's not.'

'She's my wife!' Jamie yelled.

Alice gasped, placing a hand over her mouth. 'Jamie!'

Lizzie dropped the other bag as Jamie stormed out.

163

CHAPTER 26

Jamie

Marching down the road, Jamie huffed and puffed, chastising himself with every step. He hadn't brought a coat and the cold wind whipped through his shirt, chilling his bones. Light snow fell, but he didn't care. He was too angry to care about anything much at all.

How could I be so bloody stupid?

He wanted to yell out to sea. Run to the shoreline and scream at nobody. Nothing. Only the boats bobbing in the bitter water would hear his cries, everyone else being huddled up at home.

Home. What a joke! He'd just blown his chance of having one, because he was pretty sure Alice would never speak to him again after what he'd just blurted.

Jamie paced outside the café, not knowing which way to turn. How to handle the mess he'd just created for Alice. He clutched his head and gritted his teeth. 'Argh!'

The door to the café flew open and Will ran out.

'Jamie? What's wrong?'

Jamie turned, revealing watery eyes and agitation.

Will tugged him inside and closed the door. 'Tell me what's happened. I can help. Just talk to me. Has something happened to Alice?'

Jamie slumped to a chair, burying his face in his hands. 'It's me. I messed up. I'm an idiot, Will.' He looked up. 'Why am I always the idiot?'

Will pulled up a chair and sat to his side. 'You listen to me — you're not an idiot.'

Jamie wasn't listening. 'You know, my dad used to tell me over and over how much of an idiot I was. Now I know why he would say that to me.'

'No, he was wrong to call you that.'

Jamie caught his breath. His heart was racing, and his hands shaking. 'One thing, Will. One thing, that's all I had to do. I promised. I made a vow. Just one thing, and I couldn't even do that.'

Will took Jamie's flailing arms and lowered them. 'Look at me. I need you to take a breath. Whatever has happened, I'm going to help you. But right now, I just need you to breathe.' Will took a deep breath. 'Come on, mate. Just breathe. Nice and easy.'

Jamie copied his friend, taking short breaths in and long ones out, closing his eyes for a moment, wanting to block out the world.

'It's all right, Jamie. Everything's going to be just fine.' Will's voice was soft and calm with a hint of authority. 'You're doing really well.'

Jamie started to settle, but he was still infuriated with himself, and there wasn't anything he could do to fix his mistake.

'Talk to me, Jamie.'

'I messed up.'

Will nodded. 'How?'

'I broke my promise to Alice.'

'You in trouble with the law?'

Jamie shook his head, lowering his face once more. Just thinking about what he had done was hard enough, let alone talking about it — even with Will, who he trusted.

Will patted Jamie's arm. 'I told your gran I'd look out for you, so if you need somewhere to stay for a few days, you can come home with me.'

Jamie looked up. 'Thanks. I'm not sure I'm welcome at the B&B right now.'

'You want me to go and pick up a few of your things, or do you want to tell me what's gone on and see if I can help fix it?'

'The damage is done now.'

'Start at the beginning.'

Jamie took another deep breath. What difference would it make telling Will? Soon everyone would know the truth. 'It was ten years ago. I found a lump, got scared, thought I had cancer again. Don't know if you know, but I had it as a child.'

'I heard some whispers.'

'I thought it was the end of the line. I didn't want to tell anyone but I confided in Alice. We started talking. I told her about my bucket list — all the things I wanted to do.' Jamie looked directly into Will's curious eyes. 'One of them was to get married. Pretend I had a normal life.'

Will's head bobbed slightly.

'Alice made me go to the doctor for tests, and she married me in secret before I'd even got the results back. We both thought it was going to be bad news, and we didn't want to waste time.'

'Had the cancer returned?'

Jamie sighed, leaning back in the chair. He focused on the silver star hanging in the window. 'No. It turned out to be a harmless cyst.'

'That must have been a huge relief.'

'Yes, but we were married, and Alice told me it didn't matter as long as her family never found out. We never spoke of divorce. We never talked about the marriage at all. It was that much of a secret, it kind of disappeared. We always knew, but neither of us brought it up again. It was just a bucket list thing after all, not a real marriage.'

166

'And now?'

'I just shouted it at Lizzie.'

Will sighed. 'Ah, I see.'

'Alice and I had that one day where we made the world go away. It was just the two of us all day. All night. We lied to each other, we lied to ourselves. A day of pretending. It was madness, but it was ours. Just for that one moment, we shared more than we ever had before or since, and we've been through a lot together, but not like that day. It was special.' Jamie rolled back tears. 'Nothing about my life ever feels normal.'

Will leaned forward, offering sympathy in his smile. 'There's no such thing as normal, mate. Everyone's got their shit going on. We just do the best we can with what cards we've been dealt. You're only human, and the whole cancer thing messed with you. What you and Alice did, well, that's between you two. And if you chose to stay married, then maybe there's a reason for that. One neither of you will admit out loud.'

Jamie stared out the window, wishing he could turn back time and keep his big mouth shut.

Will stood. 'How about we go see Alice now, and you can apologize? Make things right.'

'She won't want to see me. She'll be too upset.'

'I think you should at least try.'

Perhaps Will was right. What good was running off going to do? He just hoped Lizzie had gone home because he really didn't want to have to deal with her as well.

Jamie followed Will to the door. 'Am I stopping you from doing something here?'

'No, I was about to head home. I was having a tidy after the evening meals. Samuel had only just left when I spotted you outside.'

'I didn't know where to go. I just felt like running and never stopping.'

'Yeah, life gets you like that sometimes.' Will locked the door behind them. 'Best to face problems though. They get sorted that way.'

Jamie wasn't so sure, but he walked with Will around the corner to Seaview.

Lizzie and Alice's voices could be heard from the end of the pathway, causing the two men to come to a halt.

Will raised a hand. 'Wait here while I see if Alice is ready to talk to you.'

Jamie thought that was for the best too. He sat on the wall, staring across the road at the darkness of the sea.

'How could you?' came Alice's distraught voice.

Jamie stood as he turned to see her standing in the open doorway. 'I'm so sorry.' What else could he say?

'Go away, Jamie.'

Will came out and walked to the end of the path. 'Go and wait by my truck. I'll just pick up some of your things.'

With his head dipped, Jamie went back to the café where Will's dark pickup truck was parked. No doubt his friend would bring more than an overnight bag. Alice was probably clearing out all of his belongings this very minute.

It didn't take Will long to return. He had a single holdall with him.

'Did Alice say anything to you?' Jamie asked, climbing in the vehicle.

'She let me in your room, that's all.'

'I know it's a stupid question, but how was she?'

Will started the engine. 'She looked worn out, mate. I didn't want to stick around. Lizzie was fired up, and Benny had just got home. Thought it best not to fight your corner. A good breather is needed all round.' He put the windscreen wipers on as the snow got a little heavier. 'Let the air settle, Jamie. Things are always easier in the morning.'

Jamie sat back, watching chunky snowflakes hit the window. He hoped Will was right. But even if Alice did calm down, he had still let her down. Again.

'Let me just send Ginny a quick message so she knows what's going on.'

Jamie thanked him.

It wasn't long before Will was heading down the driveway of Happy Farm, where he lived with Ginny.

Jamie hadn't been to Will's home before. Even in the dark, the old farmhouse looked welcoming. 'What do you think Ginny will say?'

Will pulled up out front and glanced at the sky. 'Knowing her, she'll say, start gritting the pathways before the snow settles.'

'It is getting pretty heavy.'

'Come on, you can help me. It'll clear your head for a bit.'

They got out the truck and went to the house.

Jamie stood in the hallway with his bag, looking around the cosy rustic scene.

Ginny came down the wide stairway to greet them. 'Hello, Jamie. Ooh, you look in need of a friend.'

Will kissed her cheek. 'Spot of bother with Alice. I'll explain all the details later. Right now, the snow is settling, so we're going to toss some salt down.'

Ginny thumbed towards the kitchen. 'Robert's asleep. I'll check on Ralph.'

Jamie turned to Will as she hurried away. 'I know Robert is your son, but who's Ralph.'

Will grinned. 'Our rescue donkey. We have chickens as well, and a cat.'

'I wish my life was as sorted as yours.'

Will blew out a laugh as he showed Jamie to the cloakroom to give him a coat to wear. 'Wasn't that way for years, mate. Both Ginny and I had it tough for a while, but we found each other, and everything you see, we built together through love.'

Jamie thought of Alice. They'd been through so much together.

'Follow me,' said Will, heading outside.

The snow was falling thick and fast. Jamie blinked a few times as he made his way over to a small shed.

Will pulled out a bag of gritting salt and handed Jamie a shovel. 'Pathways and drive, then hot shower and a cuppa.'

It wasn't how Jamie had expected his night to turn out. Dancing with Alice by the tree, their Christmas dinner, the angel necklace she so proudly wore flashed through his mind as he got on with his task.

'Better make it quick,' called Will, poking a finger upwards.

The snow was fast becoming a blizzard. Jamie wiped his mind of all problems, hurrying so they could get back inside, out of the battering they were now getting from the weather.

Ginny had the kettle on by the time they finished, and the hot drink was well and truly appreciated.

'You go warm up in the shower, Jamie,' she said. 'I think we could all do with getting our PJs on and settling down.' She glanced out the kitchen window. 'Looks like this is here for the night.'

'I'll show you where everything's at,' said Will.

Jamie thanked them, then followed Will upstairs, picking up his bag along the way.

'This will be your room.' Will opened a door to reveal a small bedroom with white panelled walls and dark-wood furniture. 'Bathroom's next door, clean towels in the cupboard in there, and little man is asleep along the landing so keep the noise down, not that I expect you to start playing music or anything.'

Jamie smiled softly. 'Thanks for all this, Will.'

Will patted his arm. 'No worries, Jamie. You get yourself sorted. A good night's sleep will do you good. Things will look brighter in the morning.'

Jamie put his bag on the floor as Will walked away. He couldn't see how things would improve just because the sun came up. Alice never wanted to hurt her family and, because of him, she had. All those years he never said a word. What on earth possessed him to speak of it now?

He went to the bathroom and turned on the shower, knowing part of him wanted the whole world to know Alice was his wife. He only wished it was real.

As soon as the steam built and the water covered his face, Jamie let the tears fall. Life felt unfair once more.

CHAPTER 27

Alice

Alice felt totally exhausted. Over and over, she explained why she married Jamie, but her mother remained enraged and wasn't listening properly. Benny asked more questions than she could handle, and Luna had arrived, telling them she sensed trouble.

A snowstorm chose to enter the fray, and now Alice was trapped inside with everyone for the night because she wasn't about to chuck them out into a blizzard, even if they did just live around the corner.

'Well, I can't say I saw this one, Alice,' said Luna, snuggling over by the wood burner.

'It's a bloody joke, that's what it is,' snapped Lizzie, slumping to the sofa, showing no signs of calming anytime soon. 'Of all the stupid things.'

'I think it's nice what Alice did for Jamie,' said Benny, leaning against the door frame of his bedroom. 'They thought he was going to die.'

Lizzie's hand shot out towards Alice. 'She should have waited for his results first!'

'Well, perhaps I wanted to marry him!' yelled Alice. She clutched one side of her aching head. 'Did you think about that?'

'The lad was a walking disaster. Why would you tie yourself to something so destructive? You're making no sense, girlie.'

'It made sense at the time.'

Benny approached Luna. 'Do you want some tea, Granny?'

'I think something stronger might be in order, my boy.' Luna pointed at the small kitchenette. 'Drop of sweet sherry wouldn't go amiss.'

Lizzie scoffed. 'Yes, Mum, let's all get drunk. Perhaps then our Alice will no longer be married to a loser.'

Alice clenched her fists. 'He's not a loser.'

Lizzie spun her way. 'Why are you the only one who doesn't remember the trouble he used to get into, hmm?'

'I do remember. But that's the thing, isn't it? He *used* to do those things. He doesn't anymore. Just because you found out we're married, doesn't change anything. You should still be giving him a chance.'

'Chance? Chance!' yelled Lizzie. 'Don't talk to me about chances, Alice Dipple — though I can't call you that now, can I? Alice *Stark*! I've got one daughter left, and I didn't get the chance to see her walk down the aisle when she got wed. How do you expect me to feel about that, eh?'

'We're all upset by that, love,' said Luna softly, smiling at Benny for pouring her a drink. 'It would have been nice to have been there for your big day.'

'It wasn't a proper wedding. It was his bucket list, and that's why I didn't tell you.' Alice slumped into an armchair. 'You wouldn't have let me go through with it had you known — I wasn't stupid. I knew you didn't like him back then.' She shook her head. 'I just assumed you'd be okay with him now, seeing how he's a different person. A better person.'

'I can sense the good in him.' Luna raised her glass of sherry a touch. 'He was troubled, Liz. Still is a bit, but his head

172

and heart are in the right place now.' She glanced at Alice. 'You're a good person, a little too nice at times, and perhaps you shouldn't have married the fella, but it's done now.'

Lizzie shook her head. 'Why didn't you get a divorce? Ten years, you said, and what, no mention of it?'

Alice shrugged. 'What did it matter? Neither of us had plans to marry someone else.'

'All makes sense now, Mum,' said Lizzie. 'All these years and no boyfriends except once, and I've not got it in me to talk about Alan right now.' She waggled a hand at Alice. 'See what you've done to yourself. You could have had a lovely life with a man, but this was hanging over you, wasn't it? Holding you back.'

In some ways, Alice knew that to be true so didn't have much of an argument. There had been times when she'd thought about moving on with her life, which was why she tried to have a relationship with Alan for all of seven months, but it never felt right in her heart. She knew she was tied to Jamie, with or without the bucket-list marriage. If she didn't have such a bond with him, she'd never have stayed in contact with him while he was locked away, bucket-list marriage or not.

Benny yawned. 'I'm going to bed.' He turned to look at Alice. 'And just so you know, I don't have a problem with Jamie. I think he's nice, and from what I saw, he makes you happy.'

Alice smiled and said goodnight, losing her warmth as soon as she saw her mum's glare. 'Benny and Jamie get along.'

Lizzie folded her arms, getting comfortable on the sofa. 'At least that's one thing I don't have to worry about.'

'You don't have to worry about anything, Mum. Nothing's changed except you now know about the marriage. Jamie will still rebuild his life, I'll still be here making the best of the B&B, and we'll all just get on with our lives the way we'd planned.'

'Don't make it sound like it's not complicated.'

'You're the only one complicating things, Mum.'

Lizzie shook her head. 'This isn't normal, love. The way you are with him. The way you've always been, then doing something daft like having a bucket-list wedding when he wasn't even dying. How do you expect anyone to understand you?'

She had never expected anyone to understand the way she was with Jamie. She'd faced many questions about him over the years.

'You've got to calm down, Liz,' said Luna. 'The past is done. Alice is a grown woman now and—'

'And not much has changed with her when it comes to Jamie Stark.'

'We're not hurting anyone, Mum.'

Lizzie turned to her. 'You hurt me, girlie. I'm your mother and you weren't even going to tell me you married someone.'

'Only because I knew how you'd react.'

Lizzie blew out a sarcastic laugh. 'At least I know the truth of why he came here.' She circled a finger in the air. 'Got his half of this place now, hasn't he? You do realize that, don't you? As your husband, if you divorce or you die, he gets his home back.'

'I made a will, leaving everything to Benny.'

Luna sat up. 'I don't know what the law is like with these things, but would Jamie have that much of a say if they didn't consummate the marriage? I mean, she only married him to do him a favour. It's not like they made it *that* real. She could get an annulment, then I'm sure the business would be safe.'

Alice felt her cheeks heat, and she was glad Benny was in bed.

Lizzie sighed loudly. 'Oh, you didn't, did you?' She shook her head in disbelief. 'She slept with him, Mum.'

Luna's eyes widened. 'Ooh, you are just full of secrets, aren't you, Alice Dipple-Stark?'

Avoiding all eyes wasn't doing much for Alice, and her wedding night wasn't something she wished to discuss with her mum and nan.

Being in Jamie's arms beneath the covers that night was the most magical thing that had ever happened to her, and

174

even though she knew it was just to make their wedding real, of sorts, for him, she had held on to the moment so dearly, pulling it out of its box each time she needed comfort.

Alice inhaled slowly. 'I get that this upset you, I really do. But in all honesty — everything else is none of your business. The B&B is secure in my name and will go to Benny to do whatever he wants with when I'm gone. As for Jamie, he has his own plans for his life. We got married, and yes, we had sex — so what? We were grown-ups. We're different people now, and we're just trying to live a normal and peaceful life.'

'Tell me why you won't divorce him?' Lizzie asked so quietly, Alice barely heard.

'He's never asked for one.'

Lizzie looked her directly in the eyes. 'Why haven't you asked for one?'

'I don't want one. I'm happy how I am.'

'But you don't have a proper marriage, love.' Lizzie's tone was calmer now. Gentle.

'It's not really something I pour my energy into, Mum. I've got this place and Benny to concentrate on. I don't think about marriage.'

'You spent eight years of your life keeping that man part of your day when you didn't have to while he was locked away. So it's quite clear that work and motherhood aren't the only things you think about.' Lizzie sighed and sat back.

'I don't think about marriage. Even when I decided to start dating and met Alan, I wasn't thinking about marriage.'

Silence sat between them for a long moment.

'Your mum has had a shock, Alice,' said Luna. 'Everything will be all right soon enough.'

Lizzie wrinkled her nose. 'Will it?'

Luna sipped her sherry. 'Don't see why not. They're happy with the way things are between them. As long as that's the case, then let them get on with it, I say. Our Alice is safe and cared for, and that's what matters.'

Alice wasn't sure about much after Jamie blurted their secret. Maybe she was safe and cared for, but did he have any

175

respect for her? Did he tell her mum just to be spiteful to Lizzie? She covered her angel necklace with one hand, wondering what was going through Jamie's mind. It wasn't as though she could call him to ask — he didn't have a phone. Not that she wanted to talk to him just yet.

Taking a deep breath, she went out to the foyer to double-check the main door was locked. Even if she wanted Jamie to come home, he wouldn't be able to travel in the blizzard.

The door was fine, so she grabbed the spare key to his room and headed upstairs.

Most of Jamie's things were still there, Will only having packed some overnight bits.

Alice watched the snow for a while battering the balcony. There had been many times she'd missed the warm touch of Jamie Stark, but tonight, she felt lonelier than ever.

With a pounding head and eyes half open, Alice curled up on his bed and hugged his pillow. No, she didn't have a real marriage, and no she didn't have a man declaring his love for her each night. But she did have the memory of their one night where they were joined in every way.

Jamie had been so tender. His lips peppered kisses all along her jawline and neck. His eyes had shown affection each time he gazed at her beneath him. He had stroked her hair back and cupped her face, asked if she was okay, and held her tightly. The whole night had become frozen in time. A time she didn't want to end. And Jamie had kept her in his arms till the sun came up and a new day began.

Alice closed her eyes and fell asleep, warm with her memory. But still so angry at him for breaking his promise.

CHAPTER 28

Jamie

Jamie woke to a blanket of snow covering the fields around Happy Farm. It looked so serene and pretty that just for a moment he wasn't thinking about why he had spent the night at Will and Ginny's. Peace surrounded him, and he felt a tad free from his life.

He had a cellmate once who had lived on a farm. He would talk about rolling hills and trickling brooks. They'd swap stories of harbour life and country living, using their imagination and memories to whisk themselves off home for a while.

Staring down at the chicken coop, Jamie knew he was as enclosed as the chickens today. No one was going anywhere with the amount of snow all around.

He got washed and dressed and headed to the kitchen to see if there was anything he could help with.

'Sit yourself down, chick,' Ginny said as soon as he entered. 'We're having a fry-up. What do you fancy?'

Jamie sat at the table. 'Bacon sarnie is good enough for me, thanks.'

Will waggled the kettle his way. 'Or we've got juice.'

'Juice, please.' Jamie went to stand, but Will waved him down. 'You stay there. We've got this.'

Jamie glanced at the carrycot in the corner. 'Is he asleep again?'

Will peered over. 'Nope. Staring at his mobile. Go and take a peek.'

Jamie wasn't sure if the baby would cry on seeing a strange face, but he had a nosey at their son. 'Hello, little man. I like your farm animals.' He tapped one of the sheep on the mobile hanging over the cot.

Baby Robert gurgled, making Jamie smile.

'Roads are covered,' said Will, putting some bread on the table. 'Said so just now on the radio. We won't be opening the shops today.'

'It should clear a bit tomorrow.' Ginny plated some food. 'We've got Sophie's wedding in a few days. It might look nice with the snow, but it won't be nice if we can't get there.'

Will gave her a gentle hug. 'It'll be all right by then, Gin.'

She nodded. 'Yeah, you're right, it should be. There aren't supposed to be more blizzards heading our way, but you never can tell in this country.'

Jamie sat back down and thanked Ginny for his sandwich. 'Is there anything I can help with around here, seeing how I can't get home.' He added a small shrug. 'That's even if I'm welcome there.'

Ginny smiled warmly. 'Will told me what happened. I'm sure Alice will have calmed by now, chick. It was all a bit of a shock, wasn't it?' She widened her eyes. 'Shocked the life out of me. Can only imagine how Lizzie felt.'

Jamie felt terrible for how it had all come out. He had betrayed Alice, and it hurt so badly. He hoped she would forgive him. He needed to make things right. 'I will apologize to Lizzie as soon as I get back. Well, I'll try. I'm not exactly her favourite person right now.'

Ginny glanced over at her child. 'As a mum, all you want is the best for your kid. Lizzie knows the old version of you, and that's why she doesn't want Alice around you. I wouldn't want my Robert in with a bad lot. What parent would? But I can see you've changed. You just need to convince Lizzie of that. So, yeah, by all means apologize, but I think it's going to take more than a sorry.'

Jamie knew it would take time for Lizzie to see his changes. In the meantime, she would carry on thinking the worst.

'I can talk to Lizzie about your paid and voluntary work at the café,' said Will. 'Let her know how well you're doing.'

'And I can mention you're helping at the Hub,' said Ginny. 'Show her you're part of the community now, rather than against it.'

Jamie warmed at their kindness. 'Thanks. Who knows, maybe she'll like me one day.'

Ginny tapped her fork on the edge of her plate. 'But if she never comes around, chick, word of advice — don't spend your life trying to impress her. Just be you, do you, and focus on yourself.' She shook her head slightly. 'If you've left your past in the past, then you make sure no one drags you back there. Let them knock on old doors, you won't be there to answer.'

'Ginny's right,' said Will. 'Have a chat with Lizzie. Clear the air. But that's as far as you can go. After that, it's up to them.'

Jamie nodded. 'She did agree to give me a second chance, but that was before she found out I'm her son-in-law.'

'Why don't you give Alice a call after brekkie?' said Ginny.

'I don't have a phone.'

Ginny gestured to the hallway. 'There's one right there. All yours to use whenever.'

'Thank you, but I'm not sure she wants to talk to me.'

Will thumbed behind him. 'Only one way to find out.'

Jamie finished his breakfast, listening to Ginny and Will talk about the chickens and donkey. Robert was pretty quiet, and a black cat padded in to curl up beneath the carrycot. The whole kitchen held a cosy family vibe he wished he had.

Ginny took the baby into the living room for a feed, and Will went off to check on Ralph, leaving Jamie to pace by the telephone.

Alice had never looked so mortified, and the disappoint-
ment in her eyes last night still stung. He really had no idea
what to do for the best. She was probably busy anyway, no
doubt cleaning something. She would be snowed-in too so
would more than likely answer the phone, at least.

The phone seemed to torment him, or perhaps he was
just tormenting himself. He didn't want to talk to her that
way. Face to face was best.

He went over to the window to check how deep the snow
was. Everything they had gritted was clear, but he couldn't see
the road. Did it matter? He wasn't about to drive. But walk, he
could do that. Happy Farm wasn't too far from the harbour, and
if a bus managed to get through some parts, he would hop on.

Will was out back, so Jamie went there first.

'Hey, Will, is it okay to borrow one of your coats?'

Will nodded as he came out of the chicken enclosure.
'Sure. Why where you going?'

'I'm going to see Alice.' He looked down. 'I've got my
boots. I'll be fine — it's just a bit of snow.'

'I would drive you, but it's a bit dodgy, and as I said
earlier, a lot of the roads are closed.'

Jamie bobbed his head. 'I'll be all right walking.'

'Take a hat and scarf as well.'

Jamie thanked him, then headed off to the cloakroom to
wrap up for his journey.

Ginny came out of the living room. 'Will got you doing
stuff out back?'

'No, I'm going to walk to the B&B.'

'Ooh, you sure about that, chick? It's cold and there's
snow everywhere. How about you call first? Check she wants
to see you.'

'If I do that, we'll end up talking on the phone. She deserves
an apology to her face and I can't wait days for this snow to
melt.'

'Okay, if that's what you think is best.' Ginny followed
him to the door. 'You mind how you go out there.'

Jamie tugged a blue woolly hat down to his ears. 'I'll come back later for my bag, if that's all right?'

Ginny nodded. 'Don't you worry about that. And if you need to stay here any longer, you're more than welcome.'

'Thanks for everything.' He gave a small wave and headed off up the driveway.

Whether he'd be doing the same walk back later was up to Alice. He knew what he wanted to say, but he really had no idea how she was going to react. He'd hurt and upset her, betrayed her trust, and caused friction between her and her mother.

With every step of the long walk, he practiced the words he'd say, but nothing sounded good enough for the trouble he had caused. If she slammed the door in his face, he wouldn't blame her. Did he even have any right to turn up on her doorstep? It was all such a mess. His mess, as usual.

The snow was deep along the pavements, and in some places Jamie had to walk in the road. No traffic came by, and he could see why. The roads looked dangerous, and the chances of him catching a bus were slim to none. At least the sun was out, even though it wasn't giving off any heat.

His heart thumped in his chest when he saw an elderly man on the ground outside a cottage along a back road. He quickly opened the small blue gate and sprinted along the pathway.

The old man groaned on seeing someone.

'Are you all right?' It was clearly a stupid question, but Jamie didn't know what else to say.

'I was trying to clear the path,' said the man.

Jamie crouched to his side. 'Do you think you can get up if I help?' He was no medic so wasn't sure if moving the man was the best thing, but he could hardly leave him there freezing in the snow. The man's trousers were already soaked through.

'I'd like to try.'

With that, Jamie hooked his arms under the man's and heaved him to a sitting position first. He glanced around to see if anyone else was about to help, but the cottage had no neighbours for a mile or so.

'How's that so far?' Jamie asked, checking for scrapes or signs of bleeding, pleased to see none.

'My hip feels a bit bruised, but that's about it, I think.'

'Let's see if we can get you inside. Is there anyone in there?'

'No, just me, son. My wife died two years ago now.'

Jamie's heart went out to him.

'My boy is supposed to be along today,' the man added. 'I wanted to clear the snow for him.'

'How about we give him a call when we get you settled in the warmth?'

The man nodded, and Jamie took a deep breath before lifting him to a stand.

'How you feeling? Dizzy at all?' asked Jamie, checking him over.

'I wouldn't mind getting out of these wet clothes, son.'

'Yes, yes, of course. Let me help you inside.' Jamie took the man's arm, noticing the old fella was a bit wobbly on his feet, and got him into the hallway.

'Thanks for this. I'm normally all right walking about and doing odd jobs, but I slipped.'

'Do you want me to help you upstairs?'

'No, I can manage. Just a bit bruised, that's all.' He pointed at his telephone by the door. 'Can you call my boy? His number is written on the front of the phone.'

'Will do. What's his name?'

'Joseph.' The old man started to slowly climb the stairs, groaning on each step. 'He's a chef, you know, at the Jolly Pirate pub along the harbour.'

Jamie smiled to himself. He hadn't met any of the kitchen staff at the pub, but at least he knew he could call Demi for help if he couldn't get through to Joseph. He had memorized her number.

'What's your name, son?'

182

'Jamie Stark.'

'I'm Thomas.' He frowned for a moment. 'You're not Mabel's grandson, by any chance?'

'Yep, that's me.' Jamie squirmed on the inside, wondering what memories Thomas had of him.

Thomas hummed quietly for a second. 'I remember your mum. Lovely lady. You look like her.'

The comment warmed Jamie a touch. His mother was hardly spoken of, so it was nice to hear someone say something about her.

Thomas knitted his bushy eyebrows. 'I also remember you causing mischief.'

'I'm not like that anymore,' Jamie said softly.

'Good for you, son. I was nothing but trouble when I was a lad, then I sorted myself out, fell in love, got married, and lived a peaceful life. More so within, you know?'

Jamie knew. 'You get yourself changed before you catch your death, Thomas, and I'll call your son to let him know what's happened.'

'All right.' Thomas went off to his bedroom and Jamie made the call.

Joseph was distraught on hearing about his father's fall, and said he was on his way. Seeing how he would have to walk, he should be there in half an hour.

Jamie called up to Thomas to let him know.

'Stick the kettle on then, son,' Thomas called back. 'You'll have a cuppa with me, yeah?'

Jamie smiled. 'Will do.' He headed to the small country-style kitchen and filled the kettle. A half hour was no big deal. He'd see Alice soon enough. As for now, he was doing what he'd set out to do when he left prison. Helping people and finding ways to give back to his community.

CHAPTER 29

Alice

Alice was glad when her mum and nan went home after breakfast, not that anything else had been said since the night before. She just wanted to sit in peace and read a book or something. Her neck was up to a pain level of seven, so she had her neck brace on as soon as she got out of the bath.

Benny had gone to the newsagents, mostly to help Luna walk in the thick snow. They were sure they wouldn't get many customers, but Lizzie liked to open the shop anyway.

The mobile phone rang in Alice's pocket. She plonked down into the chair behind the desk at reception to answer, happy to hear Ginny's voice.

'Hello, chick. Will told me about you and Jamie. How you doing?'

Stressed was the word, but she couldn't be bothered to get into how the situation had caused a flare-up. 'I'm okay, thanks.' Part of her wanted to ask how Jamie was, knowing he had gone home with Will, but she chewed her lip instead.

'You want to talk about anything?'

'Not really, Gin. I feel all talked-out. Mum calmed down in the end, but I know she's still upset, which was why I never wanted her to find out.'

'It was a big secret to keep all these years, chick. Things like that can put a strain on a person.'

Alice stared over at the twinkling Christmas tree. 'It was never a problem for me. Quite the opposite.' She mumbled the last part to herself.

'Look, Al, I don't want to poke my nose in, but I also called to let you know Jamie's on his way to yours. I told him to ring you first, see how the land lies and that, but he wanted to talk to you face to face. I just thought you might appreciate a heads-up.'

'I do, thanks for letting me know.' Alice frowned at her grey loungewear, wondering if she should get changed into something not so drab.

'Will told me off for interfering, but I thought you might be annoyed at me for not warning you.' Ginny's sigh crackled the phone. 'Rock and hard place.'

'It's all right, Gin. I know where you're coming from, and I'm glad I know.' She went over to the window to peer out at the snow-covered road. 'How's he getting here?'

'It said on the radio that half the roads were closed, so Will couldn't drive him, but Jamie was determined to talk to you, so he's walking.'

She wished he had stayed indoors in the warm. 'When did he leave?'

'About twenty minutes ago.'

'Thanks for letting me know.'

'Right, I'll let you get off then. Oh, and, chick, you know where I am if you need me.'

'Love you, Gin.'

'Love you too, Alice.'

Alice started to pace the foyer, knowing Jamie would show up soon. Not knowing how she felt or what to say to him now he'd blurted their secret, she decided to potter around and do some light cleaning to help take her mind off things.

It wasn't easy polishing and dusting while her neck felt like it had whiplash, but it wasn't her first time wearing a neck brace so she just got on with her morning as best she could. There was no way she'd be able to concentrate on a book or TV show, not now Jamie was heading home.

The next time Alice checked the clock, it was almost lunch. Where on earth had Jamie got to? It was a bit of a walk from Happy Farm, but it wouldn't take that long to reach the harbour.

All sorts started to flash through her mind. Accidents in the snow were common, and he had no phone to reach anyone. She really needed to do something about that.

Alice marched to the front door and looked both ways down the street. No sign of anyone about. She stood there for a while, staring over at the bitterly cold sea.

She decided to make a cup of tea to accompany her door watch.

After another half hour, Alice could take no more waiting. She headed to her bedroom, changed into jeans and a jumper and shrugged into her warmest coat. She didn't bother with a scarf because her neck brace was warm enough, but slipped on a woolly hat and some gloves.

She figured if she walked the most obvious route to Ginny's, she'd bump into Jamie along the way, or at least see if there had been any accidents.

The outside temperature was milder than the day before, so that was helpful, but it was still cold and Alice was grateful for the grip on her winter boots.

It wasn't until she hit the first country lane that she chastised herself for not bringing her walking stick. It was folded in her large bag back home, which was little use to her now, and seeing how her right calf was starting to cramp, it annoyed her even more that she had rushed out without thinking.

Alice slowed her pace, knowing what to do when her body played up. She glanced over her shoulder, wondering if it would be best to head back before her knee went as well, something that was quite possible. Her knees were unpredictable and she couldn't always be sure her legs would stay the distance whenever she went out.

The sensible thing was to head home, but Jamie could be lying in a snowy ditch for all she knew so, leg pain or not, she had to continue.

Her luck was out. Cramp wasn't giving up, even though she'd stopped to stretch her foot against a lamp post a couple of times, and her left knee had decided to join in with frustrating her.

Alice spotted a small wooden bus shelter and hobbled her way to its seat to take a moment, fed up she had to rest at all. Time was ticking on, and she hated sitting around doing nothing. Jamie could be . . .

She peered down the road at a man heading her way. His head was dipped, his body slumped, but she was pretty sure it was Jamie.

He glanced up for a second, then went back to looking at the ground before his head shot up to face her.

It *was* Jamie. Alice had never felt so relieved, but she still had the hump with him so tried to suppress her smile.

Jamie's plod turned into a jog, reaching her side within seconds. 'Alice? Where are you going in this?'

Seeing how she was sitting at a bus stop, it would be easy for her to lie, but she was in too much pain to have the energy for fibs. 'Ginny called. Told me you were coming to see me this morning.' She tapped her wrist as though wearing a watch. 'But that was hours ago, so I got worried and came looking for you.' She ignored the slight quirk that hit the corner of his mouth.

Jamie sat by her side. 'I would have been home sooner, but I saw an old man on the ground outside his cottage and have been helping him.'

'Oh, goodness, is he all right?'

'A bit bruised, but I got him indoors and called his son, then waited until he showed up. Turned out his son is the head chef from Robson's pub.'

'Oh no, poor Thomas.'

Jamie frowned. 'How about we focus on you right now. Did you give up looking for me and decide to catch the bus home?' Before she could reply, he added, 'Not seen one come along while I've been out. I've not seen any cars either.'

She glanced at how thick the snow was covering the road. 'Actually, I was just taking a rest.'

He peered along the way she had come. 'You're only fifteen minutes from home.'

Alice huffed. 'Tell that to my legs.'

His finger pointed up at her neck, clearly just noticing the brace. 'What's happened?'

'Fibromyalgia, that's what.'

His gaze lowered. 'I'm sorry, Alice. I didn't mean to cause you stress. And after what I did, you shouldn't have come looking for me.'

'I can't help it if I worry,' she snapped.

'Yeah, I know, Angel. I worry about you too, and we need to talk — but not out here. Let's get you home and warm and where you can put your feet up.'

Alice gestured to the road. 'That would be great, but right now my knee doesn't want to walk so I'm going to have to wait for a bus.'

'We could be here a very long time.' Jamie stood, waggling fingers. 'I'll carry you.'

Alice had to laugh. 'I'm not being carried.'

'It's better than sitting here all day freezing.'

He had a point, but she felt a bit silly.

'What if you slip?' she questioned. 'We'll both end up in hospital.'

Jamie flashed one of his smooth smiles. 'I won't fall, not when I'm carrying such precious cargo.'

'Hmm. Well, perhaps I could get on your back.' It seemed better than him holding her like they were about to step over the threshold. Something they hadn't done on their wedding day.

Jamie turned so she could clamber on.

Alice wished she could bury her head further into her neck brace. She was pleased no one was around to witness the piggyback.

'You good?' he asked. 'Knee okay?'

'Yep.'

Jamie's muffled laugh vibrated through her, causing her to grin.

'Take a rest every few minutes,' was her advice, sure he couldn't go the full fifteen minutes with her on his back.

'I'll let you know if I need a break.'

'We need to get you a phone. I could have called to make sure you were all right.'

'Or you could have just stayed home where you were safe and warm.'

'I like to live dangerously, don't I?' She made sure she showed her sarcasm.

'Look, Alice, I'm sorry for telling your mum.'

'Are you?'

There was silence for a while, apart from his heavy breathing.

Alice wriggled. 'Put me down a sec, please.' She slid off his back and waited for him to face her.

'You okay?' he asked, concerned.

'I'm just confused, and my mum is upset.'

He lowered his gaze. 'Yeah, I know.'

'What possessed you?'

'Can we talk about this when we get home, please? I just want you settled back indoors.'

Alice knew he was being sensible so gave a curt nod before climbing back up, silently cursing her knee. At least the cramping in the calf had eased.

Jamie didn't slow until he'd reached Harbour End Road, and Alice wished he would take a rest. She even offered to walk, seeing how they were so close to home, but he kept telling her he was fine.

When they finally closed the door behind them and Alice was back on her own two feet, she said, 'Ooh, I'm glad to be indoors. Thanks for helping me.'

Jamie went straight to her quarters. 'No thanks needed. Right, you get into your loungewear which I know are your favourite clothes, and I'll light the wood burner and get your blanket. You can spend the day on the sofa. I'll make you something for lunch.'

Alice sighed to herself. 'And then we can talk about our marriage.' She noticed his flush cheeks pale a little before he turned for the door.

'Sure.'

CHAPTER 30

Jamie

Making lunch, all Jamie could think about was what Alice was about to say. He already had it in his head she wanted a divorce — and he couldn't blame her. He'd hurt her and her family. She had every right to wash her hands of him in every way.

He placed ham sandwiches and hot tea on a tray, then took a deep breath before going to see her.

Alice was already on the sofa, a soft blue blanket over her legs, her neck brace still in place. He wished she hadn't come looking for him.

He put the tray down on the coffee table and handed her a plate. 'Hope ham's okay?'

Alice smiled. 'Thank you, that's fine.'

'You warm enough?'

'I'm okay.'

'Your legs?'

She nodded briefly. 'A lot better.'

He sat in the armchair by her side, putting his plate on his lap. He wasn't feeling that hungry. Too many words whirled in his head, and his stomach wouldn't settle. 'Do you want a divorce?' he blurted, needing the question to be out there.

Alice lowered the sandwich she was about to bite. 'Is that what you want?' Her tone was quiet, almost sounding as broken as he felt.

'Because of the way I told your mum about us, I figured you'd hate me.'

'I don't hate you,' she said softly.

'I messed up again.'

Alice turned to face him fully. 'You made a promise.'

He nodded. 'I know, and I am sorry. I honestly don't know what else to say or what to do. I am going to talk to your mum though.'

'Perhaps leave her for now.'

'I have to speak to her at some point. It's well overdue.'

Alice shrugged.

'I want her to know I've changed,' he added. 'I need her to believe me.'

'Does it really matter what she thinks?'

'Yes, it does. She's your mother. I want her to like me.'

'Do you care that much?'

He met her eyes and smiled. 'I love you, Angel. I want us to have a happy life. A happy family.'

'When you say you love me, do you mean properly, like a lover?'

'Like your husband.'

Alice just stared at him, looking slightly speechless.

'Just to clarify,' he added, 'I'm in love with you. I don't want a divorce. I want forever.' He gave her hand a gentle squeeze. 'We've always shared so much. I can't imagine my life without you. Maybe part of me wanted everyone to know you're my wife. I don't know. But what I do know is how much I love you, Alice.'

A tear rolled down her cheek and she sniffed.

'I know I've been trouble for you,' he added quietly, 'but I won't be anymore. So if me being here is too much for you and your family, I'll leave. Whatever is best for you. I just need you to tell me what to do.'

'Stay,' she whispered.

He leaned closer. 'Stay?'

Alice raised his knuckles to her lips. 'Stay.'

Jamie gave a small nod, not sure what else to say or do.

'Should we move forward now?' she asked.

'Like we have been?'

Alice put her plate on the coffee table and gestured for him to do the same, then tugged him towards her side on the sofa. 'I was thinking more along the lines of being a proper couple.'

He smiled softly and stroked her cheek. 'I'd like that.'

'And we can kiss whenever we want.'

'I always want to kiss you.'

Alice went to kiss his hand again, but Jamie pulled it back, replacing it with his face.

'We haven't done this in a long time,' he added, inches from her lips.

'We haven't done a lot of things in a long time.'

He ran his finger down to her neck brace. 'We can catch up when you feel better.'

'I feel better now.'

Jamie grinned. 'You need to rest.'

'I can still kiss.'

He lightly nudged her nose with his own. 'You sure?'

Alice leaned closer, joining their mouths, and just for a moment Jamie stilled, absorbing her touch. She had no idea how often he had dreamed of being with her. He mumbled her name, and she raked a hand into his hair, immediately heating the kiss, and Jamie was way more than overwhelmed. He was lost in her.

After a moment, they came up for air and simply smiled at each other.

'Should we talk some more?' he asked. 'I want everything to be perfect.'

193

'Is there such a thing?' Alice pecked his cheek. 'I don't know what to say anyway.' She sat back and sighed. 'This morning I was still angry with you, then when you didn't show up, I got scared. Just thinking of you hurt or alone, destroys me. Always has.' She shook her head. 'People say we're a strange pair. Maybe we are.'

'We're just us. Who knows how other couples are really? No one can be sure what goes on behind closed doors.'

'Our marriage has been hidden away.'

'It doesn't have to be that way now.' He glanced at the door. 'Not sure who your mum has told, but Ginny and Will know, and I'm happy to shout from the rooftops that you are my wife, the best wife in the world.'

Alice blushed. 'Now you're just being soppy.'

'No, now I'm just letting you know how I feel about you. How I've felt for so long.'

'Are we strange, Jamie?'

He shrugged. 'Don't care if we are. We've always worked. We've always had a strong bond. All I know is, life feels better when you're around.' He lowered his head and inhaled deeply. 'When you used to visit me in prison, it was as though happiness itself had walked in. I can't begin to describe those moments.'

Alice lifted his chin. 'It was so hard saying goodbye. I hated it.'

'Me too.'

'I couldn't go through that again.'

'You won't have to.' He tilted one side of his mouth. 'Unless you get yourself arrested.'

'Flipping heck, I never thought of that.' She placed a hand over his heart. 'Let's both agree prison is in our past.'

'Definitely. So no more trouble from you.'

Alice blew out a small laugh, then smiled softly. 'I can't believe we're here together now.'

'Yeah, it's a little surreal at times, isn't it?'

'I'm going to talk to my mum again. If we're going to be together properly, I want her to hear it from me.'

Jamie agreed. 'But I do want to talk to her as well. Just say my piece. Let her know exactly where I stand. It'll be better coming from me, then she'll know it's not just you sticking up for me.'

'Meanwhile, will you take me to bed?'

'You getting worse?'

Alice grinned. 'No. I meant to snuggle.'

He raised his brow, amused. 'Oh, did you now. Well, I think you should rest today. Perhaps the next few days. Get you back in shape ready for Sophie and Matt's wedding.'

'I can't believe it's only a few days away.'

He stroked down her arm. 'I wish I gave you a better wedding day.'

'We did what we did. There's no point going over it now.'

'But I took away your walk down the aisle moment. Your white dress. Your friends and family. None of that kind of thing matters to me, but I reckon that's your kind of wedding.'

Alice pressed her head against his. 'We never exchanged rings.'

Jamie sighed. 'You deserved better than that.'

'It didn't matter. It was your bucket list. I thought you might die.'

'What were we like, eh?'

Alice straightened. 'Remember the tandem that was on your bucket list. We never did buy one.'

'But we will, and we'll go cycling when the weather's nice. When your legs get tired, you can put your feet up and I'll do all the work.'

Alice chuckled. 'I can just see us riding along in the sun. Me relaxing while you build up a sweat.'

Jamie kissed her cheek. 'Yeah. Something to look forward to.'

'We've got loads to look forward to. I feel like I've just been set free in a way.'

'You've had a lot on your plate over the years. I swear, you're the strongest person I know.'

Alice shook her head. 'I'm not strong. I'm the same as everyone else. We just get on with things the best we can.'

'I guess that's always been us, and now we'll continue that way.'

'But this time we won't be holding back or fighting off feelings. No more secrets. No more problems, just freedom.'

'We really are free of everything, aren't we?'

'Yep, so now will you take me to bed?'

Jamie laughed. 'I'll take you to bed every time you ask, but we're only snuggling. You're in pain, and I've added to that enough over the years. From now on, I'm only doing things that bring you peace.'

Alice gestured at the bedroom. 'Like the bed part?'

'Come on then.' He stood and scooped her up, making her giggle.

Alice latched on, peppering kisses along his neck, then whipped off her brace as he carefully placed her on the bed.

'You know we haven't had our lunch.' Jamie snuggled down beside her.'

'It can wait. We might not be able to do much today, what with all my aches and pains — sorry about that — but we can have a few minutes here in bed.'

Resting on one elbow, he looked down at her relaxed on the plump pillow. 'Firstly, never say sorry for being in pain. It's not your fault, and secondly, we can spend I reckon twenty minutes tops here before your tummy starts rumbling.'

'It will definitely rumble soon. I like the way you know my stomach so well.'

Jamie grinned and peeled back the cover, kissing her stomach. 'I know all of you very well.'

Alice laughed. 'Oh, this isn't fair. I don't want to be in pain today. I want to be with you.'

He rested his head by hers and gently pushed back her hair. 'Hey, you are with me. And we're going to spend every night in each other's arms from now on.'

She pulled his mouth onto hers, smiling on his lips, making him smile back.

'I love you so much, Angel.'

Alice kissed him hard, wrapping him in her arms, and Jamie wanted to stay there forever. He laughed as her stomach rumbled.

'You stay snuggled. I'll bring your food in.' He gave her a cheeky wink, then went off to fetch lunch, coming to a halt when he saw Benny in the living room staring at the cold cups of tea.

'You're back then,' Benny said, eyes moving to Alice's bedroom door.

'We sorted things. After lunch, we're going to talk to your nan.'

Alice was suddenly in the doorway. 'Benny, it's best you know. Jamie and I are staying married and we're going to be a proper couple.'

Benny's lips twisted to one side for a moment. 'And that's what you're going to tell Nan?'

She nodded. 'Yeah, and clear the air. Plus Jamie wants to tell her in his own words that he's changed.'

Benny sighed. 'Well, she has calmed down now.'

'And you?' asked Alice. 'What do you think?'

'I just want you to be happy, Mum.'

Alice rushed forward and hugged him. 'You're so lovely, Benny.'

'I know,' he said, chuckling on her shoulder.

'Are you really all right with us being together?' asked Jamie, knowing kids often hid their true feelings. He always had.

Benny's head bobbed slightly. 'You seem nice enough, and Alice has a lot of faith in you. I don't have a problem if she doesn't.'

Jamie thought the lad a lot more mature than he was at his age. Stable too. 'I want you to know I love Alice, and I plan nothing but happiness for our future. It's all going to be okay around here. There are no more secrets. This is it now.'

'All right.' Benny motioned towards his bedroom. 'I'm going to call Ellie.'

'I'll make you some lunch,' Alice called after him. She smiled at Jamie. 'He's such a good kid,' she added quietly, then headed to the main kitchen.

Jamie followed her, taking their lunch. 'You eat, I'll sort Benny's food.' He guided her to the table, happy to see her finally eating her sandwich.

It was a nice feeling just doing something simple while feeling part of a normal family. Alice's smiles shooting his way every minute only made him happier by the second. If only he could make peace with Lizzie, all would be well.

CHAPTER 31

Alice

Alice had thought it best to leave the chat with her mother until the next day. Besides, the snow had melted a lot more by then, so it was easier to get around.

Hand in hand with Jamie, she entered her family's shop and greeted her grandmother who was sitting behind the till reading a magazine.

'Been wondering when you'd show up.' Luna glanced up. 'Mum's in the kitchen making mince pies.'

'How are you, Nan?'

Luna closed her magazine. 'I think the question is, how are you two?'

Alice raised their linked hands. 'Still married.'

'Hmm, well, as long as you're happy.'

'Thanks, Nan.'

Luna looked at Jamie. 'You just keep making the right choices for yourself, son. Then you'll be okay.'

Alice wondered what she meant by that, as Luna often had hidden meanings in her words. Was Jamie about to face something bad? Make the wrong choice?

'I have my plans,' said Jamie, smiling at Alice.

They headed upstairs to find Lizzie singing along to a Christmas song on the radio. She looked quite festive in her holly-print apron, but all cheer disappeared as soon as she saw them enter her kitchen.

'Come to tag-team me?' Lizzie switched off the music.

'We don't want to fight,' said Alice.

Jamie moved to the table covered with round and star cookie cutters and rolled pastry. 'It's me who wants to talk the most.'

'Mum, will you please just listen.' Alice sat on a chair and gestured for Jamie to do the same.

Lizzie wiped her hands on a tea towel and leaned by the sink. 'I'm listening.'

Jamie spoke first. 'I want you to know I love Alice. I guess I always have, but now we're older, and since being locked up, I've realized just how much she means to me. I did try to hold back — I want better for her, too — but then I stopped telling myself I wasn't good enough. I've changed, in many ways; not just what I do but how I think, feel. Your daughter has been the one constant in my life, and I would never do anything to hurt her. I'm proud to call her my wife, and I'm so happy she wants to build on our marriage and give me a chance.'

Alice squeezed his hand and smiled, seeing the love in his eyes.

A moment of silence sat between them all.

'Mum, Jamie and I really are going to give this our all. We just want a quiet life, to have it be as normal as possible. Just be a couple. But I won't lie. I do want your blessing. I don't want the people I love to be at war with each other. I know I upset you, but Jamie is part of my life, and I just want you to accept that. To accept us.'

Lizzie sighed quietly. 'All right.' She gazed at Alice. 'You're my baby, and all I've ever wanted was your happiness. It's always been Jamie, I knew that. It was obvious. I have spent many a night wishing your heart was with someone less troubled, but it is what it is, and I'll not fight you anymore.'

'I don't want you to hate Jamie, though.'

Lizzie shook her head, looking at him. 'I don't hate you, Jamie. It was a bit of a shock, that's all. If I'm honest with myself, I can see you've changed. Feel your energy even, and if you two want to be left alone in peace to enjoy your marriage, then who am I to stand in the way.'

'Thank you,' said Jamie softly.

'I don't want thanks, just my daughter's happiness.'

'My past is a different chapter in my story,' said Jamie. 'More like a different book. What I have now is so precious to me and I wouldn't do anything to ruin our lives. She's my world, Liz.'

Lizzie nodded briefly. 'All right, Jamie. Let's start over.'

Alice smiled so widely, her cheeks hurt from the strain. 'Really, Mum?'

'Yes, really. We're all family, and it's time to act like it, I say. And if Jamie here has fought long and hard to change his attitude, then I can change mine.' Lizzie looked at Jamie. 'I'll be on your side now. I'll not fight either of you. You're out of prison, have grown into a different man, and you deserve the right to rebuild in peace. I promise not to bring up your past ever again. You don't live there. You live here now, and that's what matters.'

Alice leapt from her chair to swing her arms around her mother's shoulders. 'Oh, Mum, thank you so much.'

Lizzie smiled over at Jamie. 'We do family group hugs here, love. Best you start to join in.'

Alice chuckled as Jamie's arms came around her and her mother.

'Well, this is going to take some getting used to,' he said, a laugh in his tone.'

'Yep,' said Lizzie. 'But we'll get used to it the more it's done.'

They all stepped apart, Alice still beaming.

'Thank you,' said Jamie. 'I really do appreciate you giving me a chance, Liz.'

'You're family.' She shook her head as she blew out a small laugh. 'Still can't get my head around that one, but here we are, so best you wash your hands, roll your sleeves up and help with the baking.'

'I can do that.' Jamie headed for the sink as Alice switched the festive music back on.

Lizzie smiled her way. 'It's all good, girlie. We got there in the end, eh?'

Alice nodded. To her, it had taken more than days or weeks to get to where they were now. It had been years, and as hard as it had been, she was so pleased they'd all found their peace with each other.

Jamie gave her a cuddle as she approached the sink to wash her hands. 'You okay?' he asked quietly.

'More than okay. This is all I wanted.' She glanced over at her mother pottering around the other side of the table. 'We have a hole in our family since Lisa died, and I never wanted to add to my mum's sadness, so her acceptance means everything to me. Thank you for trying so hard to make friends.'

'That's because I want her as my friend. I don't want to bring any more unhappiness to your family either.'

Alice lightly brushed his cheek with one finger. 'We're good now.'

His smile was warm and filled with love. 'It's hard to believe, isn't it?'

She nodded. 'I'm so happy, Jamie.'

'Good. Me too.'

Lizzie called over. 'When you two have stopped nattering, you can make some gingerbread men while I get on with the mince pies.' She pointed at the fridge. 'The gingerbread pastry is in there ready to roll out.'

Alice made space on the table, then handed Jamie the shape cutters. 'Ooh, can we make some for the Hub?'

'That's where I was taking them,' replied Lizzie.

'I've got a shift later,' said Jamie. 'I can take them over.'

Lizzie grinned. 'There you go, teamwork already. See, we're going to be all right.'

Alice shared a look with Jamie. She wasn't quite sure whether her mum was trying to convince herself or them, but it didn't matter. The atmosphere in the kitchen had changed for the better, and when Lizzie tied a Mrs Claus apron around Jamie, the mood turned even cheerier.

It wasn't long before Alice and Jamie were taking their baked goods to the Hub to hand out to anyone who popped inside.

'What a relief, Angel.' He kissed the side of her hat. 'I feel like a weight has left my shoulders.'

'Me too. I think things will be . . .' She gasped, seeing the window to the Hub smashed, glass everywhere.

Jamie moved her back a step. 'Wait here.'

She peered through the damage as he entered, calling out to see who was inside. 'What on earth . . .' she mumbled.

Spencer appeared from out back, and Alice opened the door, juggling the tray of iced gingerbread men in her hands.

Jamie jogged over and took the tray, placing it on the table that was free from glass. 'You okay, Spence?'

Spencer splayed a hand to the shattered window. 'Yeah. I only closed for a half hour because no one was here to help and I needed to pop to my shop to bring over some poinsettias. Just came back to this.'

Alice went to the back room to fetch a broom.

'I've called the police,' added Spencer. 'Just got off the phone when you arrived.'

'I wish we had arrived earlier,' said Alice.

Jamie shook his head at her. 'I'm glad you weren't here.'

Alice turned to Spencer. 'Anything been taken?'

'I'm not sure. I haven't had a good look yet.'

Alice scanned the storage room. 'Where are the children's chocolate selection boxes? Have they been handed out already?'

Spencer leaned over her shoulder to a low shelf. 'They were in a box right there.'

Alice huffed. 'Why would someone steal those? They're for kids.'

Jamie called from the front. 'Can't see anything missing out here. Mind you, whoever did this wouldn't have had long to load up.'

Alice went to the window with a dustpan and broom. 'Good thing too. We've got loads of food now it's Christmas, and we don't need some lowlife running off with the lot.'

Jamie took the broom from her. 'Let me. Fetch a box for this glass, and I'll scoop it into there. You call someone about repairing the window.'

'Ooh, yeah. Let's hope something can be done soon.' She went to the phone book they kept in the Hub that contained all their helpers and associates.

The door to the Hub swung open, and Samuel walked in. 'What happened?'

'Someone stole the chocolate we had for the kids,' said Spencer, helping to clear the floor.

Samuel's brow lifted. 'That's just shocking.'

'I'm just calling the glazier that put the window in when this was being renovated. Hopefully, he'll be able to help.' Alice waggled the phone.

Samuel shook his head in disbelief. 'I'll check the security footage.' He opened the app on his phone.

Jamie glanced up at the ceiling, not spotting any cameras. 'I didn't know you had any here.'

Samuel was focused on his phone. 'Yep. Just outside.'

'You wouldn't think a place like this would need one, but Samuel had it installed when he joined the team,' said Spencer, tipping glass into the box Alice brought over.

'Some young bloke.' Samuel showed everyone the screen on his phone.

Alice gasped. 'That's Gregg's little brother, Karl.'

Jamie peered over her shoulder. 'I've not seen him in years, but it does look like him.'

Spencer shook his head. 'Didn't even care to hide his face. Idiot. Well, the police are on their way, so that's him caught. Not like they don't know where that family lives.'

Alice went back to making her call. The memory of when such crimes around Port Berry were committed by Jamie washed over her. She was so glad he wasn't that person anymore. And that he had nothing to do with the likes of Gregg or Karl.

CHAPTER 32

Jamie

Jamie was hanging some mistletoe around the B&B, thinking it would make Alice laugh when she had to keep stopping for a kiss with him. It was something to do now that he didn't have his shift at the Hub. The window was getting fixed, and Alice was still over there, refusing to leave.

Benny had just broken up from school for the Christmas holidays, so he was busy in his room, wrapping presents.

It had been a busy day, and Jamie still couldn't believe Lizzie was now his friend and had welcomed him into her family. There was no way he was going to let her down.

Part of him wanted to go back to the Hub to lend a hand, not that there was much to do, but Alice was there with the rest of the founders, so he knew he wasn't needed. He considered going to group therapy later. Even though Demi praised it so much, he didn't feel it was a fit for him anymore. Perhaps one more go wouldn't hurt.

Life was good. A few hiccups, but he didn't expect perfection. He couldn't wait to start his new course in January. To see in the new year with Alice. His dreams were coming true, and it felt beyond amazing.

Jamie started to whistle as he clambered down the step-ladder by the main entrance. He abruptly stopped when Gregg came strolling down the pathway.

'Can I have a word?'

It felt rude to not talk to him. After all, they were good friends before prison. Jamie moved the ladder and waved him inside, gesturing towards the dining room.

Gregg pulled out a chair from one of the tables and sat straight away, making himself at home.

'Don't tell me,' said Jamie, sitting opposite him. 'This is about Karl breaking into the Hub, right?'

Gregg shrugged. 'So you heard?'

'Saw the damage. And did you know he stole sweets that had been donated for kids?'

'Yep. Easy to sell selection boxes this time of year.'

'So, what do you want from me?'

Gregg's beady eyes bore into Jamie as he straightened in his seat. 'You've got access to their security.'

Jamie scoffed. 'Seriously? You want me to tamper with that? Erase your brother from the footage? The police already have the evidence, Gregg. There's nothing anyone can do now.'

Gregg sighed loudly. 'Then do something else.'

'Like what?'

'Help him. He's young. Not even twenty-five yet. You know he won't be able to handle a stretch. He's not like us.'

'I'm not like us.'

Gregg waved off the comment. 'This is me you're talking to, mate. I know exactly what you're like.'

'No. You knew a past version of me. You don't know me now.'

'Jay, mate, I'm asking for your help with that lot. Surely you can put in a good word or something.'

Jamie frowned. 'Put in a good word? Are you crazy? Your brother broke into the Happy to Help Hub. He stole from the food bank. From kids.'

206

Gregg shot forward, slamming his fist on the table. 'You owe me.'

'I don't owe you anything.'

'I looked after you when you were one of us. Treated you like family. Got you money.'

Jamie scoffed. 'You taught me how to pick locks, boost cars, shoplift. Now you're acting like you're some sort of role model. I've just done eight years inside. Where were you then, eh? Did you visit? Write? You vanished, mate, so don't come to my home and tell me I owe you, because I don't owe you sod all.'

Gregg stood, his lanky body leaning over the table between them. 'Short memory, Jay.'

'No, long one, Gregg. I remember it all. If you were any sort of friend of mine, you'd be happy I've turned my life around. You wouldn't be standing in my home trying to get me involved with your brother's crimes.'

'I wasn't asking for the crown jewels here. If you just explain to that Hub lot that my brother was drunk, not himself, anything, they might listen to you now you're in with them, and perhaps tell the police they don't want to press charges. It that too much to ask?'

'Yes,' snapped Jamie. 'What a bloody cheek you've got.'

Gregg smirked. 'I suppose I could just ask Alice.'

Every single part of Jamie boiled as he jumped to his feet, eyes darkening and heart thumping. 'You go anywhere near my wife, and I'll rip your throat out.'

'Now, there's the Jamie I know and love.'

Jamie chastised himself. He couldn't allow Gregg to draw him back into a world he hated. Aggression, crime, emptiness.

'Hang on,' added Gregg, chuckling. 'Married her, did you? Well, there's a turn up. Does she know about all those women you slept with while she was hanging around here with your granny?'

Jamie unclenched his fists, trying so hard not to take the bait. 'There were no women.'

'Yeah, but she doesn't know that.'

'So that's your plan, is it? You're trying to blackmail me by using lies.'

Gregg shrugged. 'Just helping my little bro.'

'Perhaps prison will help him. It certainly changed me.'

Gregg narrowed his eyes. 'I don't want him going inside.'

'And I don't want this being my business.'

'Then do something to help.'

'No.'

Gregg smiled. 'Fine, then I'll tell your missus a whole heap of crap, and we'll just let that sit on her chest for a while. See what grows of those seeds.'

Jamie took a calming breath. 'Why are you being so nasty? What did I ever do to you?'

'He was always jealous of you,' said Alice, standing in the doorway.

Jamie's stomach flipped, and not in any good way. There was no telling what lies Gregg was about to say, and Alice might believe some. He didn't know what to say. He couldn't even think straight.

'Hello, love.' Gregg winked at Alice, but she just scowled at him. 'Been there long?'

'Long enough.'

Gregg sat on the table. 'So you can see my dilemma?'

Alice shook her head. 'No. All I see is a loser trying to get my husband into trouble.'

Gregg laughed. 'Ooh, you look so tough, Dipple.'

'It's Stark. And, no, I'm not tough — I'm just not enter-taining you. Neither of us are. So you, and your brother, can rot in hell for all I care. You'll get no help here.'

'And there was me thinking you so nice.' Gregg's smile changed to a smirk.

'Get out of our home, and don't come back. You're not welcome here. Oh, and just so you know, you can make up a million lies about Jamie, I'd never believe you.'

'That's because he's got you wrapped around his little finger, as always.'

Alice smiled. 'Good. That's exactly where I want to be. Now, if you don't mind, we have a happy life to get on with. Good luck with your crappy one.'

Gregg's nose wrinkled as he stepped towards her, but Jamie moved between them, daring him with his eyes to touch her.

Alice placed her hand on Jamie's back. 'Let's just see him to the door.'

Jamie wasn't about to take his eyes off Gregg, and Gregg wasn't giving the impression he was going to leave anytime soon.

'Get out,' snapped Alice.

'Make me.' Gregg's smirk was back.

Jamie felt Alice's hands tighten on his waist.

Gregg laughed. 'If you touch me, Jay, who do you think is going straight back to the slammer?'

'If you don't leave our home, I'm calling the police to arrest you,' shouted Alice.

'Do it then, Dipple. Ooh, sorry, Mrs Stark.' Gregg's tone was immature and filled with venom.

'There's no need for that,' said a deep voice from the foyer. 'We'll make him leave, and he won't come back.'

Jamie turned to see Will, then he spotted Robson, Spencer, Matt, and Samuel.

Gregg saw them too and raised his palms as he walked towards them. 'Yeah, all right. No need for dramatics.'

'Stay away,' warned Will.

Gregg shrugged as he met the pathway. 'Never liked this place anyway.'

Jamie went to follow him, but Alice tugged his hand. 'It's all right, Angel. Give me two secs.' He kissed her cheek, then caught up with Gregg on the pavement.

'Get lost, Jay. I'm done with you.'

'That's what I came to make clear to you. I thought we could still be mates, you know, from a distance. I would never have ignored you if I saw you out and about, but after this little stunt, you're no longer a mate of mine.'

'Suits me. Don't like your type anyway.'

Jamie raised his brow. 'What's that then, nice?'

Gregg waved a hand as he walked away. 'Stick your life, Jay. Have fun with your new mates.' He glanced over his shoulder. 'Oh, and if you ever need my help, don't ask.'

'I don't need anything from you.'

As Gregg disappeared around a corner, Jamie took a deep breath. Another part of his past was gone with clear instructions not to return. The relief overwhelmed him for a moment, that and Alice overhearing and stating she wouldn't believe anything Gregg said.

Jamie stopped at the end of the pathway and stared through the open door at the men inside the B&B. He had different friends now. Ones that were good role models. Ones with compassion, encouragement and advice. He felt so blessed, and happiness washed over him as Alice came into view.

'You see that, Jamie, that's what change gave you,' he heard his grandmother whisper.

He went inside to thank everyone for their help and to let them know Gregg wouldn't be back.

'We were heading to the tearoom to get some tables and chairs for outside the Hub,' said Will. 'We heard you shouting, Alice.'

'Thanks for coming to check on me.' She smiled softly, clinging on to Jamie's arm.

Spencer gestured at the door. 'Best get back to it now we know everything's okay.'

'Why are you taking tables and chairs to the Hub?' she asked.

Samuel smiled. 'So many people have heard about the break-in already, and the carollers from the church have just arrived to sing outside with their collection buckets. We figured some seating while we served hot drinks would help liven up the street. The ones outside the café are in use.'

Alice pointed at her dining room. 'Use those ones. Ginny needs hers more than me at the moment. Come on, we'll help.'

The men got on with the task, and Jamie pulled her to one side.

'Hey, you okay?'

Alice nodded. 'Just a few chairs and a couple of tables.'

'You know I'm not talking about that.'

Alice leaned into him, making him smile. 'Your past is staying back there, Jamie, and no one is bringing it here.' She kissed his lips, then kissed him again. 'Let's go have a sing-song.'

'Benny's out back. I'll just go get him.' Jamie couldn't stop smiling as he went off to ask Benny to come see the carollers.

Within moments, they were all outside the Hub, the Christmas songs cheering the growing crowd, and Jamie had Alice wrapped in his arms.

'This is what we do here, Jamie,' she told him. 'We come together and make everything better.'

He kissed the back of her head. 'You make everything better for me. I love you, Angel.'

Alice turned in his arms and kissed his mouth. 'I love you too,' she mumbled on his lips. 'And I love it even more when you sing "Jingle Bells" at the top of your voice.'

Jamie laughed as he got the hint, then belted out the song along with the carollers and gatherers. It really was going to be the best Christmas ever.

Alice snuggled into his side and joined in with the song, then handed him a hot chocolate when Jed passed a tray of hot drinks their way. 'Cheers, love.' She tapped his cup with her own.

'Cheers, Angel.'

Will flung an arm around Jamie's shoulder while booming out the song, making Jamie laugh into his hot drink.

The collection buckets were filling, and it was safe to say parents visiting the food bank for a Christmas parcel were going to receive chocolate treats for their kids, as planned.

CHAPTER 33

Alice

Alice woke in Jamie's arms, feeling snug and warm. The worries of yesterday were gone, and all that remained was the love surrounding her. She had the idea to stay in bed all day, but Benny would think she was ill, so best stick to the plan of wrapping more presents and helping her mum with a Christmas food shop, even though none of them needed much, especially as they were having dinner that day at the pub and had already paid for their meals.

Jamie stirred, and Alice kissed him. 'Morning to you too,' he said, smiling before opening his eyes.

Alice kissed him again, not wanting to stop.

Jamie grinned on her lips. 'I'm surprised you're not tired after keeping me awake half the night.'

'Oh, I kept you awake, did I? Or was it your wandering hands?'

Jamie stroked along her side. 'You like my wandering hands.'

'I love them. And I want them right now.'

'Oh, is that right?'

'Yep. Get busy.'

Jamie chuckled, then peppered kisses along her neck.

Alice took thirty-seconds' worth before cupping his face and bringing his mouth to hers. She couldn't spend the day in bed with him, but she was sure another hour would be okay.

Her mobile phone started buzzing on the bedside table, causing them both to groan.

'Leave it,' mumbled Jamie, back on her neck.

'It's early for someone to call. It might be important.' She leaned over, surprised to see it was Sophie calling. 'Hello, Soph. Everything all right?'

Sophie sniffed down the phone before answering. 'Oh, Alice, there's been a big flood last night.'

Alice shot up. 'Where?'

'At the hotel where my wedding reception is due to take place in two days. Two days, Al. And now . . .' Sophie started crying.

Alice lowered the phone to whisper to Jamie. 'The hotel they booked for the wedding had a flood last night.'

His brow lifted. 'Oh no, that's terrible.'

Alice went back to her call to hear Sophie still sobbing. 'It's all right, Soph. I'm sure the hotel can arrange something.'

'No, they can't. There's too much damage.'

'Bloody hell.' Alice looked at Jamie as he held her hand. 'I don't know what to say.'

'Ginny's already calling other hotels to see if they have halls or rooms for hire.'

'That's good. I can ring around too if you like.' Alice could feel poor Sophie's heartache. It was stressful enough for her arranging a white wedding, let alone having a disaster take place two days before the event.

Sophie sniffed again. 'Let's see what she can find first.' She sighed. 'Bless her. She did offer use of her barn, but it's a bit draughty. Having said that, if everything is booked up for Christmas, then the barn might be our only choice.'

Alice gasped, not meaning to sound so dramatic. 'It's not your only choice, Soph. You can use the B&B for the reception. We've got the dining room, the foyer, a big kitchen. All the place needs is some decorations.' She smiled at Jamie as Sophie started mumbling to Matt in the background.

Jamie bobbed his head. 'Good idea,' he mouthed.

Sophie was back. 'You know what, Alice, we'd love to have our reception at yours. How wonderful would it be to celebrate on the same street as our shop, where we first met. Matt's nodding away. Do you really think it's possible at such short notice?'

Alice scoffed. 'Please, this is us you're talking about. We can arrange fundraising events in days. We can manage a wedding.'

'But it's Christmas.'

'Not yet, it's not.' Alice beamed. 'You leave this to us, Soph. You want a wedding party at mine — you'll have the best Port Berry has ever seen.'

Sophie stopped sniffing. 'Oh, Alice, thank you so much.'

Alice smiled down the phone. 'Right, you call Ginny and let her know you've got a venue, and I'll get Lottie and Spencer over here to see where they can put flowers. Don't you worry about a thing, Soph. We've got this.'

'That was nice of you,' said Jamie as soon as the call ended.

Alice tapped his arm. 'Come on, love. We've got a busy two days ahead.' She stood by the wardrobe, not knowing what to do first.

Jamie grinned. 'You can make some calls while I fix us brekkie, then we'll see what's in storage that can be used.'

'Yes, good plan. And we'll need a checklist.' She hurried to the bathroom, taking her phone with her so she could ring everyone to let them know of the new wedding plan.

The porridge Jamie made went down well and she was sure she'd need the energy for the long day. Lottie and Spencer were due in soon, and Ginny was on her way over, as was Robson.

'What do you want me to do?' asked Benny, grabbing an apple from the fruit bowl on the kitchen table.

'Would you be able to help your nan with a food shop?' asked Alice.

'Yep, I can do that.'

Alice ticked that off her list and told him to eat breakfast.

'I'll have something at Nan's.' Benny opened the front door, letting Robson inside.

'Ooh, Rob, you're here.' Alice splayed her hands to the foyer. 'What do you think?'

'Sophie just called to say the hotel has already refunded her, so she's giving me the money now for food and drink, so I'm going to have the food cooked in the pub, then brought round by my staff. As for the drinks, I want to set up a small bar.'

Alice waved him to the dining room. 'We have the serving hatch. What about that? You can put the drinks on tables in the kitchen and serve from there.'

'Perfect. I'll have a couple of bar staff work the night.'

'Do you think they will?'

'Yep. Everyone wants more money this time of year. I've got staff coming out of my ears at the moment wanting shifts. This will help out a couple, and Demi is going to lend a hand in the kitchen.'

Alice smiled warmly. 'We have to make it so wonderful for Sophie and Matt. She sounded heartbroken earlier.'

Robson put his arm around her. 'We will, Al.'

'We definitely will,' said Lottie, appearing in the doorway with Spencer. 'And, as Sophie was keen to mix Christmas into her day, we can fix this place up to look quite magical.'

Spencer agreed, perusing the area. 'Our flowers will fit in nicely, that's for sure, and I've called the balloon lady to let her know where we'll be now. She's going to pop by at lunch for a size-up.'

Lottie raised both hands. 'Winter wonderland meets Seaview. Christmas, wedding, love and—'

'A Nutcracker,' said Ginny, trying to heave a six-foot one through the door.

Robson sprinted over to help. 'Where did you get that?'

'It's mine, chick. Thought it would look good on the doorstep of the farm, so I bought one. Now I think he'd make a brilliant usher for the wedding.'

Everyone stared wide-eyed at the tall festive statue, that did look rather elegant.

'Impressive, Gin,' said Spencer, taking a selfie with it.

Alice pointed at the dining room. 'I'm going to need help moving the tables around, and I was thinking we could use the foyer for the DJ and music. Oh, has anyone called him?'

'Yep,' said Samuel, walking in. 'He gave me the measurements of his setup, so I'm here to see where he can fit, then I'll call him back.'

Alice looked over by the storage cupboard. 'Here's a good space.'

Samuel pulled out a measuring tape and got on with his task.

Lottie and Spencer started taking their own notes, and Robson went into the kitchen to see how he could create a bar.

'Poor Soph, eh, chick?' Ginny linked arms with Alice. 'And the owners of that hotel. And just before Christmas as well.'

Alice thought about her own B&B, grateful she didn't have that problem. 'As long as we've got each other, we'll always be okay, won't we, Gin?'

'That's right, chick. You know what we're like when we join forces. Nothing can stop us.'

Alice glanced at the ceiling. 'We need garlands up there.'

Ginny laughed. 'Well, we've certainly got enough mistletoe. Why so much?'

'Jamie did that. Thought he was funny.'

'I am funny,' he said, approaching.

Alice chuckled. 'You can kiss me anytime, you know. You don't need mistletoe.'

Jamie kissed her cheek. 'Good to know.' He frowned on seeing the Nutcracker. 'Where did that come from?'

'He's with me,' said Ginny.

Alice nodded. 'The new usher.'

Lottie called out for more assistance in the dining room, so Jamie went off to help.

'How's it going with you two?' Ginny asked, gesturing towards Jamie.

Alice smiled inside and out. 'Great. He's really settled.'

'And you?'

'Yep, me too.'

Ginny nudged her arm. 'Come on then, chick, let's get over to the pub to find out what Demi has planned. We might need to clear some fridge space in your kitchen. We can use the tearoom and café as well, if need be. Lots of fridge space in both.'

Alice went to tell Jamie she was popping to the Jolly Pirate.

'Before you go,' he said, motioning at a back wall. 'Where do you think the wedding cake should go?'

Lottie opted for the corner. 'We wouldn't want anyone knocking it over.'

'Or it could be wheeled in from the kitchen,' said Spencer.

Lottie scoffed. 'They stand more chance of toppling when on the move. Corner, I say.'

Sophie walked in with Jed. 'There's more room in here than I remember,' she said softly, her eyes red and puffy.

Jed gave his granddaughter a hug. 'I thought it best to bring our Sophie along to see what will be done. Settle her a touch.'

Alice leaned in to give her a hug as well. 'You won't recognize the place by the time we're finished.'

Jed chuckled. 'We already love the Nutcracker.'

'He's on loan,' called Ginny, making everyone laugh.

Robson came out of the kitchen. 'You go rest for your big day, Soph. Pamper session tomorrow, I hear.'

Sophie nodded. 'I think I need a week in a spa now.'

'No more worrying,' said Jed. 'You've seen for yourself now. Your mates have got it covered.'

'We certainly have,' said Lottie. 'So, do as you're told, and feet up.'

Sophie wrinkled her nose. 'Fat chance. We've got huge seafood orders to get ready for our customers, and Matt's in the shop by himself.' She tugged her grandfather's arm. 'Okay, I'm ready. Let's get back.'

Jed gave her a reassuring smile. 'That's my girl.'

Sophie stopped in the doorway. 'Thank you all so much.'

Ginny waved her off. 'No thanks needed. It's what friends are for.'

Alice and Ginny followed Sophie and Jed as far as the pub, then parted ways to go see Demi in the kitchen.

'I've got it covered,' said Demi as soon as they entered, sitting them down to talk through her menu plans.

Alice made notes, took mental notes, and arranged to collect any decorations on offer that would add to the magical theme they were going for, then headed back to the B&B.

It certainly was a full-on day, though Alice enjoyed every moment, knowing how happy Sophie and Matt would be. She only wished she'd experienced such magic on her wedding day.

Alice watched Jamie while he helped move tables. What did it matter if they'd had a secret wedding with no guests or photos? They had each other. But it didn't stop her wondering what it would have been like to walk down the aisle with him waiting for her.

As though sensing her moment of sadness, Jamie came over and put his arms around her waist. 'You all right, Angel?' he asked quietly.

'Yeah, just pacing myself.' She wasn't sure he bought that, but he didn't say anything. She got back to work, sorting through tablecloths.

Someone switched on Christmas songs, then once everyone started singing along, Alice forgot all about her own wedding day and focused on Sophie and Matt's instead. After all, it had been a marriage she wanted more than a wedding, and now she had one. So as far as she was concerned, she had nothing to grumble about.

CHAPTER 34

Jamie

It was the night before the wedding, and Jamie was in the Jolly Pirate with the other men while the women were up at Lottie's having a pampering party.

The bar and restaurant were busier than usual, with a work Christmas party taking place along with Matt's non-alcoholic get-together, that he wasn't calling a stag do.

Robson had set them up in a corner by the opened double doors. The heat inside was a bit much for everyone, and a lot of customers had spilled out onto the front beer garden, where the air was crisp but mild for the time of year.

'Sometimes I can't believe how my life turned out,' said Matt, going into the beer garden with Jamie.

Jamie smiled. 'I know the feeling.'

They sat beneath the large grill area. Robson had started to cook some burgers because he was getting requests for barbeque food.

Matt glanced up at the high ceiling, then brick pillars. 'When I first came to Port Berry, I wouldn't even go inside this pub, worried in case it affected my recovery.'

'Addiction is tough, eh, mate?'

Matt nodded. 'Yeah, but what a difference it makes when you have support. And these people around here, the Hub, and my Sophie, have been the best ever.'

Jamie's thoughts were with Alice. 'It does help.'

'I never knew I'd end up living by the coast. I like it much better than London. Did you ever think about moving away?'

'No. I was never one for plans until I was in prison, then all I did was dream and set goals.'

Matt nodded. 'When I decided to get clean from the booze, I set the goal of just walking. Not much of a goal, I know, but it just happened to me. I started walking away from all I knew, and I kept going.' He splayed a hand. 'Then I found this place. I just wish someone could have told me years back that this was my destiny. Wouldn't it be good to have at least some idea?'

The locals often went to the Dipple family whenever they wanted a sneak preview into what life might hold for them, but Jamie had grown up with little expectations for a future. Still, it would have been nice if someone had told him to stick with Alice at all times.

'It is what it is, Matt. Who knows, maybe we're supposed to go on these messed-up journeys. Learn lessons, find ourselves, that sort of thing. I look around sometimes and all I see are people living happy lives, and I wonder why I didn't have such an adventure. It can feel a little unfair, but that's comparison for you, eh?'

'Thief of joy, they say.'

Jamie blew out a small laugh. 'It definitely can be.'

Matt smiled. 'I think you and me have epic stories.'

'Epic?'

'Yeah. We both struggled as kids, we took all the wrong turns growing up, did a stint in prison, overcame trauma, made the decision to change, made peace with ourselves, and how lucky are we that we got to fall in love and be with such kind and loving women?'

Jamie inhaled the waft of barbeque food blowing his way in the light breeze. He smiled to himself at how different his life now was, thanks to the changes he'd made.

'Blessings, eh?' added Matt, getting up to get a burger.

Jamie did feel extremely blessed, more so for having the guts to walk away from all that was toxic in his life. The circle he had now was a breath of fresh air.

A queue was forming by the grill, the scent of the food encouraging more customers, so Robson was getting every-one to sing a line from a Christmas song before handing over a burger. The lively atmosphere cheered Jamie no end. He found he wanted a moment of peace though so headed across the road to the pier.

The black sky revealed all its stars, and the calm sea swished gently below. Ever since he was a kid, Jamie loved sitting on the pier come nightfall. It was always so peaceful, and the openness of the water calmed his weary soul.

He looked heavenward, wondering if his grandmother was looking back. He smiled just in case, hoping she was proud of him now. He was certainly proud of himself.

'I did it, Nan,' he whispered into the gentle wind. 'I became the person I was supposed to be.'

'Took you long enough,' he heard her chuckle out.

'Ah, you know me, I like to go around the houses.'

'You talking to yourself, Jamie?' asked Will, plonking himself down beside him.

Jamie laughed quietly. 'I was having a chat with my nan.'

'Oh, would you prefer if I left?'

'That's okay.'

Will glanced up. 'It's nice here when it's quiet.'

Jamie looked towards the pub. 'You had enough of sing-ing for one night?'

Will chuckled. 'Hey, I like singing. But I also like to sit with the sea every so often.'

'Do you miss being in the navy?'

'Sometimes. It was a big part of my life, but I'm happy with Ginny and our son up at our farm.' He sighed deeply while smiling. 'Still blows my mind when I think about the life I have now.'

'Matt was saying something similar a minute ago.'

'I guess we all look back at our old life at times and compare it to the one we live in now.'

Jamie knew he had been blessed to have had Alice in all stages of his life. 'Mine's definitely improved.'

Will laughed. 'Mine too. Good, isn't it?'

'We were saying how it would be good to have some guidance along the way. Someone to point out which direction you should go, that sort of thing.'

'But then you'd have no surprises.'

Jamie scoffed. 'I don't like surprises. I'd rather know what my map looked like.'

'Maybe there is no map, just the decisions we make.'

There had been many bad decisions Jamie had made over the years. He did reach a point where he wondered if he was just stupid, but Alice often told him he was simply human.

He inhaled the salty air, then slowly sighed. 'I've got Matt, Jed, and Sam all staying at the B&B tonight while the bridal party sleeps over at Lottie's. There's a room for you, too, if you want.'

'Thanks, but I'm picking up Robert from Ginny later to take home. I'll see everyone at the church in the morning. Good thing no one's drinking tonight.' Will tapped his shoulder. 'Right, I'm off for a burger, or, with a bit of luck, a steak if Rob's stuck some on the grill. You coming?'

'In a bit.'

Will waved one hand as he went back to the pub. Jamie stretched as he stood, glancing in the direction of Berry Hill, where Lottie lived. If he took a slow stroll that way, he'd be closer to Alice for a moment, and he wanted so much to be with her.

The climb up the steep hill had him a little breathless, and it was decided that he would up his fitness levels in the new year.

The row of pastel coastal houses looked different since Lottie and Samuel had knocked three of them together to make one big house, but the street still held its charm.

Jamie went to the other side of the road to peer over the waist-high rail that wasn't there when he was a kid. The drop down to the shingles was always a concern for the locals, so he could see why the council finally got around to making the grassy verge safer.

The boats in the distance bobbed gently in the dark sea, a faint clinking sound was all that filled the air. Ever since his release, it didn't matter which part of Port Berry he was in, it all made him smile. He was home.

'Jamie,' came a small voice behind him.

He turned to see Alice coming out of Lottie's.

'Ginny said she spotted you from the window.' Alice wrapped her white dressing gown further around her as she plodded over in her slippers. 'What you doing out here all by yourself?'

'I didn't feel by myself. I felt close to you.'

She tilted her head, seemingly studying him.

'I just missed you, Angel,' he added quietly.

Alice snuggled into his side. 'Is your energy low?'

'It's been fluctuating all day.'

'Keep holding me and I'll give you some of mine.'

He smiled, then kissed the side of her head. 'I'm not draining you of your energy.'

'Doesn't work that way when you both love each other. When you're running low, I fill us up, and when it's my turn for some emotional support, you share your energy with me.'

'What if we're both running low?'

'We eat chocolate.'

Jamie laughed. 'Oh, I do love you, Alice.'

They held each other in silence for a while, Jamie hugging her close to give her all the body heat he could.

'Do you know what's bothering you, love?'

He wasn't entirely sure. Perhaps the wedding, maybe his new life overwhelming him, or just knowing he wasn't going to be with Alice all night. 'I don't know.'

'How are you feeling now?'

'Always better with you.'

Alice rolled her head up his shoulder to face him. 'I have strong energy.'

He smiled and kissed the tip of her cold nose. 'You have everything, and as lovely as this is, you need to go have fun with your mates. I need to get a grip and go back and celebrate with Matt and the others.'

'I don't mind staying out here with you for a bit longer.'

'I know, that's how wonderful you are. But tonight isn't about us — though tomorrow night we'll have some catching up to do.'

Alice giggled on his lips. 'Look forward to that.'

He walked her to the door and kissed her once more before heading down the hill, a slight skip in his step. Alice always did have healing powers.

CHAPTER 35

Alice

Alice had never felt so beautiful. Her hair curled and tied, her makeup professionally applied, her gorgeous crimson bridesmaid dress making her feel like a princess.

She stepped out of the maroon vintage car that had brought the bridesmaids to All Saints Church, then helped Sophie with her long white dress as she climbed out of a cream vintage car with Jed, looking trim in a grey top hat and tails with crimson cravat.

'You look stunning, Soph,' Alice told her.

Sophie had the biggest smile as she took her grandfather's arm.

A photographer darted around, snapping away with his chunky camera before heading inside to get ready for the church photos.

Samuel came over with Lottie's standing electric wheelchair and helped her settle with her bouquet, then gave her a kiss on the cheek before heading inside the church.

Will pulled up in the car park with Beth and their respective children. They set up the prams and had the bridesmaids cooing over Archie and Robert's mini pageboy outfits straight away.

'You get them inside, and we'll be in next,' said Ginny, waving Will towards the entrance.

Will and Beth went into the church with the children, and the others got ready for the walk down the aisle.

Alice fanned her face with one hand. 'Do not cry,' she told herself out loud, making everyone laugh.

Lottie shook her head. 'You'd better not. Your makeup is perfect. No mascara runs allowed.'

'Not even me?' joked Jed, beaming at Sophie.

'You can cry later,' said Alice.

Ginny gave Sophie the once over. 'You ready, chick?'

Sophie grinned from ear to ear. 'Yep.'

Ginny then looked at Jed. 'Are you ready?'

Jed nodded. 'And ever so proud of my Sophie.'

Sophie nudged him. 'Stop, Grandad, or I'll be the one crying.'

Alice gestured to the entrance. 'Come on then. Your groom awaits.'

Sophie let out a small squeal of delight as they all moved forward, taking their places.

The music in the church started to play, and the guests stood.

Alice saw her family first, then caught Jamie's eye as she made her way down the aisle. If only she could have met him at the altar on their wedding day. She quickly shrugged off the thought and went back to concentrating on her friend's big day.

'Beautiful,' Jamie mouthed as she passed.

Alice smiled at him, then at Matt, Robson, and Spencer up front, wearing the same outfits as Jed, except Matt had a white cravat.

The wedding started and everyone took their seats, except the bridesmaids who were in a line beside Sophie for a while.

The church was cool and filled with everyone Sophie and Matt cared about. Dark-pink and white flowers were arranged by the alter and at the end of each pew, and the service was personalized by the Berry Buoys singing a sea shanty towards the end, which had everyone tapping their feet.

For Alice, the ceremony went far too quickly. She wanted to be in the church longer, enjoying the love on display, the joy in the air, and the way Jamie was looking at her as though she were the most beautiful person on the planet.

The bells rang out as the happy couple departed, confetti sprinkled all around. More pictures were taken, then it was off to Seaview B&B for the reception, which thanks to Sophie's friends now looked like a winter wonderland at Christmas.

Toasts were made, champagne and non-alcoholic bubbly held high, and Demi had made a feast fit for a king.

Jed shed a tear when making his speech, and Alice had to clean her mascara at that point, along with the other bridesmaids.

Then Matt got up to speak, staring only at his blushing bride. 'Sophie, you're the best thing that's ever happened to me. I certainly didn't see you coming my way, but if I had known you were here, I'd have walked a hell of a lot quicker from London.'

Everyone laughed, and Sophie blew him a kiss.

Matt turned to his audience. 'All of you have been the best. I'll never be able to thank you enough for your support since I arrived.' He glanced at Jed. 'Or for the spa day.'

Sophie reached for his hand.

Matt smiled. 'I only wish there was a Port Berry in every corner of the land because this is such a happy place. The kindness here is like nothing I've ever seen before. Thank you for coming to our wedding. For making the reception so magical for me and the missus, and thank you for simply being part of my life.' He looked down at Sophie. 'And to you, my love, for believing in me. I love you, Soph.'

'Love you too.' She leaned over to kiss his lips as he sat, and the guests cheered.

Alice held Jamie's hand beneath the cream tablecloth, smiling his way. She glanced down when she felt him stroke her bare wedding finger. The memory came back of them telling the officiate they didn't want to exchange rings. It wasn't law, and it wasn't as if they could wear them anyway.

'It's been a nice day, hasn't it?' said Jamie.

'Yes, and I'm so glad everything went well.'

They got up to help some of the others tidy the tables so they could be pushed along the walls to make more space for dancing. When the lights dimmed and Sophie and Matt had their first dance, Alice swiped away another tear.

The party was alive and buzzing, leaking out onto the small front garden, and more food was laid out on the tables, including lots of seafood from Sea Shanty Shack.

Luna came over and put her arm around Alice's waist. 'It's been quite the year, hasn't it, love?'

'It's been quite the month.'

'And it's not over yet.'

Alice smiled at her grandmother. 'Not long to the new year, which, to be honest, I'll be glad to see.'

'Ooh, don't wish your life away, Alice. Enjoy each day. So much can happen between now and next year to make this your favourite year yet.'

Alice side-eyed her nan. Was she being cryptic again or simply teaching the art of being present? Either way, now that it had been mentioned, Jamie being released from prison had made it one of her favourite years. It just had brought a lot of the past with it.

'You don't need a new year to make a fresh start, Alice. You can make that happen at any time.'

Alice watched her nan dance off into the crowd gathered in the foyer, leaving her by the reception desk, mulling over life.

Needing a moment to herself, Alice went to her bedroom and sat on the bed. It had been a challenging month, more so for her emotions. She picked up a snow globe from the bedside table and shook it to watch the fake snow sprinkle down onto a gingerbread house. Jamie was going to be with her for

Christmas, and that thought alone was just as magical as the ornament in her hand.

Sighing, she smiled softly up at the ceiling. 'How's it going, Lisa? Have you been watching?' She was never quite sure what words of wisdom her sister would say. If Lisa could see life in Port Berry, Alice was sure her sister would focus more on Benny anyway. Still, it was nice to have a chat every so often.

A gentle tapping came from the door, then Benny poked his head inside the room. 'You okay? I saw you come in and wondered if you didn't feel well.'

Alice patted the bed, gesturing for him to sit by her side. 'I'm fine. I was just giving my eardrums a rest from the music.' It was quite muffled in the bedroom but still possible to know what song was playing. 'And I was having a bit of a natter with your mum.'

Benny glanced up. 'Do you really think she hears us?'

'Who knows for sure? But if it makes us feel good to have that chat, then we should continue to do so.'

'Do you think she would like my girlfriend?'

Alice leaned gently into his arm. 'She would want happiness for you. And if Ellie is good to you, then your mum would be pleased.'

Benny smiled widely. 'Ellie is lovely.'

'That's all anyone wants in a partner. Someone nice.'

'I'm glad you have Jamie now.'

Alice blew out a small laugh. 'I've always had Jamie. I'm just glad life is more settled for him now. For us all. We've all been through tough times.' She shuffled around to face him full-on. 'Benny, I want you to know that we all make bad decisions for ourselves once in a while, so when that happens to you, or you feel you've taken the wrong road, don't be so hard on yourself. We're only human. We don't always get it right, but it'll be okay. We learn, we grow, and change is possible. So don't ever feel stuck — you can always move forward.'

Benny leaned in for a hug. 'You're starting to sound like Granny.'

Alice chuckled. 'Your granny is wise.'

'And she's a great dancer. Have you seen her moves out there?' He laughed as he stood. 'Come on, Mum. It's time we joined in.' He stopped for a moment, losing his smile. 'Or do you want to be alone?'

There had been many times she had felt alone, but she never really was, not with her loving family and many friends.

Alice creaked to a stand. 'Nah, I'm not staying here. Let's go have a knees-up with the others.'

As soon as they joined in with the dancing, Jamie's arms curled around her, making Alice's smile grow bigger. So what if it had been an unusual month, what with all that had happened. Having Jamie around made all the darkness fade to light, and Alice had never felt so happy.

CHAPTER 36

Jamie

Christmas morning felt surreal to Jamie. He couldn't help but have a moment where he thought about the friends he had made in prison. He knew what kind of day they would be having, and was so glad he wasn't there with them anymore.

No one had woken yet, which Jamie was pleased about. He wanted some time to himself to absorb the sun rising on the one day of the year when he normally felt the loneliest.

He stepped outside to the empty street, coffee in hand, enjoying how peaceful it was. Even the dark waves over the road were small with a gentle hiss.

Any view was better than the one from his old cell, but the view from Seaview B&B would always be the most spectacular to him.

Light snowflakes began to fall, but he didn't go back inside. His dressing gown was keeping him warm enough in the cold breeze, but it was the stillness of the morning that held him captivated.

Soon all the homes in the area would come alive with people opening their presents, the scent of roasting turkey would fill the air, and festive songs would start pouring out from the Jolly Pirate pub as soon as its doors opened.

It had been a nice time of year back when his mum was alive, but after her death, his father would spend most of the day drinking, then pass out by the time dinner was served.

Jamie could hear all their voices. His grandmother trying to be extra cheery, his dad grumbling to himself, Shannon moaning because she didn't get what she wanted. Then he could hear the men in prison. The ones quietly sobbing, the others singing loudly, making the best of their bad situation, the guards reminding everyone visits would commence the following day.

Sighing, he walked to the front wall and sat to drink his coffee. Inhaling the fresh air made him feel alive. Free. He couldn't help but smile, albeit a small one. It truly was a magical moment, and one he was sure he'd remember forever.

He raised his mug to the sky. 'Never again.' Who he was talking to, he wasn't sure. He just wanted to say his thoughts out loud. Make it clear that his troubled days were well and truly over.

Back inside was Alice and her family, still sleeping. Lizzie and Luna had stayed over. They had a big day ahead of them. One Jamie hoped went to plan.

'Morning, son,' said Jed, seeming to appear from nowhere.

Jamie jumped out of his thoughts. 'Oh, hello. You're out and about early.'

'Always am. Besides, I like a walk early Christmas morning. Blows away the cobwebs.' Jed gazed over at the lighthouse. 'Once upon a time, I had a different Christmas each year. One with my wife and son. It was just Sophie and me for a while, and now we have Matt. It all changes, son. Best enjoy all the glimmers when we get them.'

'Glimmers?'

'Opposite of triggers. And let's face it, we all have those from time to time.'

Jamie nodded. 'Christmas can be triggering, I know, but I'm not going to let it own me anymore.'

'Good for you.' Jed raised a hand. 'Right, best get these old knees on the move. Looking forward to seeing you later.' He winked, then headed off.

Jamie smiled to himself. It was time. Alice needed to wake and open the present he'd bought her. They were due in the pub for dinner at three, and there was so much to do before then.

'What you doing out there?' her voice came from the doorway.

He got up to greet her with a kiss under the mistletoe. 'Just having my coffee.'

Alice sipped some when he offered her the mug. 'You okay?'

'Yep. Just eager to unwrap pressies.'

Alice giggled. 'You sound like Benny. Come on, he's just got up and is already sitting by the tree.'

They closed the door just as Luna and Lizzie came down the stairs.

'Merry Christmas,' said Jamie, greeting them with a hug.

'Happy Christmas,' came the response from them both.

'Has Benny started yet?' asked Lizzie, following them into the back rooms.

'No, I'm waiting for you lot.' Benny waved them over to the twinkling Christmas tree, and Alice made everyone a hot drink before she joined them.

'I am pleased I got a new scarf,' said Lizzie, holding up the woolly red one Luna had made her.

Luna clapped quietly, then turned to Jamie. 'What's that our Alice has bought you?'

He held up his new mobile phone. 'I think I might have to do a course in how to work it.'

Benny laughed. 'Don't worry. I'll show you.'

Jamie thanked him, then reached for the gift he had bought for Alice. 'Here.' He watched her eyes widen a touch at the ring-sized box.

Alice gasped quietly as she opened it to reveal two plain gold wedding bands.

Jamie bent to one knee. 'Will you marry me again, Angel?'

Her lips curled. 'Again?'

He nodded. 'Renew our vows. Do it properly.'

Lizzie and Luna locked arms, and Benny was up on his knees.

Alice stroked the jewellery. 'I'd love that.' She leaned over and kissed his cheek. Jamie melted a little while telling himself to keep it together. 'When were you thinking?'

He swallowed hard. 'Today.'

Alice's laugh shot right in his face. 'Today? But it's Christmas.'

'People can get married on Christmas Day.'

'But don't we have to book it in advance?'

He bobbed his head. 'It is booked, Alice. We have a half hour time slot with Father Stephen up at All Saints at midday. But, just in case you don't want to, he is on standby for my call to cancel.'

Alice reached for her hair. 'But I don't have anything to wear.'

'Oh, but you do, girlie,' said Lizzie. 'You see, Jamie here arranged everything the day after Sophie's wedding, and just in case you agreed to today, we all got prepared.'

Alice's mouth gaped for a moment. 'You all knew about this?'

Jamie took her hand in his. 'I want you to have your white wedding. I want you to have your ring. Your family and friends around you. What you've always wanted. What you deserve.'

'Oh, Jamie.' She swung her arms around him, sobbing quietly into his shoulder. 'I love you so much.'

'I love you too, Angel.' He waited for her to pull away first. 'So, what do you think? You want to do this today? Remember, this is your choice. I've got everything ready just in case, but we can do this any day. You are completely in control. I mean it, any day.'

'Why did you choose Christmas Day?'

That was easy to answer. 'Because I wanted our wedding to be as magical as you.'

Alice inhaled deeply while grinning. 'Then what are we waiting for?' She giggled as she jumped up. 'I need to find something to wear.'

Lizzie quickly took her hand. 'That's all sorted as well, love. Come upstairs and I'll show you how your husband has gone above and beyond.'

Jamie kissed Alice's cheek before she was dragged away.

'Yay!' cheered Benny. 'I knew she'd say yes to today.'

Luna stood. 'Which means, we need to get some brekkie in us all to keep our strength up for the day. It's going to be a long one.'

'And the best ever,' said Benny.

Jamie knew he had taken a massive chance, but he also knew his angel. She was getting what she deserved. And just for a moment, he felt perhaps he was too.

CHAPTER 37

Alice

Alice couldn't believe it. She was going to be a proper bride. Her idea of one at least. No sneaking around. No empty seats behind them. No worrying what her mother would say if she found out.

The room that she had given to Jamie when he first arrived at the B&B was now strewn with clothes and makeup and wedding flowers. Some of her friends were downstairs, the others in the room with her, faffing and making a fuss.

'I am so glad we tried on those wedding dresses in the shop now,' said Ginny, unzipping a large garment bag hanging on the wardrobe door. 'And that the dressmaker knew your size from the bridesmaid fitting. Sophie got in touch with her straight away, she was that excited you were getting hitched.'

Lizzie gasped as the white satin-and-lace dress came into view. 'Wow, that's a beauty.'

'It was Alice's favourite in the shop,' said Ginny.

'But it cost a small fortune.' Alice stepped towards it, finding it hard to believe it was hers.

'Jamie sold those action figures he'd had since childhood,' said Lizzie. 'He wanted to give you the best day he could.'

Ginny took the dress out of the bag. 'And we've added wedding cake to our Christmas dinner menu at the pub. So, we're sorted there.'

Lizzie held Alice's arm. 'And there is a wedding car waiting downstairs to take you to the church.'

Alice rushed to the balcony to have a peek. 'Oh, it's beautiful.'

'Vintage and cream,' said Ginny. 'See, this is what happens when you talk weddings at a fitting. We got to hear how we'd all like our wedding day to be.'

'And you told Jamie.' Alice grinned as Ginny shrugged.

'Well, he did ask.'

Alice let out a little squeal of delight. 'Ooh, I can't believe this is happening.'

Ginny held the dress up to Alice. 'I've never been to a renewing of vows before. Do you know what you're going to say, chick?'

Alice stopped smiling. 'No! I haven't had time to eat, let alone think.'

'Speaking of which,' said Lizzie, bringing over a plate filled with sliced banana. She popped one in Alice's mouth. 'I'll get you fed. You've got a big day.'

'Yes, I'm normally in the pub by twelve, helping Robson.'

'Well, not today, chick.' Ginny waggled the dress hanger. 'Come on, the others will be heading for the church in a minute. Let's get you ready, and you can nibble on food and write your vows in your head.'

'We have a half an hour slot.' Alice chewed her lip. 'Best keep it short.'

'Did you say much last time?' asked Ginny.

'No. Just the usual lines. It was over within minutes, and we didn't take photos.'

Lizzie peered out the window. 'You've got a photographer this time, love. That part of the wedding is on me.'

'Aww, thanks, Mum.'

'Yeah, well, I wanted to pay for something.'

Alice smiled. 'Did you get a mother-of-the-bride outfit.'

'Too right I did. I'm off to get dressed now. See you in a bit.'

Alice beamed at Ginny as Lizzie left. 'Gin, this feels surreal.'

'Usually does when dreams come true.'

Alice sat on the bed, delaying wearing the gorgeous dress. She just wanted to stare at it a little longer. 'I never expected any of this. I didn't even know Jamie would be here for Christmas, let alone anything else.'

'But you're happy, right?'

'More than I knew was possible. I just wish Jamie and I had this happiness all throughout our relationship.' Alice scoffed. 'Not sure that's the right word to use. I don't think there is a word for us. We just have a bond that doesn't go away.'

'I think that's called love.'

Alice smiled as Ginny tugged her up to get dressed. 'All right, all right, I'll get ready. Let me take it slowly. I want to remember everything.'

Ginny helped her into the wedding dress. 'You will remember the lot. You probably remember every moment you've shared with Jamie.'

There had been many moments over the years. Even though Jamie had chosen wrong roads to travel, when he had spent time with her, there'd been a lot of smiles.

'He's part of me, Gin.'

'Yeah, I can see that.' Ginny nudged her arm, snapping her out of her daze. 'So, let's get you down the aisle.' She gave Alice the once over, nodding her approval. 'You're certainly a beaut, Alice Dipple. Oops, Stark. I'll get used to it at some point.' Ginny laughed, heading for the door. 'Get your shoes on and come down so Lottie can make you up.'

'I'll be down in a sec.'

Ginny smiled warmly before leaving.

Alice went over to the window to stare at the sea. A place she'd stood many times, not realizing she'd one day be standing there in her wedding dress feeling overwhelmed by love.

Glancing down at her bare wedding finger, she stroked over her cool skin, knowing soon a gold band would cover the area, and she could shout from the rooftops that Jamie Stark was her husband.

'Bloody hell,' she whispered.

She heard her mum call, so composed herself and went downstairs. Benny was in the foyer, wearing a dark-blue suit with a red carnation in the buttonhole.

'Oh, Benny, you look handsome.'

'I'm here to walk you down the aisle, Mum.'

Alice placed a hand over her heart. 'I was going to walk down by myself.'

'You still can if you want.'

Alice shook her head. 'No. Not now I know you're offering.'

Lottie was in the dining room with her makeup collection set out on a table. 'Get a wriggle on, Alice. We've got to leave soon to make it on time.'

Alice quickly sat, wondering where Jamie was.

As if reading her mind, Lizzie said, 'Everyone's at the church. Sam's just outside waiting to take Lottie, and Ginny's going with them, then it's you, me, and Benny in the car.'

'Where's Nan?'

'She wanted to be at the church when you arrive.' Lizzie went off to ask the photographer to take some pictures of Benny by the car.

Lottie finished Alice's makeup, then tied up some of her hair, leaving some loose strands dangling down the sides. 'I always like this look on you, Al.' She raised a hand mirror.

'Ooh, I look lovely. Thanks, Lott.'

Lottie handed over a red bouquet and smiled. 'You look beautiful. Now, let's get going, else Jamie will think you've jilted him.'

'Not sure I can if we're already married.' Alice grinned as she headed for the vintage car, stopping for photos before they all went to the church.

'It's nice that you've got some light snow for your day,' said Lizzie as they pulled up in the car park. 'Magical.'

Luna was waiting in the entrance and came over to admire Alice as she stepped out of the car, stopping for more photos. 'What a vision you are, Alice.'

'Thanks, Nan.'

'He's a lucky man, that Jamie Stark.' Luna gestured towards the aisle.

'Is he there, Nan?'

'Yep, looking as nervous as any groom.'

Alice could imagine. She waited patiently for her grandmother, mother, and friends to head inside, before taking Benny's arm and a deep breath.

'Ready, Mum?'

She smiled into his gentle blue eyes. 'I am.'

Everyone Alice cared about was there, up front, looking as excited as she felt as Benny walked her down the poinsettia-lined aisle while soft music played.

There was a dreamy expression about Jamie, standing at the altar, with Will at his side. Alice melted on seeing her husband, who was dressed similarly to Benny.

'You're beautiful, Angel,' Jamie whispered.

Alice wanted so badly to reach out and kiss him, but she turned to Father Stephen who said a few words about being blessed in the eyes of the Lord.

Jamie took her hand and slipped on the gold wedding band, and Alice felt a rush of emotion overpower her, even more so when she placed a ring on his finger. Everything about her marriage was real now, and the joy was like nothing she'd experienced before.

Ginny stood up and read out a short poem about love and commitment, warming Alice no end. Then Jamie said his vows.

'Angel, there are no words for how much I love you. Through thick and thin you've stayed by my side, showing me what true love looks like. You're my heart and soul, my best friend, and my safe place.' He dipped his head and peered up through his lashes, a glow about his cheeks. 'Alice, you're my home, and I vow to spend the rest of my life making you happy. I love you.'

No longer caring about the rights and wrongs of the service, Alice stepped forward and kissed him hard on the lips, then backed away when some cheers echoed through the church.

'Alice, do you have anything you'd like to say?' asked Father Stephen.

She nodded, turning back to Jamie. 'I haven't had time to write anything down, but I don't need to think much about how I feel about you. Jamie, you've always been part of me. I don't know why or how that happened, it's just who we are. I don't know life without you, and I don't want to. I love you so much, and I always will.'

They shared a gentle kiss, and their guests started to clap, Sophie adding in a loud cheer.

Alice and Jamie turned, Alice grinning, Jamie taking a small bow. Arm in arm, they headed outside and posed for some photographs while light snowflakes fluttered over their heads. Confetti rained over them, then Jed and Will sang out a sea shanty that had everyone linking arms and joining in while the photographer continued to snap away.

The chauffeur opened the car door for the married couple. Alice got in first, grabbing Jamie into a loving embrace as soon as he was by her side.

'I can't believe you did all this, Jamie.'

'It was worth it to see the look on your face.'

She kissed him, only pulling away when things got a little heated. Giggling, she winked. 'Later,' she whispered, and Jamie bobbed his head.

A flower arch made of red flowers, silver ribbons and gold baubles greeted them at the Jolly Pirate, and a blown-up picture of Alice and Jamie sitting on the wall outside Seaview B&B as kids was propped by a two-tier wedding cake.

Alice laughed. 'Goodness, where did that come from?'

'I took that,' said Luna. 'It was Mabel's birthday, and we were having a small tea party inside. I remembered as soon as Jamie showed me the picture.'

'Nan had it packed away with my things,' he told Alice.

'I thought a large version would look good here today,' said Luna.

'Oh, it's brilliant, Nan. Thanks.' Alice snuggled into Jamie's side as they both gazed at their childhood.

'Who knew, eh, Angel?'

'I wish I could go back and tell them. Us. Let them know everything will be okay in the end.'

Jamie placed his head close to hers. 'If I could go back to that moment, I'd do this.' He kissed her temple.

She pulled back and grinned. 'When was the first time you wanted to kiss me?'

Jamie chuckled. 'Probably when we were in our early to mid-teens.'

'I didn't pick up on that back then. I thought maybe when we were a bit older. More late teens.'

'Ah, so that's when you saw me in a new light, eh?'

Alice laughed. 'I've seen you in all lights.'

'You certainly have.'

'And I still love you.' She gave his waist a gentle squeeze.

'That's why you're my angel.' He pulled her around so she was in his arms, facing him. 'It's quite a skill you have there. Loving someone no matter their flaws.'

'We all have flaws. We're human.'

'Yeah, but you always saw good in me.' He shrugged. 'I don't know. You seemed to be able to see parts of me I couldn't.'

Alice smiled. 'My nan's psychic. It rubs off.'

Jamie smiled back. 'Perhaps we have a spiritual connection. Knew each other in a previous life.'

'You don't believe in any of that.'

'With you, I believe in everything.'

'Because I'm an angel?' she teased.

Jamie beamed, filling her heart with love. 'My angel.'

EPILOGUE

One Year Later

Christmas music was playing in the Jolly Pirate pub, cheering the customers drinking at the tinsel-adorned bar and those feasting on a turkey dinner in the restaurant area.

Sophie and Matt pulled a Christmas cracker, and Sophie encouraged him to read the joke out to everyone at the long dinner table.

Matt cleared his throat. 'Okay, can I have your attention? It's Christmas cracker joke time.'

Sophie shushed everyone.

Matt unfolded the small piece of paper. 'I'm pregnant.' He frowned, reading it again, then turned to Sophie. 'What?'

Sophie nodded. 'Surprise.'

Everyone cheered as Matt wrapped her up in his arms.

Lottie and Samuel fussed over their four-year-old daughter who they'd adopted that year, placing a paper hat on her red curls and one on her doll sitting on the table.

Will and Ginny had their son in a highchair between them, feeding him mashed roast potatoes with vegetables, which he kept spitting out.

'This table just keeps growing each year,' said Ginny, wiping Robert's mouth.

Spencer had his own son on his knee. 'Yep, and louder.' He shushed Archie's squealing, then tickled him to make him giggle.

Beth leaned over to pass their son a toy duck to keep him occupied. 'One day, our lot might take over the whole pub, Robson.'

Robson laughed, placing his arm around Demi's chair. 'I'll have to close for the day and charge you lot double.'

Everyone booed him, then laughed, and Demi kissed his cheek.

Jed stood, raising a glass of lemonade. 'Here's to our Christmas table. May it always grow and grow and know nothing but love, friendship, and sea shanties.'

Luna cheered. 'Can't let that die out.'

'We won't,' said Sophie, holding Matt's hand on her stomach.

Lizzie clapped. 'Aww, what a year we've had again. We should toast to all our achievements.'

'The success of the Happy to Help Hub,' said Spencer, raising Archie's sippy cup.

'Extra funding for the food bank,' said Samuel.

Lottie nudged him. 'And our beautiful daughter.'

Samuel nodded. 'To our Sarah.'

'And to sobriety,' said Demi, adding a small cheer.

Matt smiled her way. 'And support.'

'The kindness of strangers, who helped us newbies when we arrived here,' said Beth.

Ginny and Will held hands across the highchair, and Robert was happy to smear their fingers with food.

'To the whole of Port Berry,' said Will, smiling at Ginny.

More Christmas crackers were pulled and drinks poured as the lively chatter continued around the table.

Alice noticed Benny texting Ellie. She left him to it, turning to hold Jamie's hand instead. 'Just think, this time last year we were renewing our vows.'

'It's flown by, hasn't it?'

'Yep, and look what we've achieved. You and your new website design business.'

Jamie lifted a hand. 'Oh, yeah, and let's not forget the Seaview winning best B&B in Cornwall last summer. Give it up for the incredible Alice Stark.'

Everyone cheered, and Alice blushed, lowering his arm. 'Stop that. We celebrated enough back then.'

Jamie cuddled her. 'And we'll never stop celebrating, Angel. Look around us. Look what we have.'

Alice took in her friends and family one by one. 'It's pretty special.'

'Not everyone is fortunate enough to be part of a wonderful circle like ours.' He placed his palm on her large baby bump. 'And I'm so glad our kid will know the power of friendship.'

'Jed always says Port Berry is magical.'

Overhearing, Jed nodded. 'That's right. And I'll never stop telling folk. If you want to clear away the cobwebs, find a place to call home, know what love, support, and kindness feels like, then come along to Cornwall and visit us in Port Berry.'

THE END

ACKNOWLEDGEMENTS

This story is dedicated to everyone on a healing journey. You are powerful, resilient, problem-solving masters who know how to survive the deepest, darkest pits of hell. Remember that next time you doubt your strength.

Huge thanks goes out to the Choc Lit/Joffe Books team for their help, support, and encouragement for the Port Berry series and my author journey. Much appreciated.

Also sending a cheer to my readers who are also a constant support to my author journey. I want you all to know that I'm so completely and utterly grateful to each and every one of you.

As always, sending lots of love and light your way. Keep reading. It's good for the soul.

ABOUT THE AUTHOR

Hello, I'm K.T. Dady. I write uplifting love stories filled with friendship, family, and community set here, there, and everywhere, as love happens anywhere and under all sorts of circumstances. But whatever challenges my characters face along the way, there is always a happily ever after.

Feel free to join my newsletter over at my website, where you can download a free Pepper Bay short story that you won't find anywhere else. Newsletters go out once a month and often contain free gifts, previews, and writing tips amongst the news. Head over to my website at ktdady.com.

If you enjoyed reading my book, please leave a rating or review on Amazon or Goodreads. It really helps to bring the story to more readers. Thank you so much.

You'll also find me on my social media accounts.

Instagram: @kt_dady

Facebook: @ktdady

THE CHOC LIT STORY

Established in 2009, Choc Lit is an independent, award-winning publisher dedicated to creating a delicious selection of quality women's fiction.

We have won 18 awards, including Publisher of the Year and the Romantic Novel of the Year, and have been shortlisted for countless others. In 2023, we were shortlisted for Publisher of the Year by the Romantic Novelists' Association.

All our novels are selected by genuine readers. We are proud to publish talented first-time authors, as well as established writers whose books we love introducing to a new generation of readers.

In 2023, we became a Joffe Books company. Best known for publishing a wide range of commercial fiction, Joffe Books has its roots in women's fiction. Today it is one of the largest independent publishers in the UK.

We love to hear from you, so please email us about absolutely anything bookish at choc-lit@joffebooks.com.

If you want to receive free books every Friday and hear about all our new releases, join our mailing list here: www.joffebooks.com/freebooks.